Praise for

On the Mountain of the Lord

"*On the Mountain of the Lord* is a thriller, superimposed over biblical prophecy, history, and geography. Bodie Thoene expertly weaves an intriguing plot through current events, while Ray Bentley adds a depth of understanding to complicated Middle East issues. The combination is a good story that has meaning. I'm already looking forward to their next novel."

—**Anne Graham Lotz**, author and speaker

"*On the Mountain of the Lord* weaves the headlines of today and the pages of the Bible into a page turning thriller. It brings the most contested place on Earth—the Temple Mount—and the most heated conflict in the world to life. Bodie Thoene and Ray Bentley take you on a dramatic journey into the heart of Jerusalem, onto the streets of London and up to the ancient sites of the Promised Land to feel the heartbeat of today's most important crossroads of history and prophecy, Jerusalem. If you want to feel this heartbeat for yourself, you'll want to read *On the Mountain of the Lord*!"

—**Chris Mitchell**, CBN News Middle East Bureau Chief

"The inspiring novel *On the Mountain of the Lord* by Ray Bentley and Bodie Thoene takes you on an amazing journey connecting prophecies of the past to their modern day fulfillment. As the prophets declare, all nations will one day ascend the Mountain of the Lord to learn of His ways, and in this novel you will feel the connection as you are being drawn in, being reconnected to the Promised Land and the people of Israel."

—**Mark Biltz**, founder of El Shaddai Ministries and bestselling author

"*On the Mountain of the Lord* came like a wind and deeply penetrated to my heart. From the very start it awakened my soul to its core beyond my comprehension. I truly believe it's going to bring such understanding of truth, healing, and inspiration to millions in a very unexpected manner. I have learned, grown, and was inspired all at once reading a well-written story of the ordinary in an extraordinary way. It tells us in the deepest and darkest hours of our struggles and wounds there's dawn, there's hope and there's that glorious supernatural breakthrough. Ray Bentley and Bodie Thoene paint a masterpiece of truth: in the midst of darkness, turmoil, and terror, we can still believe in miracles. So touched. So inspired. This book is telling the world to dream dreams and never give up. People, cultures, and places are studied so well I felt I was there! From England to Tel Aviv to the Mount of Olives, I was there as if it were a movie."

—**Işik Abla**, founder and CEO of Işik Abla Ministries, evangelist (to the Muslim world), and author

"*On the Mountain of the Lord* takes us on a fascinating journey of intrigue through the Holy Land revealing fascinating biblical prophecies. Pastor Ray Bentley's thorough knowledge of the Bible combined with his passion for Israel is complemented by Bodie Thoene's captivating characters and gripping story line. What a combination these two make! Unfolding at a riveting pace, you'll be encouraged by the book and left wanting more at the end! It was hard to put down, as a matter of fact, I didn't put it down until I finished! It's a wonderful book, enjoyable, and educational!"

—**Ed Taylor**, senior pastor, Calvary Chapel of Aurora, Colorado

"Here is a novel of profound impact on Israel's current political situation. It is a fast-moving, action-packed detective narrative of its history and Islamic atrocities engulfing the whole world. It is both spellbinding and gut-wrenching. An amazing, informative thriller. A powerful and clear testimony of Israel's betrayal by the international community. Within its vast panorama, it is the keen sense of the small moments of life that endears the reader and invites him to step into the story in a remarkable and stunning way. Wow reading!"

—**Robert Mawire**, president, WRNO Radio and Gerizim Technology Group

"*On the Mountain of the Lord* is a suspenseful and captivating read. Behind the fictional story of Jack Garrison is a comprehensible mingling of history, biblical events, and prophecy connecting all three with current events. This is historical fiction at its best. If you want to gain a biblical understanding of why Israel is at the center of world conflict as well as enjoy a great read, then this is the book for you!"

—**Pastor Brian Brodersen and Cheryl Brodersen**, Calvary Chapel Costa Mesa

"Bodie Thoene and Ray Bentley's collaborative novel captures one man's struggle to understand the prophetic implications of the land of Israel. Bursting with drama and suspense from the very first page, it will have you reading late into the night. This stirring tale casts a spotlight on the place where heaven and earth meet, where modern geopolitical realities converge with ancient prophecies, and where the God of Israel chose to put his name—Jerusalem's Holy Temple. In *On the Mountain of the Lord*, we are gently reminded that the heartbeat of God remains His promised land and the eternal destiny of His people."

—**Dr. Dinah Dye**, bestselling Messianic author

"I honestly expected to painfully read *On the Mountain of the Lord* and I discovered that it truly is brilliant and I can't put it down!! I have too much to do and I'm mesmerized after chapter nine. How clever of Ray Bentley and Bodie Thoene! Take people on a tour of Israel and with one eye on the past prophecies and the other on the current realities you are weaving together a remarkable and memorable plot line. Absolutely love it!! Rosenberg, look out!!!"

> —**Lloyd Pulley,** senior pastor of Calvary Chapel Old Bridge, New Jersey, author, and host of Bridging the Gap radio program

"Lovers of *The Zion Chronicles* and *The Zion Covenant*, rejoice! Master storyteller Bodie Thoene has once again set her keen eye on Jerusalem, this time in the twenty-first century. She and Ray Bentley remind us in this compelling novel, *On the Mountain of the Lord*, that heaven's headlines certainly trump the world's skewed take on the plans for Israel, the Church, and the Jewish people."

> —**John Waage**, CBN senior editor, Israel

On the Mountain of the Lord

THE ELIJAH CHRONICLES

On the Mountain of the Lord

A Novel

Ray BENTLEY   Bodie THOENE

Research by Brock Thoene

SALEMBOOKS
an imprint of Regnery Publishing

Salem Books™ is a trademark of Salem Communications Holding Corporation
Regnery® is a registered trademark of Salem Communications Holding Corporation

Cataloging-in-Publication data on file with the Library of Congress

ISBN 978-1-62157-794-2

Published in the United States by
Salem Books
An imprint of Regnery Publishing
A Division of Salem Media Group
300 New Jersey Ave NW
Washington, DC 20001
www.SalemBooks.com

Manufactured in the United States of America

10 9 8 7 6 5 4 3 2 1

Books are available in quantity for promotional or premium use. For information on discounts and terms, please visit our website: www.Regnery.com.

To my beautiful wife Vicki and her family, who are the inspiration for the main characters in this story, Jack and Bette.

And to all the people who have kept this dream alive, "Next year in Jerusalem..."

Contents

Prologue

BRITISH OCCUPIED JERSUALEM

JUNE 14, 1946

The British Union Jack was bathed in brilliant moonlight above Jerusalem's King David Hotel, headquarters of the British Mandate.

Sol Baruch watched from the rooftop of his flat with seven members of his Haganah team as the flag slowly dimmed and turned blood-red in the shadow of a full lunar eclipse. Stars appeared as the sky darkened.

"Look. Can you see it?" Ari gestured toward the Blood Moon. "There's a shadow there—like a red horse—across the moon."

Sol studied the strange apparition. "Yes. Yes. I see it."

"Do you think it means something, Sol? I mean, tonight we finalize our plans for the attack—while this is happening above our heads."

Sol frowned and considered that he must answer Ari carefully. In two nights the forces of the Jewish Haganah, with other resistance fighters, would blow up eleven bridges linking the British Mandate of Palestine to other countries. Sol did not want his explosives teams to fear bad luck. "You mean, like a bad omen or something?"

Ari nodded, not taking his eyes from the scarlet orb. "Yes. A warning to us? Bad luck?"

Sol rubbed his hand over his copper-colored beard. "You are religious, Ari. You read today's Parsha. Yes? No? You tell me."

"The prophet Zechariah. All this week. The red horse is in there too."

"Yes. Okay. This red moon is maybe a sign, but it is a good sign for us and for the nations who bless the Jews, Ari. And a bad sign for those who curse and oppress us. The Almighty, HaShem, is warning all the nations who have injured His beloved people. They have poked their finger in God's eye. When Israel is a nation again, all the Jews who were scattered and broken will come home."

Ari still stared up with dread. "So much Jewish blood. You—you finally heard the news about your friend just today. And the Agency is still looking for my family. Those who survived the Nazis are still locked up in Displaced Persons camps. Here is a homeland for them, and now British blockades keep them out." Ari smiled slightly and nodded. "So we will blow up British bridges. And that will be our sign to all the world we will no longer be ruled by gentiles."

Pieter Kowalski, who escaped from Nazi-occupied Poland, put a hand on Ari's shoulder. "Superstition. Come on, Ari. We make our own luck. And we will fight to make our own homeland. Our job for now is to blow up the Allenby Bridge and get back alive. Vengeance. That's what I want. This is just an eclipse. Let our enemies look up and be afraid of the omen of a red moon. Superstition. Nothing more."

Ari shrugged. "Well, I say it's a good thing to be God's Chosen People. It gives one courage, don't you think?"

Pieter's eyes narrowed. "If the last few years are any indication of what it's like to be God's chosen, I wish God would choose someone besides us Jews." He bowed slightly. "And now, as for me? I want to go home and get some sleep."

Members of the team trooped down the steep steps, leaving Sol alone in his one-room flat. A scarlet glow streamed through his open window, falling upon the stack of letters tied with a ribbon on his desk. His Bible was open to the day's passage in Zechariah.

Sol switched on the lamp and read again the yellow paper telegram from the Jewish Agency, confirming his best friend, Jacob Louzada, had perished in a Nazi death camp.

He was glad to be alone. He had not had time to grieve the reality of such a loss. His gaze lingered on the words of Zechariah. Black fire upon white fire. "'Up! Up! Flee from the land of the north,' declares the Lord. 'Escape to Zion!'"

Addressing the bundle of letters Sol chided, "Why didn't you listen? You paid with your life. Too late, you listened." He shook his head.

From the prophet Zechariah he read aloud, "...to the nations that plundered you...he who touched the apple of my eye. Sing and rejoice O daughter of Zion, I will come and I will dwell in your midst, declares the Lord. And many nations shall join themselves to the Lord in that day and they shall be My people. And the Lord will inherit Judah as His portion in the Holy Land and will again choose Jerusalem."

What could this mean? Surely the time for restoration must come. The nation of Israel must be reborn or there will be no hope left for the People of the Book.

"God, I will remember this night," Sol said aloud. "It does mean something. Something important." He drew a weary breath as the gloom of the Blood Moon deepened across the ancient city. Switching off the light, he grasped his Bible tightly to his chest. Lying down on his narrow bed, he fell into a deep sleep.

Chapter One

PRESENT DAY

Christmas was American-born Professor Jack Garrison's least favorite season in London. As the world beyond Great Britain seemed to crumble, the Brits' cheerful portrayal of the Charles Dickens holiday spirit was an assault on Jack's senses. Even the late afternoon, working-class Londoners, laden with packages, smiled while crammed into the Bakerloo Line Tube train.

Jack sensed for months he was being followed. He scanned his fellow passengers. Real concern or paranoia? There was no proof; only a vague unease.

At age thirty-two, Jack believed the Underground was a cross-section study of London society: a few elite middle-aged travelers in pinstriped suits read *The Times*; middle class faces were concealed behind the latest tabloid headlines; *London Sun* and *Daily Mirror* screamed the latest outrages about the American president. Younger eyes of shop clerks and office workers were all fixed on cell phone screens.

Jack's cell phone, tucked away within the inside pocket of his navy blue, corduroy jacket, was set on airplane mode—location services off. He wondered who, among his fellow passengers, might be snapping photos of him.

The PA announced their arrival at Embankment Tube station. The train slowed and stopped. Doors slid open. Jack held back as a dozen people stepped off, then he followed.

No one exited behind him.

Unreasonable relief.

A trio of brass horn players: trumpet, trombone, and tuba performed at the bottom of the Embankment Tube station escalators. Jack paused and pretended interest as crowds from other trains pushed past.

He tossed a one-pound coin into the musicians' collection basket and joined the current of strangers pouring out from a warren of Underground tunnels and onto the escalators.

The sounds of "God Rest Ye Merry Gentlemen" followed the jostling crowds upward toward the Strand. Jack had not been merry for a very long time and God seemed very distant indeed.

It was only 4:30 p.m., drizzling, and already dark as Jack emerged from the station. A sidewalk peddler scooped warm chestnuts from a grill and poured them into a small, brown-paper bag. Jack purchased a bag, jostling the hot paper from palm to palm, and read the headlines at the news vendor's stand. Just released evening tabloids shrieked about the American president's latest tweet.

Jack ducked his head as the rain began to pelt his face and stopped to buy a paper. He handed over another pound coin.

"American?" asked the vendor, making change.

"Is it that obvious?" Jack held the paper above his head.

"Only a Yank would go out without an umbrella. No hat, nor top coat, neither."

"Quite the Sherlock Holmes."

"Easy. And you're—some sort of academic?"

Jack laughed. "You *are* good."

"No tie, y'see." The vendor tapped the headline. "Interestin' reading. Quite a chap, your Mr. Trump."

"I've been away from America a long time," Jack replied. "Cheers."

Was that an expression of admiration for Trump, or amusement on the newsie's face, Jack wondered. He hurried up the cobbled pedestrian alleyway toward the Strand, a main London thoroughfare for centuries.

A sea of black umbrellas surged over the sidewalks as Jack made his way toward the u-shaped drive sheltering the entrance to the Savoy Hotel. The usual scent of diesel-powered black cabs and red buses lingered in the air. Extravagant garlands and giant lighted angels soared above the street and reflected on the wet pavement.

Jack pushed through the revolving door of the Savoy. A string quartet played instrumental carols in the marbled lobby. The Christmas tree towered almost to the ceiling and seemed to drip golden ornaments and gleaming white twinkle lights. Around the base of the tree was a heap of fake packages trimmed in gilt ribbons.

Jack scanned round tables crowded with barristers, businessmen, tourists, and well-dressed ladies finishing high tea. Jack's old college roommate, Levi Seixas, was nowhere to be seen.

The maître d' eyed Jack's lean, rumpled, six-one stature with disapproval. Jack ran his hand self-consciously over the reddish stubble on his cheek.

He wondered what Debbie would say if she could see him now. Everything about his appearance was a portrait of lingering grief. Thick, unkempt hair. If Debbie were here, she would not have let him go so long without a shave and a haircut.

Jack was uncomfortably aware his attire was out of place amid the opulence of the afternoon business crowd. He glanced at his image in a mirror and barely recognized himself as a successful academic in worn out, blue Nike running shoes, faded jeans, and a rust-red Big Island Ironman t-shirt beneath a white, open-collar dress shirt, all of which was topped by the navy blue corduroy jacket.

The tone of the maître d' implied people who slept in their clothes were not usually welcome as Savoy guests. "May I help you, sir?"

"Dr. Jack Garrison." Jack brushed cat fur from his sleeve. The kitty had long since adopted Jack's neighbors, but left reminders behind of her first home.

The maître d' scanned his reservation list. His accent and demeanor reminded Jack of the iconic butler, Mr. Carson, in the Downton Abbey series. "You are—meeting Doctor Garrison, sir?"

"No. I *am* Doctor Garrison."

"Ah." The man arched his eyebrows in surprise as he spotted Jack's name. "American?"

"My secretary called ahead—Garrison. Professor—London, King's College."

"I see. Well, then—of course." The maître d' seemed relieved to learn Jack was an academic, and not an MD. "Neck ties are required at the Savoy, sir. However—not to worry. I have several just here. So many American tourists arrive unacquainted with our traditions." He opened a cupboard and retrieved a loaner clip-on navy blue tie.

Jack buttoned his top button and attached the neckpiece. It pinched. "Meeting an old friend. But he's not here. Probably stuck in traffic. Lev Seixas is his name. "

"American as well?"

"Yes. American."

"I'll let him know you're here—Doctor Garrison. Your table is just there as requested. Follow me, sir."

"Sure. Thanks." Tucking his chin self-consciously Jack wove through the throng to the table against a dark-paneled wall. Jack and Lev sat at this very table the last time they saw one another. That meeting did not end well. Now, Jack wondered if it was possible for two former friends to have such different views of the world and still be friends.

He propped his bristly chin on one hand, tossed the unopened bag of chestnuts on the table, frowned at the empty chair, and ordered tea. *So, what did Lev want?* Funny. He recognized Lev's voice over the phone right off, even though it had been several years. It was a lousy time of day to schedule a meeting with a guy he hadn't seen since Obama was first elected president.

Jack and Lev, both on the college wrestling team, graduated with degrees from Baylor University. Thereafter their paths took them in completely different directions.

Jack won a Rhodes Scholarship to Oxford and then earned his PhD in political science. A full professorship at King's College was followed by his appointment to an advisory chair on the ECMP—the European Committee for Mid-East Policy—as a specialist on refugee issues.

His first marriage ended in divorce. Then came Debbie and their boy. For a time the world looked bright and wonderful. All things seemed possible.

Lev's yearly newsletters kept Jack up to speed on the life of his old friend. Lev Seixas, a Messianic Jew, was descended from the first American-born rabbi, Gershom Seixas. The summer after college, Lev flew to Ireland to intern as a youth pastor. There he married a nice Irish girl named Katy, who played the fiddle and toured with Riverdance. She gave it all up for Lev. They had four red-haired kids, one after another—boom, boom, boom, boom. Lev was now a committed Zionist and the pastor of an impoverished evangelical church that occupied space in an industrial complex in San Diego, California.

Jack glanced toward the revolving door as Lev pushed through. Levi Gershom Seixas attended Baylor on scholarship as a lightweight varsity wrestler. He was still a legend among the Bears. He ripened into a powerfully built man. Unlike Jack, he was dressed appropriately for a meeting at the Savoy. With his navy business suit, Lev sported a muted, green-and-gold Baylor alumni tie. Broad shoulders and a thick neck made him seem larger than his five-nine height. A thick thatch of dark hair did not conceal the cauliflower ears, proof of hard fought victories on the wrestling mat. Wide-set, brown eyes scanned the Savoy Grill room for Jack.

The maître d' inquired Lev's name, then pointed in Jack's direction. Lev's craggy face split in a wide grin as he waved. Jack stood and motioned for Lev to join him.

The string quartet played a familiar Christmas carol. Though the lyrics remained unsung, and probably unremembered, by the average citizen, Jack knew the words of the Issac Watts hymn. The Christian message behind the music blared in his memory.

Joy to the World!

The Lord is come!

Let earth receive her King

Let every heart

Prepare Him room

And heaven and nature sing...

The too-bright melody squeezed Jack's heart. He wished all Christmas carols were banned; he wished he didn't know the verses.

He wished he could have a drink. . .

There was no king on the way; no hope of heaven and nature singing. No joy to the world anymore. Like the fake packages around the tree, Jack's life was empty.

Lev strode through the crush of tables and, ignoring Jack's outstretched hand, hugged him and clapped him on the back. "Hey, Jack! So, Dr. Garrison. Look at you!" He tapped Jack's tie. "Still an Iron Man?"

"It's been a while. A couple years. You have to keep up with it to compete."

"I was coaching junior wrestling back home. That's about as competitive as I want to be." Lev sat down, then gave a low whistle as he spotted the tree. "Where I come from we call that a Hanukkah bush."

"Yeah. The Brits know how to do Christmas."

A moment of awkward silence was broken as the waiter approached. Lev ordered a glass of Pinot Noir.

Jack leaned across the table. "Seems we have had this conversation before—like an awkward script: small talk and then. . ."

Lev nodded, "Politics. Eight years ago. "

Jack continued, ". . . then Obama's Mid-East policy—Israel's right to occupy."

"Israel's right to *survive*." Lev's eyes flashed. "But—that's long enough, isn't it? I mean long enough for us to stay angry because we disagreed?" Silence. "Jack, I heard about Debbie and your boy, and I'm sorry. I wanted you to know. . ."

"Thanks." Jack's tone was bitter. "Is that why you wanted to meet with me today?"

"No. Well, partly—I wanted you to know I am praying for you and—"

"Save your prayers."

"Jack, I am here for you if you need to talk. I feel—I mean it was wrong to destroy a friendship over. . ."

"Over land for peace? And now this madness of an American president declaring Jerusalem as the capital of Israel? Despite every warning! Every objection. Telling the whole world he intends to move the U.S. embassy to Jerusalem? Have you changed your mind? Because I haven't changed mine. You're a Jew. Naturally you favor what you perceive is the best thing for Israel. But what's best for the rest of the world is still a matter of debate. You and I hold vastly different opinions about where the world is heading, Lev."

"I don't have to change my opinions in order to remember you were once my closest friend."

"I'm not sure any friendship can survive a difference of opinion on Middle East policies. The expanse between us is as wide as the Persian Gulf! You are religious—I am not. You would say I lost my faith, I would say I found my faith. My faith is in men working out their problems. Negotiation. Compromise—I believe dogmatic religion divides people and nations. It does not unify."

"The British withdrawal from the European Union? Brexit? How does that affect your position on ECMP?"

"It doesn't. We're a think tank. We consult, investigate and report as neutral observers. . ."

"Hardly neutral." Lev shook his head.

Jack sat back in his chair. "Look, Lev—we have to agree to disagree or. . ."

The music played, sans lyrics, but both men knew the words:

Oh Come, Oh come Emmanuel,

And ransom captive Israel

Which mourns in lonely exile here

Until the Son of God appear...

Lev paused to choose his words carefully. "I've been thinking about that day, our conversation—our argument—thinking about it a lot. "

Jack waved his hand at the music in irritation. "I haven't thought about it at all. People who actually believe the Bible or ancient prophecies have anything to do with current world politics are just..." Again a dismissive wave. "Well, preachers and prophets and holy rollers are not on my short list of people who can change the world. Neither President Obama nor his State Department are interested in Jewish Messiah myths or the Bible. Here in Europe, the Committee consults me about refugees. I tell them the Palestinian conflict is as old as history itself and may never be settled—unless there is great compromise."

Lev did not reply to the insults. His wide mouth curved in an enigmatic smile. Jack recognized the meaning of that smile. Lev always smiled like that when he had some secret wrestling move he was going to use to pin his opponent in the first five seconds of a match.

Lev replied quietly, "You'll be in Israel soon, I hear. Policy discussions."

"You hear? From whom?"

Lev shrugged. "This stop in London is just a layover. I'll be leaving for Israel next Wednesday. It's a small country. Very small. "

Jack cautiously conceded, "I won't be traveling to Israel as a tourist."

"Neither will I. We're making Aliyah; moving to Israel permanently. My wife and I—the kids—were called to Jerusalem."

"Called? Who called you?"

"The Lord."

"Ah. The Lord. I see."

Lev drew himself erect. "I am descended from Gershom Seixas. A Sephardic Jew, and a Levite. Jack, my family was exiled from Israel in the first century. We lived in Portugal, Holland, England, Philadelphia... but the new millennium is beginning. Time for this Seixas to return home to Israel, where my family's journey began."

"So. You are moving to Israel in the name of your ancestors?"

"Returning. Yes. Permanently."

"We have ancestry.com to blame for this madness. That would be like me moving back to—France, say—somewhere on my grandmother's branch of the tree."

"France wouldn't want you, and I may be the only Jew in Israel who will be glad to see you arrive. So? I wanted to let you know you will be welcome at my table in Jerusalem—any time."

That explained the smile. Lev slid a business card with his Jerusalem phone number, address, and email across the table. "Partners with Zion," the business name read.

Jack sat back in his chair and laughed. "What are you, Mossad, or something?"

Lev shrugged. "No. I'm not the Israeli Secret Service. I'm just your friend. Still your friend. We were brothers, Jack, and I have not forgotten."

"Alright, then. So maybe we'll have coffee in Jerusalem. We'll talk about the old college days. We'll steer clear of discussing two state solutions, and Israeli settlements, and the Golan?" Jack glanced at Lev's Old City address. Near Christ Church. "But hey, just a warning. If some Israeli official thinks you can change my mind? Or thinks I will influence the Committee because we are friends? Tell him to forget it. You're not going to change my mind, Lev."

"I don't have to change your mind. I will leave such business to God."

The rest of Jack's conversation with Lev was about old friends: "Whatever happened to...?"

Then abruptly—awkwardly—it was over. Jack left Lev with the promise to see him in Jerusalem. He barely avoided making a joke out of "next year in Jerusalem." If Lev was taking his Jewish heritage seriously he might not appreciate Jack making fun of the Jewish longing for their so-called ancestral home.

Accepting Lev's offer to pay for the wine and tea, Jack stood and left the Savoy. At the passage into the lobby he glanced back. Lev was studying him thoughtfully, raising a hand in silent farewell.

The rain slashed down harder than before. It was impossible to see across to the other side of the Strand. The doorman inquired if Jack wanted a taxi, indicating a line of waiting black cabs. For a moment Jack considered it, then decided he didn't need the extra expense. Waving away the suggestion, Jack returned to Embankment Tube station and plunged down a succession of escalators into the bowels of the earth.

The heat on the platform was oppressive. Even after years in the UK, Jack still didn't understand the British aversion to fresh air. The entire nation had a morbid fear of cold, which translated into boiler room temperatures on the Tube all year round. And if that weren't enough, the Brits holidayed in places like the Canary Islands and Crete—in midsummer.

This journey was so automatic Jack found his way to his accustomed place on the northbound platform, noted the next train was two minutes away, and reminded himself to pick up a pint of milk before walking home—all without conscious thought.

Instead he was still pondering Lev's comment about not needing to convince Jack, but leaving that up to God.

Jack snorted and covered the sound with a fake cough, which made two fellow travelers edge away from him. As if there really were some cosmic deity. And even if there were, what interest could he possibly have in Jack? Life was what the seven billion inhabitants of planet Earth made of it—nothing more.

It made Jack irritated with himself that, while certain of his position, he still wondered what Lev meant. Convince him of what? Convince him of Israel's right to exist and to build settlements on Palestinian territory? Convince him the modern Jewish state was promised its land by God?

They really were somehow a chosen people with a divine destiny both foreshadowed and confirmed by magic prophecies?

It was all nonsense an educated, twenty-first-century human could not—should not—tolerate.

Glancing toward the countdown clock, now registering only one more minute to wait, Jack's gaze slid across a hundred faces without really seeing any of them. Black was the predominant color of clothing. Everyone had an umbrella and toted a plastic bag of groceries and a newspaper. They all sported vacant, introspective expressions; the same demeanor Jack was certain he wore.

It took something unusual to draw his attention: a Japanese music student lugging a cello case bigger than he was; the bearded man balancing an empty bird cage in one arm and, Jack smiled, a roasted chicken in a plastic container in the other; the woman from whose overcoat three pairs of legs sprouted as two children were all but hidden from sight below her waist.

Of the man wearing black-framed glasses and a tweed hat and coat standing three places to Jack's right he took no notice at all.

Chapter Two

The Bakerloo train lurched out of the Oxford Circus station. Barely anyone got off, but it seemed a million shoppers and clerks, eager to get home for supper, pressed aboard. A cloud of steam rose from the late arrivals. The entire carload of soggy wool coats and wool sweaters and wool mufflers smelled like wet dog in the most oppressive way.

Jack rode standing, holding the upright support. Regents Park, Baker Street, Marylebone, Edgware Road, Paddington, and then finally Warwick Avenue and home. Jack ticked off the number of stops remaining. He made this journey so many times he believed he could have fallen asleep and still awakened after the correct number of stations. He never actually dozed, instead mentally subtracting one each time as if he might somehow miss the right exit.

OCD, he thought. *I really am. Debbie teased me about it. I wish I had her around to tease me now.*

No anxiety about the proper station apparently bothered the Goth kid across the aisle from Jack. Paratrooper boots crossed at the ankle, the student leaned back in his seat, head tapping slightly on the window. He was snoring. His mouth hung open, displaying a large, silver tongue stud.

The sight was singularly unattractive and Jack turned away—just in time to see a man in dark-framed glasses look down abruptly as if caught staring at Jack.

Jack studied the man. It was no one he recognized. Brown tweed coat with upturned collar and matching hat. Necktie loosened and askew at the shirt collar. Swarthy complexion, though little of the face could be seen.

OCD and paranoid, Jack thought. *Wouldn't Debbie have made something out of that?* Jack shrugged. Overwork was what was behind this nonsense. Maybe he was the one needing a trip to Crete or Tenerife.

At the stop for Marylebone station, once again more passengers crushed in while way too few got out. Now it was really hard to breathe. Jack looked over the top of the Goth kid's head at a travel poster curved to fit the wall of the Tube tunnel. "Visit Turkey," it suggested. "Istanbul for L69 one way." The poster displayed an image of the Hagia Sophia. Once a Christian cathedral, then a mosque, and now a museum. That was the way the modern world should treat ancient superstitions, Jack thought.

The train jerked again and Jack's gaze once more flicked across the car.

The man in tweed was staring at him. He looked away at once, but Jack had no doubt about it: he was being studied intently.

Now what? Jack wondered. *Do I approach him and ask? What exactly am I accusing him of? There are over a hundred bodies stuffed in this metal cylinder. He has to be looking somewhere—doesn't he?*

Edgware Road came and went without Jack doing anything or even deciding if there was anything to be done. Even so, it was a relief when the train rattled into Paddington station and tweed coat got off with the crowd exiting the car.

Jack chided himself for being stupid. Paddington was a main rail station and also the connection to Heathrow airport via the Heathrow Express. Tweed coat was a businessman getting out of the city—or flying off somewhere. Nothing to do with him at all. The anticipation of seeing Lev had put him on edge. Their inability to break through the political tension and get back to their old, easy familiarity made the meeting a frustrating disappointment.

A glass of wine was called for; that was the answer. Home was now just one stop and a short walk away.

Jack was the only rider to exit from his car at Warwick Avenue. He tramped up the stairs, noting with satisfaction the rain had stopped.

He was just a block from home when he remembered the milk. The market was back the other way, but he was suddenly hungry. There was nothing much in the flat to eat. So, it was back to the market to pick up a roast chicken and some ice cream too.

Something moved in the gloom of the shadow where the bulk of St Saviour's Church blocked the light from the street lamp. A figure in a tweed coat darted around the angle of a wrought-iron railing and disappeared from sight.

Now what? Jack thought. *Do I go after him, demand to know why he's following me? Do I call the cops?* Glancing down, Jack saw he already held his cell phone in his hand. He didn't remember pulling it out of his jacket pocket.

The London police had enough on their plate already. Suicide bombers and knife-wielding truck assassins were real threats. This wasn't even a threat—yet.

On the other hand, why was Jack being followed? If tweed coat ducked off the Tube train only to change cars so he could pursue Jack unobserved, that argued something sinister, didn't it? It didn't seem wise to lead the man directly back to his flat. *Now what?* he asked himself again.

The answer presented itself in the form of a street sign pointing the opposite direction from home: Clifton Gardens. Jack strolled the avenue leading toward the Clifton Nursery. The goal was simple: find out if he was really being followed or if this was all imaginary. If tweed coat reappeared there was still the phone and a 999 call to the authorities. Maida Vale police station was less than a half-mile away.

Looking back over his shoulder—several times—produced nothing except a profound sense of foolishness. *And I accused Lev of being Mossad,* he thought. *Here I am, acting like a secret agent in the worst pot-boiler spy fiction ever.*

There was no point retracing his steps. It was just as close to walk home right from there, so Jack advanced toward the nursery at the far end of the street.

The place was a touchstone of sorts for his best memories. He and Debbie went there often in springs past. The window boxes above the yellow door of the little row house in Elnathan Mews blossomed under Debbie's touch. Each season of new life brought bright colors and new experiments: orange and golden marigolds one year, red dahlias the next.

Though the Brits who ran the shop were too polite to object, Jack was certain borrowing the nursery cart to trundle their purchases home was not usually allowed. Debbie insisted—and Jack agreed—but he returned the cart as rapidly as possible, while feeling guilty the entire trip. Americans were already regarded as so pushy and demanding; Jack never wanted to give the Brits additional confirmation.

The nursery was closed for the evening when Jack stepped off the sidewalk onto the gravel path that crunched under his feet. One more look around convinced him his fears were all nonsense. Even if tweed coat was on the same train he had a perfect right to get off at Warwick Avenue and pass St Saviour's Church.

The notion of why the man changed cars was still troubling, but now mainly an annoying unanswered question. More out of anger at himself for his silliness than for any conscious reason, Jack reached out and grasped the handle of the nursery gate. To his surprise it was unlocked. The latch clicked and the gate swung inward to reveal the dim grayscale of the silent garden space.

Jack hesitated on the threshold. A light drizzle was falling again. Even a mug of soup sounded inviting. But he was here and the place was full of memories of her—so he entered. He would just linger a minute, savoring past joys gone to vapor.

Of course it wasn't spring yet. Great, square, wooden boxes held leafless trees, their skeletal branches arching over mossy walkways. Ten more steps inward and the darkness deepened around concrete birdbaths and fountains looming like funeral monuments. This was not the pleasant relived moment Jack envisioned. He turned to go.

A face peered at Jack out of a boxwood hedge lining a fence. Alarmed, Jack fumbled with his phone and dropped it amid a pallet of bare root roses. A ceramic plaque of the Green Man, laughing face swathed in tendrils and leaves, mocked Jack's folly.

Cursing under his breath, Jack stooped to retrieve his phone and jammed his thumb into a rose thorn. No blossoms and no leaves, but the thorns made their presence known. Jack thought about using his phone's screen to illuminate the search. *I must be getting dumber by the minute.*

Cautiously, with great deliberation, Jack slipped his hand down amongst a trio of roses in the direction the device must have landed. His fingertips brushed the edge of the case just as the sound of gravel crushed under heavy footsteps came from the gate.

Jack froze, then seized the phone and pulled it free, heedless of thorns ripping sleeve and skin. His fingers stabbing at the keys, he missed the 9 button two times out of three tries.

"Is someone there?" a voice called from the entry path. "I will call the police if you don't answer."

Relief mingled with embarrassment. "Hold on," Jack called. "I'm coming out."

A flashlight beam probed the path between the plant tables, located Jack's feet, then slid up his frame to blind him.

"Dr. Garrison?" the voice queried.

"Yep. Me," Jack agreed stupidly. "Who's that?"

"Sayid Khan," replied Jack's Afghan Muslim neighbor who worked at the nursery. "I couldn't remember if I locked the front gate when I left work tonight and when I came to check I saw it standing open. But why are you here?"

"I—ah—I was just walking home and found the place unlocked— like you said. Old memories, you know. Debbie—she loved this place. Just came in for a minute."

"Of course," Sayid said. "I remember."

"Then I dropped my phone." Jack held it up into the light to show drips of blood running across his hand. "The roses. We should go."

"Yes," Sayid agreed. "You'll need to put something on that."

Chapter Three

J ack's bedroom was on the top floor of three. The ground floor contained a single car garage used to store file boxes, a tiny kitchen, and a formal dining room Jack used as an office. Up one flight of stairs was a double reception room/living room, in Jack's American way of thinking, and one bedroom. It was planned as a nursery but since. . .

The remaining flight of very steep steps opened on a landing beside a bathroom and the door to the master bedroom. The space was as big as the living room, but was partly taken up with another bath.

The mews house dated from the 1800s. Originally built as servants' quarters over stables behind the larger, grander homes fronting the major avenues, Elnathan Mews felt like a hidden gem when Jack and Debbie moved there. Handy to all parts of London through the nearby Tube station, it was also a short walk from the canal basin that gave the neighborhood its Little Venice nickname.

Jack ate a cup of microwaved chicken noodle soup and a fistful of soda crackers while staring at Sky News on the telly. There was another knife attack in Brussels, another bombing that killed forty in Kabul, Afghanistan, and another kidnapping of a Christian missionary couple in the Philippines. In other words, a routine day's events for worldwide Islamic jihad. Jack heard little of it and paid attention even less as he nodded over a goblet of something French.

Nor were Jack's thoughts occupied with his meeting with Lev, or with the anxiety-ridden journey home, about which he only felt shame.

As always, Jack's reflections were all about Debbie. He looked around the room. The stumps of long-dead flowers were still visible beyond the curtains she chose. The mahogany-framed mirror, gathered in like a treasure during a deep discount sale at Harrod's, hung unpolished over the mantle. The scenes of English cathedrals—Salisbury and Winchester—flanking the fireplace were purchased by her on two different expeditions to Storey's, the antique print seller in Cecil Court.

It was like that everywhere he turned. Padding upstairs to bed he knew her clothes still hung in the wardrobe in the corner, just as her Bible was still on the nightstand on her side of the bed. The ribbon still marked the passage—Gospel of John, chapter 14—she was reading the night before she—left.

Jack tried, unsuccessfully, to bury himself in his work. Mostly there was just a dull, unrelenting ache, brought into even sharper pain by this season of the year. Maybe the trip to Israel would be good for him. At least it would get him away from being immersed in Debbie's absence all the time. They traveled around Europe together, but were in Israel as a couple.

Sitting up in bed he glanced at her Bible, then thumbed open the Kindle app on his iPad to continue reading a P. G. Wodehouse novel. Jack read all the Jeeves and Wooster novels countless times and the plots were interchangeable anyway. That was why he kept them as his steady diet: they were mindless, pointless, required no effort, and could be abandoned at any point without harm. No getting to the end of a chapter was ever required with Wodehouse.

Tonight was true to the pattern. The wine kicked in, the Wodehouse patter grew irritating, the light switch was close at hand—and Jack was asleep.

◆◆◆

"I'm dreaming," Jack said aloud as Debbie wrapped packages beside a Christmas tree. "You're not really here. I didn't put up a tree this year."

She smiled and looked up at him with pity. "It doesn't matter, Jack. It's Christmas anyway."

"Not without you."

"Why waste your life on bitterness?"

"You took the light with you. Even the cat left me after you were gone. I see her perched in the window of the neighbor's house."

"You never really liked her. She knew it." Debbie folded gold paper carefully around an old shoebox and taped it shut.

"What are you doing there? The shoebox. Mom's old pictures?"

"We're all here together, Jack. Happy." She slid the package beneath the tree. "I just wanted you to know. You have to let me go."

"I can't."

"I'm happy." She began to fade.

"I'm not."

"Here's a gift for you…"

"Don't leave—Deb!"

As she spoke, a mist came and surrounded her. Her voice became a soft sigh. "He asked me to tell you, Jack, whatever comes—not to be surprised—He says, I will pour out my Spirit on all people—men will dream dreams and see visions…"

And then she was gone.

Jack opened his eyes. She was gone. No Christmas tree. No gold-wrapped package.

No cat.

◆◆◆

A blast of cold morning air slapped Jack in the face as he emerged and locked the yellow door of number 4 behind him. Few were awake at this early hour. The memory of the dream played over in his thoughts. Like Scrooge in Dickens' *Christmas Carol*, he told himself the vision was caused by something he ate.

But this morning it was almost as if Debbie walked beside him as he took the long way toward the Warwick Avenue Tube station.

"Why are you wasting your life on bitterness?" she asked.

He answered the question now in a whisper. "Because it's Christmas in London and you aren't here."

Oh, how Debbie loved this quaint neighborhood where old transport canals from the early 1800s merged. Her favorite place was Browning's Pool, a triangular basin where the poets Elizabeth Barrett and Robert Browning lived and wrote poems to one another. "How do I love thee— let me count the ways. . ."

A small island in the center of the pool was crowned with a willow tree. It remained as it had been more than a century before. "Pure romance," Debbie said when she described the scene to her students.

Generations of lovers lived and died in London's "Little Venice" since those long ago days. Debbie, a professor of English literature with the American College, expected she and Jack would grow old together in their nineteenth-century cottage.

But it was not to be.

Jack paused a moment beside her favorite bench but did not sit. He walked along the embankment where cherished canal boats, converted into pristine dwellings, were moored. The vessels, berthed along the waterways, and decorated for fierce holiday competitions, sported garlands of holly and bunches of mistletoe. St. Nicholas, captain's hat replacing his stocking cap, navigated the channel from atop a lean craft named *Loralei*.

Cocooned within shiny, black-enameled hulls painted with daisies and roses lived actors and artists and writers. Jack recognized the houseboat where once-impoverished entrepreneur Richard Branson dreamed Virgin Airlines into existence.

Looking down on the idyllic scene were tall, white-plastered, Regency-period town houses. Christmas trees and colored lights were framed in the windows.

How could all of this remain so cheerfully intact and unchanged without Debbie? Little Venice was like a set on the stage of an empty theater. There was no love story, no conversation, no actors. The script they imagined for their lives was lost in one unthinkable moment.

Chapter Four

T he third act of Thornton Wilder's play, *Our Town*, unfolded on the bare stage of the Royal National Theater.

It was Debbie's favorite. "Best American play ever written," she told Jack. But he had never seen it before tonight.

Jack bought his ticket at the half-price ticket booth on a whim. Maybe it was a way to avoid going home alone. Or maybe it was a way to learn something more about the only woman he ever loved, even though she was gone.

He was not prepared for the devastating final act—"Death and Eternity."

Jack gripped the arms of his seat as the spotlight focused only on Emily as she said goodbye to Grovers Corners and her beloved George.

"*I can't! I can't go on! It goes so fast! We don't have time to look at one another.*"

The actress sank to the stage and sobbed.

Jack glanced toward the exit. The green-lit WAY OUT sign was too far away for him to escape.

"*I didn't realize. All that was going on in life and we never noticed…*"

Jack blinked back tears. Was this written just for him?

"*One more look…Goodbye. Goodbye, Grovers Corners. Mama and Papa. Goodbye to clocks ticking and Mama's sunflowers. And food and coffee. And new ironed dresses. Hot baths and sleeping and waking up. Oh earth! You're too wonderful for anybody to realize you!*"

The actress seemed to look through the glare of the footlight and speak only to him. *"Do any human beings ever realize life while they live it?—Every, every minute?"*

Jack shook his head slowly, "No," in reply.

Her gaze lingered on him a moment, as if Jack were the only person in the audience. She sighed and turned away.

Jack wished he had not come. He wondered why Debbie loved this story so much. She was one of the rare humans who seemed to notice and cherish every moment. No joy escaped her attention. Ah, but Jack, on the other hand, missed blue-sky days and starry nights as he played the chess game of politics and policies.

Angry, Jack wiped his eyes with the back of his hand.

Why? Why did she love this play so much? It was an accusation, not entertainment.

The play ended quietly. Applause erupted and the lights came up. Standing ovation. Jack escaped the still-clapping crowd and fled into the cold London night.

◆◆◆

The breeze up the Thames stung Jack's face as he charged up the metal steps and onto the Hungerford footbridge that crossed the great river. A half dozen beggars and buskers positioned themselves along the span to appeal to theatergoers for spare change as they made their way home. Jack did not make eye contact, but fixed his gaze on the bright lights of London. To his right, in the distance, was the dome of St. Paul's Cathedral. To his left were the illuminated Houses of Parliament and Big Ben shining like a set in *Peter Pan.*

Two minutes 'til midnight. Jack paused in the center of Hungerford to wait for Big Ben to ring out. He leaned on the railing and blinked down at dancing lights reflected in the swift current.

One minute 'til midnight. The hands on the clock face clicked. The four melodious quarters of the Westminster chimes washed over Jack. There was a momentary pause. The first stroke of the hour bell rang out and echoed across London and then—silence. The wind suddenly ceased.

All was still. The water reflected light as clearly as a mirror. Jack gasped. The hands of the clock ticked back—one minute. Jack stepped into another time. *He heard a roar and the screams of many voices. His eyes widened as geysers of flame erupted from Westminster Bridge and Parliament, then spouted from left to right throughout the entire city! Tall buildings were engulfed in flame. Bodies lay strewn on the pavement of bridges.*

This was not the ancient London fire of 1666, nor was it the Blitz of World War II. Jack knew, somehow, he was seeing what was to come upon this city in the future, and he was experiencing it all in one moment.

The flashing lights of ambulances and fire trucks and police cars reflected on the pond-like water.

Terror!

"What. Is. Happening?" Jack heard his own voice speaking as though it was someone else.

And then, just as suddenly, he returned to the present. The boom of Big Ben continued. The freezing wind resumed. Fires vanished. The beggars shook their begging bowls and cried for mercy. All was as it had been.

Jack rubbed his eyes and shook his head. What was that? What caused his waking dream?

But it was not a dream. He had just witnessed something catastrophic that never happened; a vision of future terror in the great city he had come to love. He was there in real time and yet he had not moved from this place or time.

The last stroke of the bell ceased. Jack waited until the last note died away before releasing his grip on the cold metal railing. Then he walked on as if nothing happened.

◆◆◆

All was dark and quiet as Jack again entered the little house with the yellow door at number 4 Elnathan Mews.

It was too quiet, Jack thought, as he slid the bolt in place. Tossing keys on the table, he stood listening for a long moment in the dark foyer.

Someone in the neighborhood was playing old Bing Crosby Christmas carols. A party. Had Debbie been alive the party would have been here in number 4. Heaping platters of food and homemade Christmas cookies would have been laid out on the dining room table. The yellow door would have been open and students would have jammed the living room as the 1938 version of Dickens' *A Christmas Carol* played on the television.

That was last year. Debbie was a happy dream but her absence was the sad reality.

Tonight Jack's empty house was the only one on the block not decorated. Neighbors noticed his loneliness and had pity. Cards and invitations slipped through the mail slot were in a heap, unopened on the table.

Jack padded into the kitchen, switched on the light, and turned on the red electric kettle. Water rumbled to a boil and he made himself a cup of tea. He wished he had a cookie.

He looked away from the dark nursery as he passed it on the stair landing. The memory of Debbie painting pastel walls in the sunlight and hanging Winnie the Pooh wallpaper was all too fresh in his mind. Such hope was there, within reach. What might this Christmas have been? If only.

Nothing ever worked out the way it was supposed to. Across the road Bing Crosby sang "White Christmas." Jack drew the curtains and switched on Sky News to drown out the sound of other people's joy.

A grim-faced journalist, standing beside an ambulance, reported yet another Muslim terrorist in a stolen lorry had barreled through a Christmas market in Belgium, mowing down dozens of innocents. A homegrown radical this time, not a refugee.

Jack could hardly breathe. So much sorrow. Too much. Too close to home. Switching the channel he found the old black-and-white version of *A Christmas Carol* and sat down to watch as the ghost of Marley warned Scrooge of what was to come. Three terrible Christmas spirits; past regret, present longing, and future dread.

It seemed a mirror of his own heart. He regretted the past; that one instant which might have changed everything. He longed for a present that could not exist. He dreaded his future alone.

Could anything be changed, he wondered? Were happy endings possible in such a world?

He drifted off to sleep, longing for the Spirit of Christmas Past to carry him back where he was once happy.

Chapter Five

Heading to work on the first day after the Christmas break, Jack changed trains at Baker Street station before arriving at the Liverpool Street Underground platform. From there it was just a three-minute walk to his office—time he set aside each day to resolve all other thoughts and focus on business.

The offices of the European Committee on Mid-East Policy were on the east side of the City of London at 30 St. Mary Axe—the building commonly referred to as "the Gherkin." Completed in 2004, its bulging, then tapering cylindrical shape was supposed to suggest a spaceship but looked more like an upright pickle.

The floor above the ECMP housed the London headquarters of two U.S.-based law firms. The floor below contained a local cable television studio, and Levantine, an international shipping firm tying the UK to Jordan, Qatar, and Uganda.

Today he let the elevator bypass his usual stop to go directly to the thirty-eighth floor. When out-of-country members assembled for a general session, the ECMP often used one of the private dining rooms on that higher floor for a breakfast gathering. After that meeting concluded they would adjourn to conduct smaller working meetings in their own conference rooms below.

When Jack arrived the room was already bulging with participants. Each representative had an entourage of assistants and secretaries and sometimes translators. It was a way for the members to pad their payrolls since meetings were always conducted in English and all these diplomats and businessmen spoke it anyway.

Jack noted the members from Germany, France, Belgium, Spain, Italy, and the Czech Republic. The participants sipped coffee and munched croissants in a group most notable because they stood apart from, but kept looking at, the delegate from Denmark, Anders Ibsen.

Ibsen belonged to the conservative end of the Danish political spectrum. He was opposed to open borders for refugees from the Middle East, citing Sweden's massive increase in assault crimes. The other nations represented at the ECMP admired Sweden's reputation as the most welcoming country in Europe—or perhaps, the world. Therefore Ibsen was something of an outcast, and a contentious outcast at that. Jack wondered if his ECMP appointment was a reward for the man, or merely a means to keep him out of Denmark as much as possible.

Today's gathering was not about the Syrian refugee crisis, or about the Kurdish desire for a homeland. It was not about the Shia/Sunni feud pitting Iran and its proxies against Saudi Arabia and the Gulf states, or about the beheading of Christians in Egypt.

Today's urgent discussion was about the status of Jerusalem.

This year's outgoing chairman—the office rotated among the member states—was Signore Alphonso D'Angelo of Italy. He gaveled the meeting to order and the representatives assembled around four sides of an open square.

Jack, as an employee and consultant to the panel, sat behind his boss, executive director of ECMP, Lord Terence Halvorsham.

"Before we take up our main purpose for today," began D'Angelo, "It has come to our attention the Israelis are expanding their settlements in the area of Huwara, south of Nablus in the West Bank. This has already resulted in rock-throwing incidents and will certainly escalate violence if not stopped. The first order of business should be to deliver a strongly worded protest to the prime minister."

There being no objection, the matter was referred to the executive office to draft a letter for Halvorsham's approval and then for its immediate dispatch to Jerusalem.

The next topic of discussion was about the status of Jerusalem. None of the nations represented at ECMP acknowledged Jerusalem as the capital of Israel, though the Israelis claimed it as such. "There is rumbling again in the United States that America will recognize Jerusalem and move their embassy from Tel Aviv."

"Ridiculous," muttered Otto Gernich, member from Germany. "Such a move would undermine any credibility the U.S. has to be an honest broker for peace."

"Will Dr. Garrison please give us the historical context?"

This was the question for which Jack was preparing. A secretary handed out printed copies of his remarks even before he started to speak.

"As you all know, the United Nations voted in 1947 to partition the British Mandate of Palestine into two states—one Jewish and the other Arab. The evacuation of British troops in May of 1948 and the declaration of Israel's statehood caused the outbreak of war with five Arab armies. The United States, under President Harry Truman, was the first nation to recognize the new state of Israel, followed by other members of the UN. The city of Jerusalem remained the frontline of the conflict, with Jordan retaining control of what is called the Old City, and Israel the western portion. In December 1949, the UN declared Jerusalem to be a 'corpus separatum,' a separate body, subject to special treatment from the rest of Israel, and under direct UN control."

"Something which neither Jordan nor Israel accepted," Halvorsham added.

Jack nodded. "Despite early insistence by the Jewish state that Jerusalem belonged to Israel, the division of the city remained thus until 1967. During what's called The Six Day War, Israeli forces captured the Old City. Since consolidating their hold on Jerusalem the Israelis moved ever closer to declaring it the capital, first in 1950, and then again in 1980, passing a law in the Knesset designating it that way."

"A law branded by the UN as illegal," Halvorsham noted.

"And so it is," said Gernich loudly. "Despite the actions of the dangerously foolish American president, Jerusalem was meant to be an international city. The UN should again name it as such and send the blue helmets there to enforce it!"

A babble of voices responded, most in agreement.

Halvorsham cleared his throat and gestured for quiet. "Please continue, Dr. Garrison."

"Since the Palestinians also demand Jerusalem as their capital it is easy to see how the debate contributes to conflict. Presidents Clinton, Bush, and Obama have all entertained the idea of moving the embassy, but all have backed away from actually doing so, citing security concerns. Now that the United States and a handful of misguided nations formally recognize Jerusalem as Israel's capital—and some may move their embassies there—there will be yet another outburst of violence, even a renewed Intifada uprising."

"Thank you, doctor," offered Halvorsham.

Jack sat down.

"Nor is the rumored relocation of the U.S. embassy the only concern," Halvorsham added. "Periodically it is reported certain Jewish factions intend to rebuild a Jewish Temple on the so-called Temple Mount."

"Nonsense," Gernich burst out. "The Muslim Dome of the Rock, the Al-Aqsa Mosque, the Muslim religious authorities who have controlled that space for hundreds of years—it is a Muslim holy space."

"And continues to be so with the permission of the Israelis," the Danish representative Ibsen interrupted. "Since it is they who captured the mount in '67, and since they have actual control over the space, and anyway since they have a prior claim."

Gernich looked daggers at Ibsen and Signore D'Angelo gaveled for silence. "Gentleman, please! It is difficult to see how we can offer concrete suggestions to promote peace if we cannot achieve civility in our own meetings!"

There was little else to be said, but that didn't mean an end to the wrangling. A near unanimous voice vote declared firm opposition to both the moving of the Jewish capital, and to the Jews even touching any part of the Muslim Haram esh Sharif—the Noble Sanctuary—and expressing support for making Jerusalem an international city. A voice vote conveyed the sense of the gathering—in the midst of which only Anders Ibsen's loudly ringing "No!" recorded disagreement.

Like any well-intentioned and poorly functioning congress, the rest of the day was taken up trying to come to consensus on how to properly express in writing what they already approved.

Only one concrete step was concluded that morning: Dr. Jack Garrison was to fly to Israel to investigate settlement activity and explore the rumors about any scheme to build a Jewish temple on Palestinian Muslim property. He would then report back to the Committee.

As the morning session broke up Lord Halvorsham once again got their attention. "Let me remind the delegates this afternoon we will gather at London's famous Guildhall for our annual photo."

Jack returned to his own office to check e-mail and phone messages. When he entered the chamber, his eye fell on the hiking staff he hadn't used in over a year. In the corner formed by a low, metal credenza and a tall, black metal bookshelf stood a walnut pole topped by ten inches of fallow deer antler. On holiday in the Cotswalds Debbie noticed how much Jack admired the walking stick and secretly went back and bought it from the craftsman.

After that trip, Jack used it every time he and Deb went on a hiking excursion: up in the Highlands, alongside the Avon in Stratford, beside the white cliffs of Dover. The staff came to represent all their romantic adventures together—which is why Jack hadn't touched it since Debbie left. This day, as with every time he saw it, Jack felt the customary stab of grief and guilt, then buried both emotions deep under the press of work.

Chapter Six

Morning light illuminated Huwara, the West Bank town near Nablus. On the main road between Nablus and Ramallah, the town of some 6,000 lay near the base of Mount Gerizim, the Hill of Blessing. Twenty-seven-year-old Elizabeth "Bette" Deekmann directed her Toyota Corolla into the parking area of the Sonol petrol station and convenience store at the crossroads of Highway 60 and the road leading west toward Tel Aviv.

Since 2008 the Jewish settlement where her friend Aly lived with her husband and two young sons had been on the list to be evacuated and handed over to the Palestinian Authority, but new homes were recently built there. Aly and Zach had just moved in and the house needed "Everything!" Aly gushed. "Help me!" she pleaded with Bette.

Today, while Aly's husband babysat the kids, Bette was taking her friend on a shopping expedition to the Azrieli Complex shopping center on the coast. "Why are we stopping here?" Aly complained.

"It's still too early!" Bette returned. "I need more coffee. Remember: it was your idea to leave this early."

"Before the kids wake up," Aly reminded Bette. "Before Zach calls, desperate for help. I don't get many chances to get away and I mean to make the most of this one."

At the curb beside the station was another Corolla, the identical year as Bette's, except this one was torched—windows smashed and burned so its paint color was no longer distinguishable. It sat on its rims and what remained of melted tires. The aroma of destruction still hung heavy over the area.

Leaving Aly in the car, talking on her cell phone to another friend who was going to meet them in Tel Aviv, Bette entered the Quick Stop market and filled a Styrofoam cup from a thermos of coffee. The same sign declaring a price of eight shekels per small cup or ten for a large also promised the coffee was "Freshly Brewed on the Hour!"

Joining the back of a three-person line waiting for the lone attendant, Bette sipped the java and made a face. *Well, they didn't say* which *hour,* she thought.

The man at the front of the queue was not buying anything. Young, bearded, with curly peyot sidelocks framing his face below his kippah and wire-rimmed spectacles, he shook a collection canister at the counterman. "Spare some change for Yad Eliezer?" he asked, naming a Jewish anti-hunger charity.

Just ahead of Bette was a short, plump woman in a faded rose-colored headscarf holding a gallon of milk and impatiently tapping her foot.

Bette noted all the details without really intending to do so, but old habits die hard. She turned her face away from the line of shoppers.

In the snack aisle a few paces away, beside candy bars and other treats, something wasn't right. Another young man, scruffy beard and wearing no hat but with a long coat over khaki shirt and trousers, idly lifted a bag of chips then replaced it without looking at it. Next his fingers wandered over a pack of cookies with the same detached disinterest.

Getting ready to steal something, Bette thought, *Or...*

From beneath his coat the Palestinian produced a butcher knife. With a cry of strangled rage he leapt toward the charity collector, sweeping the blade over his head and then downward into the Jewish man's shoulder.

As the blow landed a number of other things happened.

"Look out!" Bette yelled. Bette's left hand swept the woman customer aside, knocking her to the floor and bursting the milk carton. At the same moment Bette threw the scalding coffee in the attacker's face, she drew an ESP collapsible baton from her pocket and flicked it open.

As the terrorist snarled and mopped drops of coffee from his eyes, he turned toward Bette and lunged at her.

The first flick of her baton snapped smartly against the attacker's wrist and deflected his aim. Her backhand swipe broke his nose. The next downward swing knocked the knife free from his grip and it clattered to the ground. She followed this move by lowering her shoulder and crashing against the terrorist so both of them smashed into the checkout counter.

A moment later he was on the ground. Her baton was across his throat and her knee in his back. "Hold still," she ordered. "Don't give me a reason to break your neck." To the clerk she commanded sharply, "Call security. Do it!"

Captain Elizabeth Deekmann, Golani Brigade veteran and now a member of the Yamam anti-terror task force, addressed herself to the charity collector. "Are you all right?"

The young man fingered the slash in his jacket over his left shoulder. "I—I think so," he replied in a shaky voice. The tips of his fingers showed blood.

"Take your coat off," Bette instructed. "This nice lady," she said to the cowering matron, "will get the first aid kit from behind the counter and help you."

Five minutes later Israeli security took charge of the scene. Five minutes after that, Bette had given her statement and she and Aly were again on their way toward Tel Aviv. "I'm never stopping there again," Bette observed. "They burn their coffee."

♦♦♦

"Welcome, gentlemen, welcome," intoned the white-haired docent in his navy blazer and necktie bearing the imprint of London's coat-of-arms. "Welcome to 'istoric Guild'all." Greeting the ECMP members at a private entrance he whisked them into the medieval great hall which lent its name to the entire building.

Moving smoothly into his well-rehearsed talk, the guide allowed the European delegates to prowl the premises while he spoke: "Back hin the

Roman era there was an amphitheater 'ere and sommut later the Saxons built the first Guild'all on this very spot. The building hin which we are standin' was begun hin 1411 during the reign of 'Enry the Fourth."

Jack, who visited the site many years before with Debbie, tuned out much of the talk and pondered what the day's meeting meant to him on a personal level. He was indeed about to be dispatched to Jerusalem to investigate claims about the reconstruction of the Jewish temple. The idea of this trip was privately discussed between Lord Halvorsham and himself in preparation for this gathering, but nothing was officially concluded until today—and no one should have leaked their conversation.

So how did Lev speak of the upcoming journey with such confidence and authority?

"We are hin," the guide continued, "the only non-ecclesiastical stone buildin' survivin' from that era to this. It 'as been the location of many notorious trials, includin' Lady Jane Grey, the Nine Days' Queen, and the Gunpowder Plot conspirators after they tried to blow hup Parliament in 1605."

Jack couldn't help it. Though he tried to ignore the patter, the outburst of history swept him back to a longing for Debbie again. How the two of them loved learning about the lives of the people in the past. Before their marriage, while at a formal dance with him and Debbie dressed to the nines, they spent the entire evening leaning across a table toward each other, sharing insights about the life and wives of Henry VIII and his impact on the world. When Jack and Debbie at last emerged from the 1500s to find two hours gone, they danced one dance together. They left for their homes perfectly content with the evening and convinced they were perfect for each other.

"We are very fortunate that the Guild 'all escaped with only some damage from the Great Fire of 1666—but it was severely 'urt by German bombs on the night of 29 December, 1940."

"Gentlemen, if you please." Lord Halvorsham interrupted the history lesson. "If you'll please gather here at this end of the hall for our photograph and then we will adjourn to a cocktail reception in the historic crypt."

The group jockeyed for position beneath a gallery overlooked by a pair of carved wooden effigies. The figures were dressed in a combination of Roman and Medieval armor and carried spears and shields.

"Who are they supposed to be?" inquired the German Otto Gernich.

Before Lord Halvorsham could reply, the docent lifted his chin and pronounced, "Right you are to hask. The one on the left is Gog and on the right Magog. Some says they represents a race of giants defeated when London was first founded. Wicker copies of them are carried through London on the day of the Lord Mayor's Show—guardian spirits of London, one might say."

"And others say," Anders Ibsen said loudly enough for everyone to hear, "they represent the forces of darkness which must be defeated in the last great battle between good and evil. A battle which will take place in Israel, I might add."

"Surely no one believes such a myth!" Gernich snorted. "No one sane. No one rational."

"They are mentioned in the Bible," Jack said, recalling a late night dorm-room conversation with Lev.

Ibsen eyed Jack curiously as if surprised to find an ally in this crowd.

Lord Halvorsham was also eyeing Jack. The historian hastily bowed to the German and offered, "But of course you're right. Very few take such an apocalyptic view of a couple old statues."

"It's not about the statues," Ibsen said forcefully, apparently feeling ganged up on. "It's about the enemy of all that's good."

"To whom do you think the prophecies refer?" inquired Signore D'Angelo.

"Forty years ago I was convinced it referred to Russia—which will still have a role to play. But more recently I think the reference includes the resurgent forces of Islamic jihad."

"Preposterous," retorted Gernich. "Positively Islamophobic."

Mutters of agreement swirled around the room.

"Gentlemen," Ibsen continued, "I intended to reserve this announcement until after tonight's dinner, but now I see it cannot wait. I am resigning from the committee effective immediately. I see no point in joining you in a photo. I wish you good success in the committee's work—but I am not hopeful." The Dane bowed his way out of the chamber, leaving a momentary silence behind.

"Good riddance," Gernich said. "He was always obstructionist and pro-Zionist. Probably secretly Jewish. In any case, as I said, no one believes such nonsense anymore."

Feeling a tug on his sleeve, Jack turned to find the diminutive French delegate, Yves Tornay, waiting to speak with him. Tornay said not one word all day that Jack recalled. "Monsieur Gernich is wrong," Tornay said. "I was there in President Jacques Chirac's office in 2003 when President George W. Bush called to speak about France supporting the invasion of Iraq. The U.S. president very clearly said—I heard him with these, my own ears—he said, 'Gog and Magog are at work in the Middle East. This confrontation is willed by God—to erase His people's enemies before a new age begins.'"

"There you have it," Otto Gernich applauded. "Just what I said: No sane, rational person believes such things any more. President Bush! Ha!"

◆◆◆

The headquarters of the Levantine Shipping Company, one floor below ECMP, were expensively furnished but starkly modern. Chrome and black leather chairs received no warmth from the pale birch paneling. The walls were hung with art of acrylic paint on burnished metal so the images resembled asteroid strikes.

Lord Halvorsham stood in front of the company's owner, Brahim Rahman. "The meeting went exactly as expected," Halvorsham reported to Rahman. "The Dane has resigned. He will give us no further trouble. The Committee will remain an impartial, unbiased voice, urging European governments to support Palestinian statehood while deploring illegal Jewish settlements."

"And Garrison?"

"He will soon be leaving for his 'fact finding' trip."

Rahman plucked at the pocket handkerchief in his Hugo Boss suit. "I meant, are you concerned at all about his attitude? It troubles me he has a close Jew friend. Why did we not know this before hiring Garrison?"

"Seixas? They aren't really close; haven't been for years. Besides, Seixas is not political. He's some sort of preacher."

Rahman regarded Halvorsham from under thick, dark eyebrows. "Did Garrison see Faisal following him?"

"As you suggested: only enough to make him *wonder* if he's being followed. Keep him off balance. Garrison's academic credentials are impeccable. When he returns, his report to the Committee will be exactly what we want it to be."

"Which is?" Rahman prodded.

"That Israeli settlement activity is a barrier to peace in the region. Any Israeli pretension to the Haram will cause a renewed intifada. That Israel is a fictional modern state deliberately harming the legitimate aspirations of the Palestinians."

"Nicely rehearsed," Rahman remarked drily. "This Seixas is also a Christian? Don't you find that a dangerous development? Christians and Jews must not be allowed to make common cause against my people. Christian Jew is not just an oxymoron. Such a mixed-breed cur is dangerous."

Halvorsham made a dismissive gesture. "Only extreme evangelical types equate the modern Jewish state to Biblical Israel. Mainstream Christians are just like secular Americans—except more anti-Jewish, perhaps. University students marching for Boycott, Divest, and Sanction against Israel are supported by Christian churches who are convinced the Israelis are a cruel occupying force, applying apartheid restrictions to Palestine. Garrison is a useful voice for us, especially since he is American."

"Keep an eye on him," Rahman ordered.

"Even while he's in Palestine?"

"Especially while he's in Palestine. It won't be difficult. We have cloned his cell phone, so we can listen in on his conversations and plans."

♦♦♦

Two days after the incident in Huwara, Bette stood at attention in front of the desk, hands clasped behind her back, eyes fixed at a point on the wall over her commanding officer's right shoulder. Commander

S.—his real surname was never used—said sternly, "You chose to use less than lethal force to neutralize the threat, even though mortal danger to civilians was imminent. Why?"

"Sir," Bette said. "I assessed the likely angle of attack and judged the use of my weapon created more hazard to the civilians than the approach I chose."

"How close?"

Bette's gaze flicked downward, then up to a neutral spot again. "There was a civilian immediately in front of me, sir, closer than I am to your desk, and the attacker's target, and the clerk, just in front of the woman. Since I had to clear my field of fire before discharging my weapon both male civilians would then have been in jeopardy."

"Show me your weapon," Commander S. demanded.

Bette produced a sidearm from beneath her sweater, dumped the magazine, ejected a round from the chamber, and passed it over.

"Glock 43," the officer observed.

"Yes, sir. Concealed carry. In keeping with my undercover role. If I may add, sir, our directive is to take terrorists alive for interrogation whenever possible. . ."

"Consistent with protecting civilian lives, yes," Commander S. agreed. He stared at her until she finally dropped her eyes again and met his stare. Then his formal demeanor parted with a crooked smile. "Official inquiry is over. Sit down, Bette. You did well."

Bette felt her shoulders drop a couple inches and she exhaled a long, silent breath. She took a seat in the stiff metal chair in front of her boss, the head of Yamam.

Yamam—short for Yehida Merkazit Meyuhedet—was an elite counter-terrorism division of the Israeli Border Police. Charged with hostage rescue operations and sometimes offensive action, Yamam consisted of only a couple hundred officers in all Israel. A framed copy of the Yamam crest rested on the corner of the commander's desk. It displayed a winged star and a strong tower surrounded by a laurel wreath. This central icon was flanked by the images of commandos fast-roping from a helicopter and a lone commando in full SWAT gear.

"Do you have any reason to think this was part of a coordinated attack or the opening of a new terror campaign?"

"Given the lack of preparation or any evident training by the perp, I think the answer is no. This was a lone wolf event."

"Is there any reason to think you were the actual target, or that your identity was compromised?"

"None, sir."

"Good. We're pleased with your progress, Bette. Adding female officers, particularly those who have undercover experience, was a big part of my goal when I took over this job."

Bette relaxed still further.

"In keeping with your success I have a new—temporary—assignment for you."

Bette was pleased. She volunteered for military service, was with the anti-guerilla unit of the famed Golani Brigade, then spent several years honing her special forces skills with Magav, the Israeli Border Police, before winning this coveted position. "May I know what it is?"

"Yes, since it begins soon. You will provide escort and liaison for a member of the European Committee for Mid-East Policy. American, actually: Dr. Jack Garrison."

Bette was incensed, and struggled not to show it. Escort and liaison? Bodyguard? This was not what all her training and experience was supposed to produce! "Am I—is this disciplinary?"

"Have I ever been that secretive about discipline?" Commander S. demanded. "No, Bette, not at all. Put that idea out of your head. You were specially chosen for this duty before the terror incident."

"But—why? Surely some member of the regular protective detail would. . ."

"If I am not hard to read about discipline, neither do I expect to be questioned. Look, Bette: I lobbied hard for our unit to get this assignment. This man—and the Committee behind him—want to explore the hardest questions facing Israel's future. He is not a tourist. He needs to go places and ask important questions that may place him in danger. His guide needs to be able to get him successfully in and out of those locations. We need someone who also can analyze what he sees and hears so we can assess its probable impact on the state. He must be provided with the best officer we have. Did you want to suggest I locate someone else?"

Now Bette was smiling. "Not at all, sir. Thank you."

Chapter Seven

Unlike flying to and from the states, Jack was not at all groggy when the El Al Boeing 777 arrived at Tel Aviv's Ben Gurion airport and taxied to Terminal 3. The flight took less than five hours to complete, in a comfortable business class seat no less. Despite the fact local time was 10:15 p.m., it was two hours earlier back in London; not a late night arrival at all.

Before any of the rest of the 275 passengers were allowed to deplane, an attractive, petite, dark-haired, dark-eyed Israeli appeared beside seat 14B and called him by name. "Dr. Garrison? Or do you prefer Professor?"

"Dr. Garrison. And you are?"

"Elizabeth Deekmann, Bette, if you like, here to take you to your hotel."

"Why the special treatment?" Jack asked, gesturing toward the other passengers.

"As you are the representative of the ECMP the government of Israel wants to extend you every courtesy. You are staying at the King David Hotel, is that right?"

"Correct."

Jack's luggage was already being loaded into the Mercedes E-class limo when Bette opened the rear door for Jack to seat himself. To his surprise there was already someone behind the wheel and Bette seated herself next to Jack in the rear compartment.

"Excuse me one moment," she said, then addressed the driver in Hebrew. Jack recognized his own name and the destination as the King David Hotel, but nothing else. The chauffeur nodded and they sped off.

"My apologies," Jack said. "When you said you were taking me to my hotel I thought you were the limo driver sent to collect me."

What was the motive behind that fleeting, quirky smile? Jack wondered.

"No," Bette corrected. "Perhaps you should think of me as your guide to see that your trip goes smoothly. This is Ghassan, our driver, at least for the evening."

"Arab?" Jack asked, commenting on the driver's name.

"Druze," Bette explained. "Ghassan Arslan."

Looking up at the sound of his name, Ghassan glanced at the mirror and gave a quick wave of his hand.

"It will take us about," Bette studied her wristwatch, "about forty minutes to reach your hotel at this time of day. Do you want to talk about your plans for tomorrow? I did not receive an itinerary."

"No, and you weren't supposed to," Jack returned. "We didn't announce my destinations in advance because I didn't want anyone to arrange what I'd see."

Bette frowned. "You think the Israeli government would censor your visit—in advance of your arrival?"

Put that way Jack's statement sounded both suspicious and pompous. "Sorry. I didn't mean that to be offensive. The truth is I don't know where I need to go and what I need to see until I start to go and see. Does that make sense?"

"In Israel," Bette agreed, "It makes perfect sense."

"By the way," Jack added. "Ghassan is military, yes?"

Bette nodded.

"But what about you?"

"I'm with the police," she said, "but I'm not a regular serving officer."

Jack smiled. "I thought it'd be something like that. So—tomorrow. Will you be joining me again?"

"Ghassan and I will both be with you tomorrow," Bette returned. "What time did you wish?

"I'm an early riser. Shall we say eight o'clock?"

"Eight it is," Bette confirmed.

♦♦♦

Buried in coach, twelve rows behind Dr. Jack Garrison, Faisal Husseini could only watch with frustration as his quarry was met and escorted from the El Al flight. The anger cooled quickly. That woman was some kind of Israeli government employee, which meant an official car would be picking up Dr. Garrison at the airport. It didn't really matter. Faisal knew about the reservation at the King David Hotel.

All travel arrangements for ECMP members and staff were vetted by Levantine Shipping.

♦♦♦

Jack's room in the King David hotel was plush, as befitted a five-star establishment, but not lavish. The staff was effusive in its welcome, but the place had an air of faded glory. If not luxurious the King David was still awash in history. Built of pink limestone in 1931, the inn witnessed all the struggles over Jerusalem ever since. In 1946, before there was a modern state of Israel, the hotel was the headquarters of the British Mandatory authorities—and the recipient of a bombing that killed ninety-one people.

Pulling back the curtain, Jack stared east across a dark swath of central Jerusalem at the brightly-lit Temple Mount and the golden gleam of the Dome of the Rock. *Right, there it is*, he thought. *The focus of my visit and arguably the focus of strife in this part of the world. If there were no Israel how much less trouble would there be in the world?*

Jack studied the object of his inquiry. It was no more than a couple miles away, if that. Even nearer was the blocky outline of the Tower of David that marked the western edge of Old City Jerusalem—straight down the hill and on a line northeast from Jack's window.

Calling up a map on his smart phone Jack asked it to indicate a walking path between the two Davids. There it was: "Fifteen minutes," it said.

Why not? Jack thought. *I made such a point of being unpredictable; of choosing my own path. I think I'll start now.*

After the flight and the limo ride it felt good for Jack to stretch his legs. Right on Paul Emile Botta street, down the slope, then left on Eliyahu Shama. "Use caution," the map advised.

Here in the depths of this valley it was dark and deserted. This was a park or garden in the center of Jerusalem. Some parking areas were illuminated with the orange glow of street lamps, but great shadowed spaces existed between them.

With a swirl of east wind one of the shadows moved. Jack felt the hair on the back of his neck prickle and he hesitated before taking another step. He had almost reached the bottom of a set of stairs at the lowest point of his journey. The form of his goal was just ahead. For a moment Jack relived the sense of being followed toward Clifton Gardens, then reminded himself how absurdly that fear resolved itself. He left his hotel room seven minutes before. There was his destination, seven minutes ahead. *No threat,* he decided. *Just palm fronds stirred by the breeze.* He continued forward.

"Jack Garrison." A figure stepped from concealment at the base of a palm tree. The man who addressed Jack was not asking a question. He knew Jack's identity before he spoke.

"Yes, and who are you? Did that policewoman send you?"

The figure did not answer the question. "You may call me Eliyahu."

"Eliyahu Shama? Like the name of the street? What do you want?"

"I have been sent to instruct you."

"Instruct me? In what? By whom?"

"I have installed my king in Zion, says the Lord; on my holy mountain."

"What's that supposed to mean? You're quoting Scripture to me? Listen: I don't buy it. I won't believe any more in your so-called Lord until I'm convinced of three things: the Bible really does contain accurate, real prophecies, Israel is still somehow important in some cosmic sense—not just 2,000 years ago but now, today. And three: all those speeches by long dead men are actually relevant to today—to tomorrow, in fact."

Where had that outburst come from? Angry. Jack felt angry. He was irritated at the absurdity of arguing with this—this—theatrical phantom. He was annoyed with himself for getting angry over—nonsense.

"Well?" he demanded, but Eliyahu made no reply except to say, "On the Mountain of the Lord it shall be provided."

"Who are you?" Jack said again.

He heard steps approaching him from behind and whirled around.

"Professor?" It was Ghassan, the driver.

"Did you arrange this high school drama production?"

"Who were you speaking with?" Ghassan inquired.

"Don't give me that!" Turning with his index finger outstretched, Jack gestured toward an empty circle of lamp glow. "Where'd he go?"

"Who?"

"Don't play games with me! Why'd you follow me?"

"I saw you leave the lobby. It's my job to keep you safe. But if you insist on walking about in the middle of the night you should warn me first."

"And you didn't...hey! You speak English! In the car you and Ms. Deekmann spoke in Hebrew."

"Yes, and I speak three other languages as well and I'm learning Mandarin. So?"

Thoroughly disgruntled, Jack was in no mood to continue toward the Old City accompanied by this—this lying shadow. "We'll see about this—tomorrow," he said. Passing Ghassan without another word Jack retraced his steps to the King David Hotel and his room and shortly fell into a fitful sleep.

♦♦♦

It was a place of unutterable beauty. The high mountain meadow exhibited thick grass and lush moss. It was ringed with tall, swaying pines, and majestic redwoods whispering to each other in the silken breeze. Though the air was bracing, the elevation was not so great as to eliminate spring and rebirth. Jack scented the mingled aromas of jasmine blooms and orange blossoms.

In the next moment the direction of the wind switched, bringing the warmth of summer and the scents of ripening strawberries. New mown hay accompanied the suggestion of figs, plums, apricots, and peaches.

"What an odd place," Jack said aloud. "Summer and spring, new life and harvest are all mixed up here. And yet—and yet it feels exactly right. Like home."

"Everyone who sees this place mentions something like that," Eli-yahu said, standing beside Jack's elbow.

Jack had not seen him there, but he was neither surprised nor alarmed.

Seen in soft morning light Eliyahu was an impressive figure. Slightly taller than Jack, though thinner; older, but not elderly. His beard and hair were streaked with silver. He leaned on a wooden staff planted in the soft earth beside leather-sandaled feet. He wore a simple brown robe, and over his sturdy shoulders was a sky-blue mantle exactly matching his cheerful eyes.

"Where are we?" Jack asked.

"Gan Eden," Eliyahu explained.

"The Garden of Eden?" Jack returned. "So this is a dream?"

"No," Eliyahu corrected. "You are dreaming—but this is real. Walk with me."

Eliyahu led the way beside a crisply flowing stream across the meadow to a circular clearing where shorter grass surrounded a pool of crystalline water. Dotted around the basin were a dozen boulders. Each large enough to sit on, they were not granite or limestone or even quartz. One was banded with browns and tan—agate, perhaps? Another was translucent green, shot through with golden sparks. Another Jack rec-ognized as turquoise, but Jack had never seen a chunk this big before. Lapus lazuli was succeeded by a fiery opal.

Eliyahu waved Jack toward a seat on a deep purple crystal that could only be amethyst, while he rested on a stone of dark red with black veins. "So—Gan Eden," he said again. "The place to which all long to return even though they don't know it; a cry just below the surface of conscious thought. When you are quiet enough you can hear its sound. It is a song that bubbles forth from our inner spirit, calling us home. Though few know this truth, this 'home' for which we long is the same for everyone. So here we are, on the holy mountain of God."

"Wait," Jack urged. "This garden is also a mountain?"

Eliyahu nodded. "Think of what you know of Gan Eden: four rivers flow from it, yes?"

Jack remembered. "The river that watered the garden split to become the headwaters of four rivers...."

"Just so," Eliyahu agreed. "The spring at your feet is one of them, but this pool is the source of all four. So: we are on a summit and all four rivers flow down from here."

"It is so beautiful and peaceful here," Jack said. "Why not stay here forever?"

"Why not, indeed," Eliyahu agreed. "Shall I show you the answer?"

Jack nodded.

The ring of trees surrounding the pool and pasture began to spin until the outline blurred. Against the swirling colors a new vision appeared: a man and a woman and a third figure clothed in brightness, walking in absolute harmony beside the basin.

Next the woman appeared, speaking with another being; handsome, beguiling in face and form, offering her something—the woman and man furtively sharing a meal, then hiding from the being of light, whose calls to them resonated with sorrow, not anger.

The scene changed. At the sole entry to the encircling forest appeared a winged creature with a flaming sword. The man and woman, clothed in animal skins, stumbled despondently down a slope, casting longing glances over their shoulders while the seraphim sternly blocked them from turning back.

Beside them—not with them, but paralleling their every pace, slithered a serpent, loathsome and fascinating by turns.

With each succeeding step the couple took, green grass withered and in its place arose brambles and thorn bushes. Apple tree leaves yellowed and fluttered downward, leaving barren branches.

Gemlike boulders resembling the ones on which Jack and Eliyahu sat lined the trail. As the couple passed each glistening jewel turned inward like flowers closing for a long night. Now the visible exteriors were dull, grays and browns, rough, and impenetrable to the eye.

Jack cried. Tears of loss and grief rolled down his cheeks, joining the rivulet at his feet. "Never to return?" Jack said. "Is there no way back?"

"Only one," Eliyahu said firmly as the whirling panorama ceased. "The single entry, now blocked by the warrior with the blazing blade, can only be passed by the One found worthy to return. Only He can reopen the gate of Paradise."

Jack felt himself stirring. His cheek was indeed moist, but the meadow and the trees faded into a hotel room's walls.

Yet Eliyahu continued to speak. "Remember," he said in a fading whisper. "Mountains. On the mountain of the Lord, it will be provided."

◆◆◆

Awake and unable to stay alone with his thoughts another moment, Jack dressed and went down to the Presidents' Hall buffet. He took a table for one, then toyed with a plate of scrambled eggs pushed around the plate by a croissant. When neither sparked any interest, he settled for a cup of fruit.

It was only 7:30 when Bette crossed through the line waiting for omelets and appeared beside Jack's table. "You're early," he said, glancing up. "How'd you know I was here? Your little spy tell you?"

"No spy needed. When you didn't answer your room phone I cleverly deduced you might be at breakfast. Now; shall I sit down or would you prefer I wait out in the car?"

Realizing he was being churlish—probably a result of the weird Jerusalem-inspired dream—Jack ducked his head and gestured toward the chair across from him. "Please," he said. "Coffee?"

A white-jacketed waiter appeared with a silver coffee pot and a fresh cup almost before Bette said, "Yes, thanks."

"Anyway, if I'm grumpy," Jack continued, "it's your fault—or your boss's anyway. What was that stunt about last night?"

Stirring the cream in her coffee Bette said, "You know I was going to ask you the same thing?"

"What are you talking about?"

"Going out in the middle of the night and traipsing across Jerusalem without telling anyone. And then refusing to tell Ghassan who you were speaking with."

Jack dabbed a croissant crumb from his lip. "Look, I don't know why you're playing this game. Why have someone meet me and call me by name and then refuse to tell me why?"

Leaning back in her chair Bette narrowed her eyes. "I assure you, the only one around the hotel was Ghassan, and I admit he followed you to make sure you were safe. We sent no one else. Who else knows you're here?"

Jack folded his arms across his chest. "How should I know? The only person I know in Israel is Lev Seixas. He knew I was coming, but not when."

"And it was not he you met last night?"

"No! This person was, well, old seeming."

"Describe him to me."

Jack struggled to separate the imaginary figure in his dream from the real man in the valley. "Well, he was—about my height—medium build...." Jack stopped, consternation evident in his expression.

"Bearded?"

"I don't recall."

"Dressed modern or traditional? Hat or coat?"

"I didn't get a good look."

"Arab? Jewish? Western?"

Putting his hand down on the table more forcefully than he intended, Jack jostled his coffee cup. The attendant waiter mopped the drips, spread a napkin over the stain on the table cloth, bowed respectfully, and retired.

"I didn't really get a close look," Jack insisted.

"You say he called you by name? What did he want?"

"I—look, I don't know that either." Jack did not know what this was all about but he intended to learn more for himself before he answered any more questions.

Bette rested her elbows on the table and put her chin atop her folded hands. "Are you feeling alright this morning?"

"Confused and tired but otherwise okay, yes. Why?"

"The last thing I want to do is offend you," Bette said, "but have you ever heard of the Jerusalem Syndrome?"

"Like a messiah complex?"

"Not exactly," Bette corrected. "About 100 tourists each year suffer—a kind of religious mania. A fervent desire sparked by arriving in Jerusalem that seems to—cause them to need to warn the world of impending doom, for instance."

"You think I was hallucinating?" Jack retorted, perilously close to spilling more coffee.

"No," Bette replied cautiously. "But—this city does have a profound effect, especially on first time visitors. Occurrences like you describe have happened to others."

"Terrific! Not only am I being followed but you think I'm crazy. Is that a way to discredit me and my report? Tell people I'm nuts?"

Bette seemed to decide argument was useless. Quietly she said, "You still haven't told me where you wish to go today."

"I only just decided," Jack said firmly. "I want to speak with Lev Seixas. I want to do that first."

Chapter Eight

The Etz Café on Yanai Street was a couple hundred yards from Jaffa Gate and due west of the Church of the Holy Sepulchre, just across the wall around Old City Jerusalem.

Lev and Jack sat at an outside table in bright, though chilly, sunlight.

"Glad you were able to meet me so soon," Jack said.

"Glad you saved my phone number," Lev returned. "After we met at the Savoy, I didn't know if you'd call or not. Anyway, glad this worked out. Yesterday I was in Bethlehem and tomorrow I'm heading up to Nazareth."

Though Bette and Ghassan walked with Jack from the hotel, he wanted to speak with Lev alone. After introductions they withdrew, though Jack suspected they had not gone far. In fact, he thought he spotted the Druze a block away, pretending to be absorbed in a newspaper.

"I could have come to your hotel," Lev chided.

"This is better," Jack returned. "Listen: there are things going on here I don't understand and—well, it's better this way. I need to ask some questions of someone I trust."

Lev nodded. "I'm honored, Jack. Okay. Just so I don't have to pretend about what I know and don't know, tell me officially why you're here."

Sipping a glass of freshly squeezed orange juice, Jack explained. "The ECMP wants me to investigate certain conditions here which we—the Committee—believe will damage any prospects for peace: Settlements.

Any country recognizing Jerusalem as the capital of Israel and the last—" lowering his voice to a hoarse whisper, Jack added, "rebuilding the Jewish temple."

Lev ducked his head and smiled. "You don't need to be so furtive," he said. "Building the Third Temple has been discussed around here—and around the world—for almost 2,000 years."

Jack frowned. "I'm serious! Can you imagine the chaos that would follow?"

He was surprised to hear Lev agree. "Yes, I can, but that doesn't mean it shouldn't happen—or won't happen." Lev laid his hand on Jack's arm. "Be easy. I know you don't want to hear me preach. Anyway, to show up looking for me on the morning of your first day in Israel—there must be more to it than something you could research online by Googling the Temple Mount Faithful."

Pressing his palms together and holding his fingers across his lips, Jack wondered once more how much to reveal. How crazy was this going to sound? But this was Lev, after all. Jack plunged ahead. "I had a—well—an encounter last night and I need some explanations. Just let me get this out before you ask any questions, okay?"

He had already decided not to mention the dream of Eden. Mixed with meeting the man in the valley, it would sound *too* crazy.

Lev flicked his fingers to say, "Get on with it, then."

Jack retold the story of his interrupted journey toward David's Tower without pausing or even stopping for another sip of juice. "Maybe I dreamed it," he concluded. "But that can't be right. My Druze bodyguard—or whatever he is—asked me who I was talking to, so he heard it too."

"And this man said his name was Eliyahu?"

"Yeah, just like the street I came down before meeting him: Eliyahu Shama."

"How's your Hebrew, Jack?" Lev inquired.

"El is a word for God, right?"

Lev nodded. "Eliyahu: 'The Lord is my God.' Shama: 'He hears' or 'He has heard.' So: 'My Lord is the God Who has Heard,' or, 'My Lord is the God Who Hears.'"

"He didn't agree to the Shama part," Jack objected. "I just suggested that."

"In Israel," Lev corrected, "you learn to think like this; 'Everything means something.'"

"And what this Eliyahu character said? He's here to instruct me? On the mountain of the Lord, it—something—will be provided? What about that?" After what his friend just remarked, Jack was surprised at the startled look on Lev's face when he mentioned the Scripture quote.

"I think—I think we need to take a walk," Lev said. "Are you up for it?"

"Sure," Jack agreed. "Just one detail first. Do you think I'm crazy? Jerusalem Syndrome?"

Tossing a trio of ten shekel coins on the table to pay the tab, Lev grinned more broadly than before. "Answer me this: Do you have a desire to turn bed sheets into a toga? Do you feel convicted to stand on a corner and preach? Have you been sent with a message to save the world?"

"Not yet, no."

"So, you're safe for the moment." Then more seriously Lev added, "But Jerusalem is a special place in the world, Jack. Don't be surprised if it changes you."

"That's the second time I've heard that this morning," Jack admitted. "Okay, I'm still sane—for the moment. Where're we going?"

"Follow me."

At Lev's suggestion, Jack invited Bette and Ghassan to join them. "That way you won't have to wonder if they suspect us of plotting something," Lev said to Jack with a laugh. "Or wonder if they're following you."

Bette agreed, but Ghassan said he would move the car to a closer spot for when they were ready to change locations again. "So where are you headed?"

"No surprise there," Lev returned. "Where all first time pilgrims should go on their first day here: the Western Wall."

Jack was enough of a historian and student of the Middle East to know how compact the Old City of Jerusalem was, but even so, he was surprised at how quickly centuries of history could be traversed. Past the Tourist Information Center and shops thronged with haggling visitors, their route lay straight along David Street, before veering south toward Ha-Kotel ha-Ma'aravi, the Western Wall. They walked in silence for ten minutes, then arrived at the back of the plaza. It is expansive enough to handle 400,000 worshippers at once. Jack estimated the number before them at a couple thousand, dwarfed by the towering courses of limestone blocks.

Reaching into his jacket pocket Lev withdrew a plain blue kippah, twin to the cap he already wore on his own head, and handed it to Jack who unfolded it and put it on.

"Jack," Lev said, "I don't mean to insult your training and your résumé by sounding like a tour guide, but let me begin like one and then unspool it from there."

"Fair enough," Jack agreed.

"What you see there is just the visible portion of the retaining wall built by King Herod when he expanded the Temple previously rebuilt in the days of Ezra and Nehemiah. The structure continues beneath the base of the wall we can see and extends behind those structures," he said, sweeping his arm from pavement to sky and from south to north. "Some people say Jews come here to pray because it's the holiest site in Judaism. That's not exactly correct. The most sacred spot is the location of the Holy of Holies where the Ark of the Covenant rested atop the Temple Mount—up there." Once again, Lev indicated the place where both the First and Second Temples once stood. "The Temple where Yeshua ha'Mashiach worshipped and taught was up there. Since Jews may not worship on the Mount—it belongs to the Muslim Waqf, the religious authorities—Jews come here to pray instead."

Jack indicated this was history with which he was already familiar. "But why contend for a piece of earth?" he said with a challenge in his tone. "If a rebuilt temple is so important to Jewish worship, why not find an uncontested spot, consecrate the ground, and build away?"

"And there you have summed up the conundrum that is Jerusalem," Lev returned. "Another spot cannot be chosen, cannot be consecrated, cannot be used for worship, because this one was chosen by HaShem—the Almighty Himself—right up there."

"That's an argument that only works if you believe in religious myths," Jack said with a shrug.

"Yes, but I'm not the one who brought it up to you first," Lev argued. "You know what that Eliyahu character said to you: 'On the mountain of the Lord it will be provided?' It's from the book of Genesis, chapter twenty-two. You remember the story of Abraham being told by God to sacrifice his son, Isaac? Well, the place Abraham was directed to complete the sacrifice was also right up there—Mount Moriah. And it was there he found the ram caught in the thicket that became the substitute sacrifice for Abraham's use. To us believers in Yeshua it is also the foreshadowed image of His death for us."

"Okay, I get the connection. . ."

"Four thousand year old connection," Lev clarified.

"Okay, four thousand, whatever. Still a religious argument."

"That's not the point. Whatever Eliyahu was trying to convey he started with this same location, just like me. Listen to Genesis 22:14: 'So Abraham called that place The Lord Will Provide and to this day it is said, "On the mountain of the Lord it will be provided."' That," he concluded, gesturing toward the courses of stone, "is the mountain of the Lord—or one of them, anyway."

Jack stopped arguing long enough to let it all sink in. "So, what will be provided? I'm not looking to carry out a sacrifice. I already sacrificed enough," he said bitterly. Then cutting off Lev's expression of consolation with an angry slice of his hand, he addressed Bette. "How about you? You buy into this. . ." stopping himself just before saying something ugly and offensive he substituted, ". . .this—legend?"

Bette shrugged. "I'm not religious," she said.

"I knew I liked you," Jack said. "All right, now what? My job is to figure out this place and explain it to my bosses back in London."

"What demands did you make of Eliyahu?" Lev said. "What did you tell him you'd have to be convinced of?"

"Him again? Jerusalem Syndrome candidate if ever there was one!"

At Lev's encouragement Jack grudgingly agreed to recall his questions. "The first thing I said was I'd have to be convinced the so-called prophecies were actually accurate—not just vague crystal-ball, smoke-and-mirrors—and the things predicted actually mattered; were of some consequence."

"There it is, then," Lev summarized. "The plan of your investigation."

"Hang on, hang on," Jack urged. "I'm here to learn what I can about promoting peace in this part of the world. Everyone thinks expanding Israeli settlements undermines the peace process. Rebuilding a temple at ground zero would dynamite it permanently!"

Jack saw Bette was frowning, but he didn't care. This religious mumbo-jumbo had gone far enough.

"What if you were convinced the land belongs to the Jews? Would that change your thinking?" Lev asked.

"Doubt it," Jack pronounced before admitting, "It might—some."

"Then what you heard last night and what you thought you came here to study are not really separate ideas at all."

"And you have no doubt about any of this?" Jack said accusingly to Lev. "You're 100 percent in favor of rebuilding the Jewish Temple, no matter how much turmoil it causes?"

"I didn't say that," Lev corrected cheerfully. "Actually, my position is much simpler than that. I believe the Temple is going to be rebuilt—no matter what—no matter whether I, or anyone else, approves the idea or not."

Glancing at his phone, Jack reported, "I just got a text message from London, confirming an appointment I requested for today. Want to come with me?" he asked Lev.

His friend shook his head. "Can't do it, I'm afraid. Nazareth tomorrow, remember. Have to get ready. Want to drive to the Galil with me? You'd be welcome—you and Bette and Ghassan also."

"Sure," Jack returned. "My mandate is bigger than just Jerusalem."

"Why don't we pick up Dr. Garrison first, and then you?" Bette offered.

"Great! So where is this next appointment, Jack?"

"I'm going to see the Grand Mufti of Jerusalem."

Lev looked impressed. "Let me know how it goes."

♦♦♦

The headquarters of the Jerusalem Waqf, the Muslim council that supervises Islamic religious structures, was located only a fifteen-minute walk from the Western Wall. The offices in the Islamic Quarter of the Old City were housed in a 700-year-old former monastery. It once belonged to the Sufi sect—the branch of Islam that practices mysticism.

Jack was asked to produce his ECMP credentials by three secretaries in succession as he passed farther inside. Bette's police identification card was examined once and then she was told to "Wait outside."

The man who rose from behind the oak desk in the inner room was slightly built. He wore an olive drab robe over an olive drab necktie and a white dress shirt. His face possessed perpetually arched eyebrows and a thin, white beard.

"Dr. Garrison, welcome," the man said, extending his hand.

"Thank you, Grand Mufti Hussein."

"No, no," the man corrected. "I am Ahmad, the Grand Mufti's deputy. He was called away unexpectedly at the last minute. He hopes I will be able to answer questions for you. Please, be seated."

When Jack was installed in the armchair across from the deputy mufti, the deputy gestured toward a brass tray containing a coffee pot and tiny brass cups.

"Please," Jack said, mentally acknowledging the need to be courteous and secretly suspecting he should have skipped the earlier cups with Bette and Lev.

The last of the three secretaries poured the dark, syrupy brew, distributed the cups, then closed the door after himself as he exited.

"First," began Ahmad, "let me begin by saying how much we appreciate the efforts of the ECMP to achieve peace. It is the mark of a true follower of the Prophet, blessings be on him, to strive for peace at all times."

"Thank you," Jack returned. "Very kind. We believe the lack of a durable peace here is both harmful to this region and dangerous to the entire world."

"Very true. Now, how can I help?"

"I have been sent, in part, to investigate the likely outcome of any attempt to rebuild the Jewish temple. . ."

Ahmad's free hand shot up, his palm demanding silence. "Let me correct a misunderstanding right away. The correct question must be about *building* a Jewish temple. There never was such a place here to be *re*built. The Noble Sanctuary—the Haram esh-Sharif—has always been and will always be sacred to Islam."

"I see," said Jack, thinking this was not starting well at all. On the wall beside Ahmad hung a portrait Jack recognized as Haj Amin el Husseini, the former Grand Mufti who made common cause with Adolf Hitler. "Is it not true a Waqf historian named Aref al Aref, writing in 1929, confirmed the existence of the Jewish temple?"

Ahmad said coldly, "He was mistaken. Later, more exhaustive research disproved any such claim."

Jack felt his blood pressure rising. Political expediency was one thing but an outright denial of historical fact was a direct challenge to his profession. "And the artifacts recently recovered from sifting the debris of excavations under the southeast corner of the. . ."

"Lies! Deliberate fraudulent attempts to claim a Jewish presence."

"But the finds have been authenticated as coming from the First Temple period."

"Ah! From *when* but from *where*? There is no proof. They were not investigated *in situ* as proper archeology protocols require."

"It's my understanding many prominent, well-credentialed scientists were not allowed to examine the excavations undertaken by the Waqf until after the material was dumped in the Kidron Valley."

"Again, either deliberate falsification or clumsy misunderstanding," Ahmad suggested. "There never was a Jewish presence on the Haram esh-Sharif. As you know, the Qubbat al-Sakhrah is the place from which the Prophet, blessings be on him, took his night flight to heaven."

"Is it not true the builder of the Dome, Caliph al-Malik, interpreted a reference to a distant location from where the prophet. . ."

"Blessings be on him," Ahmad interjected.

"As you say. That the good caliph interpreted the ambiguous location as referring to Jerusalem, and then designated this location as much for political as for religious reasons?"

"Are you a Zionist? " Ahmad demanded. "Are you an *agent provocateur*?"

"As much as I am a seeker for peace I am also a seeker for truth," Jack responded. "One without the other is deception and not true peace at all."

"I see," Ahmad returned. "Well, if there is nothing else, I bid you good day. I hope you will return a true report about how abused my people are by the forces of occupation."

"Thank you for your time," Jack said. "I promise to be both truthful and fair."

♦♦♦

Back in his hotel room, Jack Garrison struggled to make sense of what he saw and heard that day. Clearly Lev Seixas had bought into the "modern Israel is the fulfillment of Biblical prophecy" narrative. In Lev's view of the world, the Bible was the inerrant word of an almighty God. This omnipotent being constructed a covenant with His chosen people, the Jews, and was bent on keeping every promise ever made to them. Such promises related all the way back to the mythological Father Abraham from whom all Jews were supposedly descended and from whom they inherited the land from Lebanon to Egypt and across the Jordan to the Euphrates river, their Promised Land.

How do you argue with someone who takes that view of the universe? For Lev, a real man named Abraham nearly slaughtered a real son named Isaac until God intervened. That demonstration of Abraham's faith, carried out right up there on the summit Jack saw out his window, sealed the bargain to Jewish ownership of this land—forever. How could you debate opposing views with someone who concluded, "It doesn't matter what you or I think. God says the Jewish Temple will be rebuilt and that settles it"?

Pouring himself a diet soda, Jack swirled the glass. The tinkling of the ice cubes was an audible reflection of the way Jack's thoughts bounced around in his head. Lev was an educated, insightful, modern man. How did such conclusions come to someone who otherwise seemed so reasonable?

On the other hand, Jack pondered the irritation he felt in the offices of the Waqf; the outright lies in the face of the overwhelming historical and archaeological evidence of the Jewish Temple; the portrait of a Hitler-embracing Haj Amin el Husseini on the wall.

And the present occupant of the office of Grand Mufti. Muhammad Hussein said suicide bombings were a legitimate tactic of resistance against Israeli occupation. In a television broadcast in January 2012, Hussein quoted one of the most inflammatory passages from the Quran. "Then the stones or trees will call: O Muslim, servant of Allah, there is a Jew behind me, come and kill him."

Despicable. Not a man of peace at all.

Sinking back in an armchair Jack closed his eyes and tried to assemble his thoughts in some kind of organized pattern. How did you balance political expediency and religious fervor?

Jack had blurted out his need to actually be convinced of the accuracy of Bible prophecy, but after today that seemed not just unlikely but utterly impossible.

The reflection of a spotlight beside the Dome of the Rock was refracted by the window glass until it threw a pattern resembling shards of glass on the wall of Jack's room. Some unexpected movement there drew his attention.

Was someone moving the beam like a searchlight?

That wasn't it. Some image on the wall, framed within the fragments of light, moved sideways across the plaster.

It was the outline of a man's hand—a right hand, moving from right to left on the wall as if inscribing Hebrew script.

Jack's first response was not surprise or fear but amusement. *The handwriting on the wall*, he thought. *Book of Daniel. What a biblical allusion.* As soon as he thought of that phrase he turned it into a pun: a biblical *illusion*. Debbie always hated his puns.

I will turn aside and see this sight, he thought. *Take that, Moses; you and your burning bush! I know biblical illusions when I see them.*

Despite his feeble humor, Jack was intrigued by the moving hand. Was it writing something? If so, what?

Setting down the glass he attempted to stand—and couldn't get out of the chair. Now he was alarmed. What was happening? Had someone slipped something into his drink?

A voice Jack recognized as Eliyahu's—how was that even possible after only one hearing?—spoke to him. *Everyone can see the handwriting on the wall. The whole world knows things do not continue as they were before. Though they may not admit it, everyone knows history is racing toward some sort of climax, but they need it explained. They need to be warned. Everyone can see the writing, but only those like the prophet Daniel who seek to understand the divine plan will be able to interpret the words.*

Jack tried again to rise and almost vaulted out of the chair, spraying his drink across the floor in the process. He stepped down hard on an ice cube with a bare foot as he neared the wall.

There was no hand—no writing—no longer any fragments of refracted light.

No longer any voice addressing him.

Jack fumbled with the television remote and snapped on an Israeli news program. It was in Hebrew, but it was really just noise and real people Jack craved. Otherwise he might start to believe he was succumbing to this Jerusalem Syndrome thing for real.

Chapter Nine

Jack was surprised to see that instead of the limo, Bette Deekmann showed up in a white Toyota he guessed was her personal vehicle. "Did you get demoted—or did I?" Jack quipped as he climbed in and she motored away from the King David.

"Ghassan isn't with us today and I think my boss doesn't trust me with an expensive car," Bette returned. "My department doesn't have a big budget. Around Jerusalem is one thing but out-of-town trips are another."

Jack wondered if there was also a security concern that remained unmentioned. After all, a black limo was more conspicuous than a white Corolla. *Am I under some kind of threat?* He decided against putting Officer Deekmann on the spot by mentioning it. Anyway, maybe he'd rather not know.

"How long will our trip north take?"

"About two hours," Bette returned, "after we collect your friend. Back west the way we came from the airport, then north on Yitzhak Rabin Highway for sixty or seventy kilometers and about an hour more after that."

"Is that all? I thought it was clear across the country."

Bette looked amused. "Nazareth is not all the way north; not like the Golan or Kiryat Shmona. But most first time visitors don't realize how tiny Israel really is: eight million people in a space about the size of New Jersey."

"You speak of New Jersey as if you know it. Are you from there?"

"I have family there. But I'm Sabra—born in Israel. About three-quarters of Israelis living today were born here."

"I heard you say Kiryat Shmona. It was on the nose of the plane I arrived on. It's a city, you say."

Bette frowned and shrugged a half-hearted nod.

"You wanted to say more."

"It was named for the eight Jewish defenders who died in a battle with Shiite militiamen in 1920," she said. "But that's not the only reason we honor Kiryat Shmona. In 1974 three assassins of the PFLP killed eighteen civilians there and it has been the target of PLO and later Hezbollah rocket attacks. My father lost a brother there in 1986—my uncle, but before I was born."

Jack was quiet for a long moment. "Then the name on the plane at the gate next to mine—Sderot—that's more than just a city name also?"

"A city in the Negev—about a mile from Gaza. Did you know, for six months in 2007 three or four Hamas rockets fell there every day? The playgrounds all have bomb shelters."

"So all the planes are named for cities that have been in wars?"

Bette snorted, then smiled. "Try and name an Israeli city which has not seen a shooting, or a knifing or a bomb."

"All the more reason we must find a way to a lasting peace."

Bette studied him sadly. "Yes," she said, turning back to her driving and smoothly changing lanes. "Yes, we must."

Partners with Zion was the name of the organization with which Lev Seixas was working and staying while in Israel. Their headquarters, which also provided housing for visiting pastors and their families from around the world, was located just off Yermiyahu Street. It was not far from Jerusalem's International Convention Center.

Bette drove past an area where giant earth-moving equipment scraped and burrowed in the ground beside heaps of steel construction material. Squadrons of workers in neon-green safety vests scurried over the site.

"I confess," Jack said, pointing toward the excavation, "my thoughts of Jerusalem were all about 2,000 years out of date. This is a bustling, modern city too."

"They broke ground here last fall. Skyscrapers, hotels—50,000 jobs. But know this: in Israel, past and present don't just live alongside each other—we live *with* the past every day. Ancient hatreds, ancient fears—modern weapons."

Lev was waiting for them. Beside him stood a tall man with close-cropped dark hair, swarthy skin, and sunglasses. The man looked exactly like the actor Liev Schreiber. Lev introduced him as his friend Amir.

"Amir is the director of Partners with Zion," Lev explained. "He's an Israeli Arab—former Muslim, now a Christian—former Hamas-backer, committed to the destruction of Israel—now one of the best promoters of building bridges for peace and understanding."

While Jack greeted Amir he noted Bette had a look of suspicious reluctance. She barely overcame it in time to shake hands.

"If it isn't too much of an imposition," Lev said, "I've invited Amir to travel with us to Nazareth. Jack, I think you'll find he can shed some light on things, maybe better than anyone here can."

Jack saw Bette was not happy with the addition, but determined not to be ungracious. It was, after all, Jack's decision. "We have room," she said. "Why not?"

On the road again, Jack and Amir sat in the back seat for easier conversation. "Plenty of room," Jack joked as Lev slid his seat forward to remove Jack's knees from his back. "Amir, I am very interested in your personal story, but perhaps you should tell me about your program first. I guess the partnership between Christians and Jews is a recent phenomenon?"

Amir laughed. "I suppose it depends on how you define 'recent.' After all, the first Christians were all Jews, eh?"

"Point taken," Jack agreed. "I guess I meant the idea of Christian support for the modern Jewish state."

"No," Amir corrected. "You'd be wrong there. Theodor Herzl. . ."

Jack nodded his recognition of the name.

Bette waved her left hand toward a tree-covered slope south of the highway. "His grave is up there."

"Herzl," Amir continued, "Who many regard as the father of the modern Jewish state, said the greatest encouragement and support he received was from an Anglican priest named William Hechler. That was in the 1890s. German father, English mother, born in India, missionary in Africa. Hard to imagine a more global perspective, or a less likely Zionist."

Lev and Jack both laughed. Bette glanced back, conveying this was new information to her. Though she remained quiet, her shoulders relaxed a little.

"So we like to think of Hechler as the spiritual father of our work. We invite Christian pastors from around the world to come and stay with us—to see Israel as it really is—successes and failures, history, and modern needs—and then to carry this message home to their congregations."

"And where do they come from? Besides Lev here, I mean."

"You're right that more than half come from America," Amir agreed. "But you might be surprised at the rest. Right now in Hechler House we have pastors from Nigeria, the Philippines, Korea, and Argentina. Next month a group from Sweden is coming, as is one pastor whose country cannot be named because he would almost certainly be martyred back home if his time here were known."

"Surprising," Jack admitted. "Much more diverse than I expected. So tell me, Amir. You bring a unique perspective to any discussion about Israel. What's the greatest threat to peace in the region? Temple? Settlements? Gaza?"

Without hesitation Amir responded, "Damascus."

"I beg your pardon?"

"Syria," Amir elaborated. "The situation in Syria is a crisis the West does not comprehend. Five million refugees have fled the country. Another six million internally displaced. More than half the pre-civil war population is affected. Refugee camps are breeding grounds for radicalization. And as we know, Bashar al-Assad does not hesitate to use poison gas against his own people. What if he decides to attack Israel?

Also, Syria is being fought as a proxy war between Sunni Islam and its radical branch, ISIS, and Shia Islam, backed by Iran. None of them have any love for Israel. However this plays out, it's dangerous. Very dangerous."

"Surely Assad has enough trouble without provoking Israel into a military response?" Jack wondered aloud.

"You'd think so, but recall that Assad has the backing of Russia. Now what? And there's this; remember the Arab Spring?"

"Sure," Jack agreed. "Popular uprisings in 2011 and 2012 that tossed out the governments of Tunisia, Egypt, and Libya."

"Yes, and do you know about the Law of Unintended Consequences? When Qaddafi in Libya fell, his weapons were not destroyed. They were sold to the highest bidder: surface-to-air shoulder-fired rockets were purchased by Hamas. Same Hamas whose rockets fall on Sderot. What happens when they start shooting at planes? Or what happens when ISIS gets some of Assad's poison gas?"

This eventuality was so grim to contemplate they rode in silence for a time.

Lev pointed to an exit and remarked, "Ein Kerem. Some say it was the birthplace of John the Baptist; where Baby John leapt in his mother's womb to greet the Messiah in Mary's womb."

The pleasantry fell flat.

"Maybe now I should ask for your story," Jack said to Amir.

"Of course. I was born here. I felt the plight of Palestinian longing for a homeland. I saw their despair and I felt Hamas was right to struggle against Israeli oppression."

This was more what Jack expected to hear from an Arab viewpoint.

"Go on," he urged.

Amir rubbed his stubbly beard. "I was a journalist. I discovered the Palestinian leaders kept money, food, and medical supplies for themselves or to use as leverage to remain in power. I learned of millions of dollars of foreign aid intended for building Palestinian hospitals and affordable housing diverted to terror training camps. And still I thought the Palestinians had no choice."

"And how did that change?" Jack asked quietly. "Your views, I mean." He noticed Bette was listening intently.

"I saw a Hamas group launch a Qassam rocket from a schoolyard in Gaza. Later I saw where it landed: on a playground in Sderot. They are criminals," he said passionately. "They use children as human shields while they launch attacks designed to kill children!"

"And then?" Jack asked.

"I decided to kill myself," Amir revealed. "I was ready to die, I thought. The very night I intended to take my life a friend invited me to hear a Messianic Jew speak. This one," he said, leaning forward to pat Lev's shoulder. "It was the ultimate irony, I thought. I will die just after hearing a turncoat Jew speak on behalf of a gentile God. But that night—something changed in me forever. I heard of a Jewish Messiah who loved all people. He didn't say, 'Kill others to free some.' No! He said, 'Be willing to lay down your life for a friend.' I have been trying to follow Him ever since."

♦♦♦

On the drive north Amir suggested they head up to the Golan Heights. "It would help put things in perspective," he said, "if you visited the Golan first."

Jack agreed.

Jack, Lev, and Bette stood in a row below a ten-foot-high earthen bank. Amir was a dozen feet in advance of them, on the edge of a precipitous cliff. "Do you know what that is over there?" Amir asked Jack, beckoning Jack to step up for a better view. "Right there? Those hills?"

Jack nodded but didn't approach. "This is Golan. We're looking east, so that must be Syria."

"Correct," Bette confirmed. "Behind us is Israel, which is why we cannot give up this high ground to enemies with missiles and artillery. They are just three miles over that way."

"Much closer than that," Amir corrected, pushing his sunglasses back up on his nose. "A mile and a half, I think. And not Syrian troops. No, no. ISIS fighters."

Involuntarily Jack took a step back. His heel collided with a stone of the dirt rampart.

"We're perfectly safe," Amir said. "The hand of God is over His land and His people and this place."

"Your God, maybe," Jack said. "He and I aren't on speaking terms right now."

"I'm sorry to hear that," Amir said. "So okay, at least let me tell you why we're here. Over there Syrians are fighting Syrians. Like we talked about, yes? They can't attack Israel right now. We don't know about chemical weapons or, God forbid, Iran with a nuclear bomb, but also Israel has peace with Jordan and Egypt, who used to be great enemies. This is a time of relative peace and prosperity for Israel. You know Psalm 83?"

"Remind me," Jack said.

Lev picked up the opportunity to offer his paraphrase. "It records the enemies of Israel saying, 'Come, let us destroy them as a nation, so Israel's name is remembered no more.' In 1948 that's what Jordan and Egypt and Syria and Iraq all said. But you see, not right now."

There was a distant crump, like the sound of an automobile collision heard from a distance. That was followed moments later by a hollow booming sound.

"Artillery," Bette confirmed. "Syrians shelling ISIS positions."

"My point," Amir agreed. "You know about the ISIS terror attack on the Coptic Christians? It got sadly very little attention in the European and American press. So Egypt sent warplanes to bomb ISIS positions. Too little, too late, I'm afraid, but the right response."

Another whomping noise as another artillery shell landed was followed by a staccato burst of machine gun fire. "You don't mind summarizing, do you?" Jack requested.

"Here it is," Amir said. "The Palestinians extort Israel: 'Give in to our demands or your Arab neighbors will never recognize you,' eh? But each demand is not followed by peace but by more demands."

"These are classic Israeli hardline talking points," Jack argued.

"But things have changed. Now the Saudis and others also feel the threat from Islamic radicals. Now it's Israel's turn to say to Saudi Arabia and the Emirates and the others: 'First recognize us and then we will solve the Palestinian issue.' And the new American president will back them up in that. He told the Arabs so himself, didn't he? He called it Islamic terrorism and laid it on their doorstep. Do you see? Then there can be peace—for a time."

"What do you mean, 'for a time?' Isn't that what this whole discussion is about?"

Amir shook his head. "There will be a time of peace but only until the war of Ezekiel."

"The War of Gog and Magog," Lev added.

"The—what?" Jack asked, wondering if his expression betrayed how startled he was to hear that phrase used again here after having it called to mind in the Guildhall in London. Could the two things actually be linked? Did a vision of terror attacks in London foreshadow something prophesied more than 2,000 years ago? Remembering the carved wooden statues, Jack dismissed the notion as silliness.

"Ezekiel, chapter 38," Amir quoted. "'This is what will happen in that day; when Gog attacks the land of Israel, my hot anger will be aroused, declares the Sovereign Lord.' It is coming. There will be no true peace until Messiah comes."

"Please don't preach at me," Jack said sternly. "I appreciate your opinion and your analysis and even your fervor—but I'm not one of your flock, pastor, so leave the preaching out of it!"

"This is the land where prophecy is fulfilled," Lev said. "Where the temporary and the eternal meet. Can't understand the things of today without studying the words of yesterday."

"Yeah, okay, thanks. We should go now."

"Agreed," Amir said. "Now you must see Nazareth."

◆◆◆

It was just an hour's drive back to Nazareth. Despite the abundance of churches, synagogues, museums, ruins, caves, wells, and even a winery, it was to a steep, barren hillside Amir suggested they go.

On the hike up to the terraced area above a precipice they passed a file of Dutch pilgrims streaming back to their tour bus. Half the party was dressed in khaki trousers and Birkenstocks and the other half in denim jeans and hiking boots. When the quartet of Jack, Lev, Amir, and Bette arrived at the summit it was deserted.

Amir let Lev take the lead in describing the scene. "This is called Mount Precipice," Lev explained. "In antiquity it was a quarry site, but its claim to fame is this is where Jesus' neighbors tried to throw him off a cliff."

Jack knew the story but Bette did not. "Why?" she asked. "What had he done?"

To prove he was not totally ignorant when it came to Scripture, Jack offered, "The people of Nazareth didn't believe Jesus could be a prophet or a miracle worker because they had known him since he was a child. That's when he said, 'A prophet is not without honor, except in his own country.' Anyway, it says it made them furious so they rushed him up here, intending to throw him off."

"But what happened?" Bette asked.

Lev made a gesture by pressing his palms together and then pulling them apart.

Jack said, "He walked right through them and went on his way. It wasn't his time and this wasn't his place—if you believe that sort of thing."

"And not like the sign says," Amir offered, summoning them over to a bronze plaque. He read it aloud to them. "It says he jumped from here but was unhurt. Somehow that's easier to believe than the other?"

"But I'm guessing you didn't bring me up here to debate interpretations of Bible verses," Jack said. "What am I supposed to see?"

"Ah," Amir said, taking over the lesson. "Scripture alone is not the only key to this place. It is the vantage point of thousands of years of history. You see this valley?" Removing his sunglasses Amir swept them from left to right over the haze-obscured landscape. "The Canaanites fought the Egyptians here. Joshua fought here. Deborah rightly got the credit for the battle Barak fought here. Gideon's three hundred put an end to Midianite rule at a battle near here."

"Genghis Khan was stopped on his invasion just before reaching here," Lev contributed. "Napoleon Bonaparte said this was the most perfect field of battle he ever saw."

"Ah," Bette said eagerly. "I've heard that quote before. Then this must also be where the English General Allenby—the one the Arabs called 'al-Nabithe Conqueror'—was when he defeated the Turks in 1917."

"Israel fought battles against Arab armies here in the War of Independence," Amir added. "And more recently still, Katyusha rockets landed there because of the Israeli Air Force F-16 base."

"Okay, so a lot of blood's been shed for a small, kind of unimpressive bit of real estate. Why's it so important?" Jack probed.

"Because that small peak over there is Har Megiddo," Amir pointed out. "And this is the Valley of Armageddon. The staging place for the last great battle between Good and Evil."

"You mean, where the last great battle is supposed to happen," Jack corrected.

"That's what most everyone thinks," Amir said. "People even talk about the Battle of Armageddon, but that's wrong. Revelation 16:16 says, they 'gathered the kings together to the place that in Hebrew is called Armageddon.'"

"If not here, then where?"

"Jerusalem," Lev said. "It's always been the focus. It always will be."

"So—what's the point of showing me this, then?" Jack demanded.

Lev looked at Amir, who nodded. Lev continued, "Jack, you concede that all the battles we have mentioned have been real, verifiable historical realities?"

"Yeah, sure. So?"

"So—the gathering of forces here in the Valley of Har Megiddo will be just as real. It will happen—and Amir and I believe the four of us will, God willing, live to see it."

Jack started to object, then thought about how close the front lines were on the Golan Heights. He studied the valley sprawled at his feet and thought what a natural gap it was for armies to utilize. "And how about Gog and Magog?"

"Some teach," Lev explained, "that Armageddon and the War of Gog and Magog are the same thing. Others, that they are two different events. The point is the same as what I told you about the Temple: war *is* coming to this place. The best we can achieve is a temporary peace—and whatever peace we seek must guarantee Israel's safety in the meantime."

"If it's all gonna turn out okay," Jack joked, "why bother?"

More seriously than expected Lev replied, "Because of what God promised Abraham: 'I will bless those who bless you, and curse those who curse you.' That's not an equation you ever want to be on the wrong side of."

♦♦♦

The steep, winding, cobblestone pavement snaking past the entry to the al-Sabah bed-and-breakfast was technically a street. Jack wondered what happened when two cars happened to meet, since it was barely big enough for one. A lot of Old City Nazareth was like that.

The hostelry, whose name meant "The Morning," was run by a Christian Arab family; part of the one third of Nazareth's non-Muslim population. The only entry was an arched wooden door opening directly from the cobblestones. Parking was about a quarter mile away.

The lobby was up one flight of stairs. A balcony off the white-washed and blue-trimmed chamber gave panoramic views over the city.

While Bette went to her room, and Amir and Lev went to call on a pastor friend, Jack decided to remain seated on the terrace and think.

What had he learned? Everything in Israel was close together; impossibly so, sometimes. Take the Golan: Syrian forces able to call on poison gas weapons were literally a stone's throw from ISIS butchers, and both were within an arrow's flight of Israel. How did people live with twenty-first century weapons in a place where the world was no broader than it was in 1900 AD or 1000 AD or the year 1? Jack knew if the UN's boundaries of Israel remained as originally proposed there would be a place where the Jewish state was eight miles wide. Eight miles. From Jack's home in Little Venice to the East End of London was about eight miles. Jack could do that by bicycle in less than an hour.

The other aspect of life in Israel which most struck him was the side-by-side relationship of ancient past and modern present. Nazareth was home to shrines commemorating the boyhood of Jesus and the carpentry workshop of St. Joseph. Tour buses pulled up outside the synagogue where Jesus preached and from where his angry neighbors nearly tossed him over the cliff.

The view from the al-Sabah terrace included the Church of the Annunciation, which celebrated the visit by the Angel Gabriel to a teenage virgin named Mary. He had a message for her: if she was willing, she would give birth to the Son of God.

Jack massaged his forehead with his fingertips. What did all of this have to do with his assignment to research and report on the prospects for peace? For that matter, what did *any* of this have to do with him? And yet, as soon as he raised that objection, Jack knew there was much he was still trying to comprehend; that it was important.

Closing his eyes to concentrate, Jack wondered if he was about to have another vision. What better place for a supernatural occurrence than Nazareth, with so many connections to the life of Jesus? Besides, Nazareth had a ringside seat in the venue of so many wars of eons past and future wars still to be fought. He idly brushed a fly away from his right ear.

"Shalom?" asked a voice from the terrace doorway. "I'm sorry. Were you asleep?"

It was a young girl—thirteen or fourteen, Jack guessed. She wore a blue headscarf and a long-sleeved blue dress.

Somehow Jack was not at all surprised. "No, no. Just thinking. And your name is Mary?"

The girl smiled and laughed. "What made you say that? My name is Rebekah."

Jack pulled the slouch out of his spine and sat up. Rebekah held a can of Coca Cola. Not a vision then after all.

"Sorry," Jack apologized. "My name's Jack. Do you live here?"

"No," Rebekah said. "I'm looking for someone. I heard he had come. Pastor Lev Seixas?"

"He's staying here," Jack agreed, "but he's out right now. I came with him. Can I give him a message for you?"

Rebekah frowned with disappointment. "I can't miss my bus. I have to get back home," she said. Then she brightened. "But since you're his friend I guess I can tell you. Tell him I had another dream about Jesus."

There was a pause while Jack struggled to process what she said. "I beg your pardon?" Jack felt as if Israel was bent on turning his every expectation inside-out.

"I live in Tobga," Rebekah said. "Over by Capernaum. I'm Jewish, you see. I always hear Christians talking about Jesus and singing about Jesus—I like it when they sing.

"I grew up knowing all the stories about how Jesus came from Nazareth and he lived all around here and taught around here and..." She lowered her voice. "Did miracles around Galilee—except I'm not supposed to talk about that part."

"No?"

"No. My parents don't like it. A Christian pilgrim gave me a Bible to read. I like the stories about Jesus. He seems wonderful!"

Her face fell. "But my parents found it and took it away."

Jack didn't know what to say. Fortunately, Rebekah didn't seem to mind being the only one speaking. "Then I had a dream. A Jewish priest dressed all in white. Like a *cohen* from the old days, yes? In my dream he told me to not be afraid. That Jesus really was the Messiah. I asked him how I would know for sure and he said I should keep reading whenever I could.

"Then I had another dream. The priest told me I should go to where the Christians are and learn all I could. So now whenever I can I come to Nazareth, or I go to Capernaum, and I listen to people talk about Jesus—like Pastor Seixas. I love it that he's Jewish and also believes in Yeshua ha-Mashiach. Anyway, my friend called me and told me he was back. She has had dreams too, but she's afraid to talk about them except to me. Okay, then. Tell Pastor Seixas I'll see him next trip. Bye!"

Before Jack could frame a coherent question out of the hundreds swirling in his head, she was gone.

What did I just learn? Jack asked himself. "I guess it's this: if a Jewish teenager isn't afraid to tell a total stranger she's been having dreams about Jesus—then why am *I* holding back from telling Lev?"

♦♦♦

Jack and Lev strolled through Nazareth in the early evening to the plaza located between the Basilica of the Annunciation and the Church of St. Joseph. "Really a carpenter's workshop?" remarked Jack, pointing to the arched windows over the entry and the square bell tower alongside.

"Who knows?" Lev admitted cheerfully. "There is a grotto beneath the church that was once used as living quarters or a shop sometime around Jesus' day. Later there was a Byzantine church there and then a church that was destroyed during the Crusades. In the 1700s the Franciscan fathers bought the property from the Turks and rebuilt over the ruins."

"So what you're saying is, nobody really knows."

Lev shrugged. "I guess that's not the point. Joseph and Mary and young Jesus really did live somewhere in Nazareth. Remembering that reality is worth celebrating, even if the location is not exact."

Jack struggled to stay a modern, skeptical, nay-sayer—and couldn't manage it. "Look, Lev," he said. "I didn't ask to talk because I wanted to go back to arguing. What I really want to talk to you about is—visions."

"You mean Rebekah's?"

"No—mine."

"You already told me about meeting—what did you say his name was—Elijah?"

"Eliyahu, but no. That's just the beginning. You remember when I asked you about the Jerusalem Syndrome?"

"Still no bed sheets tied into togas, right?" Lev inquired.

"Please," Jack said. "I'm serious. I've seen—things. I know I wasn't dreaming, okay? Or maybe I was, but I still think they mean something." Jack's tone betrayed some anxiety that Lev would not believe him.

"Whoa! Okay, serious. We've known each other for—what—fourteen, fifteen years? In all that time I've never known you to be anything other than sensible and level-headed—maybe hard-headed is in there too—but if I was going to pick someone as a reliable witness, it'd be you."

Grasping both Lev's wrists Jack said, "Thank you! I needed to hear that. Okay—here goes."

Jack proceeded to tell Lev what he saw of Adam and Eve being expelled from the Garden of Eden. "I saw grass wither and gemstones turn into geodes, like everything pretty just folded in on itself. Eliyahu said the way back in the garden was closed until someone was found who could reopen the way. He meant Jesus, right?"

"If Adam couldn't even keep just one rule, then justice wouldn't be fulfilled until someone came who kept all the rules and paid for every sin from Adam down to today. Yep—Jesus."

"Okay, so I get that," Jack said. "Then I saw the handwriting on the wall."

Lev waited for the punch line to the joke until Jack corrected him. "I mean, I really saw a hand, writing on my wall. I couldn't read it, but I heard Eliyahu's voice—I didn't see him this time—telling me it means history is coming to a climax. Or something like that. And he told me some other stuff too. What's it mean?"

"Slow down. You're still not crazy, okay? Let's start with that. Next, let me tell you the same thing I told Rebekah: you are not the only one seeing visions or dreaming dreams. It's happening all over the world, but especially here in the Middle East—to Muslims, especially."

Jack took that in slowly. "Don't ask me to believe every story like mine—I can't. We might be talking alien spacecraft and Bigfoot! You can always find true believers for just about anything."

"So let's just concentrate on the handwriting," Lev suggested. "Here's what I think it might mean: you remember when we heard that chapel speaker at Baylor who talked about the End of the World?"

Jack had not been impressed with that speaker. He dismissed the man's talking points as quackery.

Recognizing the resistance building in his friend, Lev said, "Stay with me here. Is it true that before the first atomic bomb, humans had no way to kill off the whole race?"

"True."

"And now how many nuclear-armed countries are there? And whose finger is on what button?"

Jack remained silent, listening.

"And is the whole world interdependent like never before?" Lev continued. "I mean, the price of crude oil in Saudi Arabia determines whether a farmer in Iowa makes money or loses money on his corn, true?"

"I think your economic theory is a little rusty, but go ahead."

"How much food is in a grocery store if it doesn't get resupplied? I know, 'cause I asked: three days, except for canned stuff. A couple weeks 'til everything down to anchovy paste is gone and the shelves are bare."

"Your point being?"

"The point is—the handwriting is on the wall," Lev restated. "Politicians know it. Economists know it. It's in no one's interest to cause panic, but here's the bottom line: the world has never been in as desperately dangerous a situation as it is right now. How many places around the world could be called 'powder kegs?' Here? Iran? North Korea? China, flexing its muscles in the South China Sea? Russia invading Ukraine?"

Jack stopped objecting and just sat trying to take it all in. He also debated whether to share one more vision or not.

"Look, Jack," Lev said. "So far everything you've told me squares with Scripture and with what I know of the world. If you have no more visions then you can chalk it up to the Jerusalem—Experience we'll call it. But maybe these messages aren't just for you. I guess I'm saying, don't discount them lightly. Pay attention and think them through—if you have more, that is."

"I—I've already had one more," Jack admitted, and he proceeded to unfold the view from the Hungerford Bridge. "I thought it was grief or stress or I don't know what. But it was horrible. London was in flames everywhere I looked. Up river. Down river. By St. Paul's Cathedral. And individual, separate fires—like terrorist bombs."

"Nothing that's happened yet," Lev conceded. "A view of a future event. Jack, what else did Eliyahu say to you about the handwriting on the wall?"

Jack screwed up his face with effort to recall the exact words. "He said, 'Only those like the Prophet Daniel who seek to understand the divine plan will be able to interpret the words.'"

Lev clapped his friend on the shoulder. "It sounds to me like you have been given some rare insights. So here's what I know: you being here in Israel is part of the divine plan—whether you know it yet, or admit it yet, or not. Keep watching what unfolds, Jack. Just keep watching."

Chapter Ten

I
t was a few days after their return to Jerusalem from Nazareth when Bette stopped by the King David to tell Jack she would not be accompanying him that day; she had a meeting.

"Do you have time for a Starbucks?"

"There are no Starbucks in Israel," Bette laughed as they exited the hotel.

The fact she was a policewoman seemed an utter contradiction to the playful smile of this beautiful woman. "Not possible." Jack glared at his iPhone's Starbucks locator app. "How can there not be a Starbucks in Israel? Anywhere?"

"Israelis don't believe coffee should be served in paper cups, or slurped through plastic anti-spill lids while you walk around. Well, there is some of that," she admitted. "But in Israel, proper coffee is an excuse to sit for hours and talk about. . ."

"Politics?"

"No! Life. Love. Children. Start-up companies. Theater. Music. Jack, your American-ness is showing on your face like a week without shaving." She laughed. "Okay. So you want real coffee? Americano? Or Israeli, the way God created it? Come on. I'll show you coffee."

Bette lengthened her stride and wove through the crowds in the open market place. Her eyes continuously scanned the crowds and her walk projected self-assurance. It was, "No-big-deal-but-don't-mess-with-me."

Jack was grinning for the first time in a long time. She led him away from the babble of shoppers and through an alleyway to a tiny hole-in-the-wall café. The air of the courtyard was heavy with the smell of coffee grounds and intrigue. Bearded old Jews played chess at a small table in the shade of a large tree. Their espresso cups were ceramic and the thick black liquid had long ago cooled. The opponents stared, unmoving, at the chessboards. Maybe they had been there all day. Maybe longer.

Bette pointed at an empty table in the shade. "My treat. Border Police discount. Sit, tourist," she commanded. She disappeared into the café, which was a shallow vendor's stall. When she emerged with two steaming cups a few minutes later, neither of the chess players had moved.

Bette nudged the cup toward Jack. "Here you are."

He gingerly sipped the strong, bitter brew. Grounds settled in the bottom of the cup. "Hmmm. Strong. Really..."

She lifted her chin slightly and challenged, "Mud in the bottom. Israeli-style. If you gulp it down fast it gives you the shakes. So—" she inclined her head toward the serene chess players. "You can tell they've been here several hours."

"Well, it's different, for sure. But I didn't know there was a country in the world left without Starbucks."

"We have McDonalds. We have American-style shopping malls. But Israeli brew has truth serum in it. You don't finish a cup without a personal reveal. A game we play. You tell one truth and one lie. Then your opponent guesses what is true."

He raised his eyebrows and smiled sheepishly. "I—don't know..."

"Okay. I'll go first." It was clear she enjoyed watching Jack squirm. "I am Wonder Woman's cousin. I lived in the United States for a year. Okay? Guess which is truth."

Jack shrugged. "Wonder Woman's cousin? I'd have to guess that's a lie."

She gave a hearty laugh. "Wrong. Second Cousin, to be exact."

"I'm impressed. I should have known. Really. You have a family resemblance."

"In my family I am called the shorter version of Miss Israel. Second cousins. Family is important. My family: father, mother, and two younger brothers, are in Singapore. My dad's on a diplomatic mission there. Okay. So your turn."

Jack sipped the brew and winced. "I like Israeli coffee. I think Wonder Woman's cousin is—beautiful and a bit intimidating."

She softened. "Well, Jack, intimidating is good. Depending on who I intimidate. I hope one day you will learn to like our muddy water. And there is another version of this game. I ask you a question and you can either lie or tell me the truth. And I guess which."

The uneasy feeling returned to the pit of his stomach. "I'm feeling a little nervous."

"Caffeine. That's all. Makes you nervous. You are drinking too fast."

"All right, I'm in. Shoot."

"No ring. Have you ever been married?"

"Yes."

There was a long pause.

"That's it?" she probed. "No detail?"

"One question at a time. My turn—so can you introduce me to Wonder Woman?"

"I'll even get you her autograph."

"I like this game."

"And why aren't you married now, Jack?"

"My wife—and our baby boy—they were. . .an accident."

"Oh, Jack." The smile faded. "I'm—so very sorry. Pushy. I am pushy. That's truth for sure. I didn't mean to. . ."

"Yes, you did mean to. And it's fine. It is a terrible truth in my life. One I don't talk about—hardly ever—but you're assigned to me. You need to know a little personal stuff. I guess."

She checked her watch. "I am truly sorry and I'm late for a meeting. Sorry again. I shouldn't have."

"Maybe you are pushy. Okay, wait. Gotta give me my turn."

"Sure. Ask me."

"What's a nice girl like you doing in this racket? Bodyguard? Or tour guide? I mean you're carrying a what? A Beretta?"

Bette tucked her chin and the slight smile of superiority returned. "Glock, Jack. And someone had to train Wonder Woman. Okay, gotta go."

♦♦♦

High, thin, blade-shaped clouds pierced the pale blue skies above Jerusalem. There was no perceptible breeze at ground level, but aloft the spearheads flung themselves at the Mountains of Moab.

Walking in a garden area along Sultan Suleiman Street, Jack was deep in thought as he paced beside the walls of Old City Jerusalem. He left after Bette's departure without giving much regard to where he was going.

Jack needed some alone time. He had heard a great deal about prophecy and the Jewish claim to this land and this specific place, but he remained unsure what his report should contain. *Just because religious Jews and some Christians think God gave Abraham the deed to this hunk of earth doesn't make it so,* he mused. *The history of this tiny fragment of the world shows it's always been an object of conquest. And whoever holds it makes the rules, until somebody bigger and stronger takes it away from them. But is that how it must always be? Is that how it **should** be in the Third Millennium?* Despite dreams and visions and voices, Jack remained unconvinced that prophecy was a factor valid enough to be considered. *I better not let Lev hear me say that. He would want to lecture me again.*

Jack was approaching Damascus Gate. The stone structure, easily recognized by its square, crenellated battlements atop the arched portico, was a tangible supporter of Jack's thoughts. Rebuilt by Muslim overlords in the 1500s, it was a Crusader passage dedicated to the martyrdom of Saint Stephen, and before that a main Roman-era entry to their provincial capitol, Aelia Capitolina. Only back. . .way back. . .before all that conquest and possession had it been remotely Jewish. *'Til 1948,* Jack thought. *Or was it '67?* He'd have to look that one up.

Damascus Gate was not only one of the primary entries to the Old City, it also marked a boundary between the Muslim Quarter to the east and the Christian Quarter on the west. Not far from the portal was an Arab street market. The pavement thronged with a mixture of tourists and Old City residents out to do their shopping, like the young Palestinian man toting a shopping bag just ahead. The man checked his wristwatch.

A staccato popping sound came from beyond where the gate loomed. It interrupted Jack's thoughts, but it wasn't until he saw a uniformed female Border Police officer racing toward the noise that he recognized it as gunfire. Jack stood frozen in place, unsure which way to turn. There were no doorways nearby to duck into.

As the Israeli officer passed by, the Palestinian male thrust his hand into the shopping bag. It emerged with a lime green, ceramic knife clutched in his fist. He attacked the policewoman, shouting incoherently, and stabbing her in the back and neck.

At that same moment Jack was tackled from behind. Would his next sensation be the pain of a blade across his throat and then blackness?

"Keep down!" hissed Ghassan.

"Help her! Help her!" Jack urged as he saw blood streaming from the prostrate form of the young woman. The assailant continued a frenzy of slashing and stabbing.

"Down!" Ghassan ordered.

An enormous boom next to Jack's right ear deafened him.

Out of the corner of his eye Jack saw Ghassan firing his pistol at the terrorist. A trio of Israeli Border Police raced forward, heedless of their own safety.

A bullet ricocheted off a nearby stone wall and struck a Palestinian woman. She cried out and fell in a heap of spilled bread and scattered dates and olives, clutching her leg.

Another shot whined overhead. Ghassan fired until his clip emptied.

Just as suddenly as it began, the attack ended.

The Palestinian was dead, shot multiple times.

His knife lay on the pavement next to his victim. She was the pallor of the stones amid jagged scarlet wounds and pools of crimson gore.

"Help her!" Jack cried. "Please, help her!"

Roughly Ghassan dragged Jack to his feet and hustled him back toward the hotel. "Help her!" Jack ordered feebly. His legs didn't seem to work well and he was suddenly grateful Ghassan was helping him stay upright.

"We don't know if this is over or not," Ghassan growled through gritted teeth. "My duty is your safety. Anyway, others are already tending to her."

♦♦♦

Later that day the television news reported the female officer was seriously wounded at the hands of an eighteen-year-old attacker. Two more terrorists sprayed the area near Zedikiah's Cave with bullets before they were killed.

In a prepared statement Hamas, the Palestinian government of Gaza, denied the action was carried out by ISIS. Hamas took full credit for the deed. "The attack in Jerusalem is new proof the Palestinian people continue their revolution against the occupiers and the intifada will continue until complete freedom is achieved."

"A glass of wine, sir?" the cocktail waiter finally inquired. Jack had been brooding over the drinks menu for a good five minutes while the increasingly nervous server hovered.

"I—yes—no—gin-and-tonic," Jack muttered.

"Brand, sir?"

"Sure. What did you say?"

Sitting at Jack's right hand Lev answered for him. "Tanqueray, make it a double." And then as the waiter hesitated he said, "Nothing for me. And you, Bette?"

The policewoman shook her head and the waiter scurried off.

The three were seated in a quiet corner of the Oriental Bar in the King David Hotel. Since witnessing the attack in the street Jack showered and changed clothes before joining the other two, but still he sat mute and brooding. He stared at wall sconces shaped like menorahs, or at faux wall columns designed to suggest palm trees, but saw neither.

Bette and Lev talked quietly before Jack came in, but now they too kept silence.

Lev reached out and laid his hand on Jack's arm. Jack shuddered. His eyes flicked to Bette and away. What he saw was a pretty, young woman lying on the stones of Jerusalem, marred, shattered, her life flowing inexorably away. And for what? For what?

"And I couldn't do anything to help her!" Jack said fiercely, speaking his thoughts aloud without preamble. "And even if Ghassan hadn't been holding me down—I was already frozen. I saw the terrorist before…before. He was just ahead. If that policewoman hadn't been running by, it could have been….maybe she…I have to know her name," he demanded abruptly. "What's her name?"

"I'll find out," Bette said. Standing and stepping away from the table, Bette made a call.

"Where's Ghassan?" Jack asked Lev. "He wasn't hurt, was he?"

Lev shook his head. "He's fine. Bette said he had to go to headquarters to make his report. The commander wanted to interview you, but Bette said she'd handle it."

The waiter returned with Jack's drink, set it down hurriedly, and disappeared again when Lev waved him away.

Jack took a large gulp, then looked up expectantly as Bette returned.

"Her name was Hadas Malka," Bette reported.

"She didn't make it, did she? I mean she's. . ."

Bette confirmed the girl's death. "Hadassah hospital. They are the best, but. . ."

"How old?"

"Twenty-three."

"Did you know her?"

"No, not really," Bette replied. "I met her at her graduation from the academy, but I think that's the only time."

Jack nodded gravely as if this was important information, then drained half the remaining gin. "Who was he?" Jack said. "The terrorist?"

"Eighteen-year-old, from a West Bank village," Bette explained. "There were three altogether. The other two were from a different village, but they coordinated their attack. They're all dead."

Jack took a deep breath and turned toward Bette. He focused his eyes as if just arriving in the room. "Anyone else?"

Bette shook her head. "No one else killed. Four injured—police and two bystanders wounded—none seriously."

Jack's phone, lying on the table by his elbow, rang: Beethoven's Fur Elise. Jack regarded it as if wrestling with whether to answer it or not, then jabbed the button to take the call.

The thin, distant voice of Lord Halvorsham on speaker asked, "Jack? We've only just heard about another attack in Jerusalem. Where are you? Are you all right?"

Jack confirmed he was okay, then added, "But I was there. I saw it."

"It must have been terrible. BBC report says three Palestinians killed by Israeli police. Horrible."

Jack waited, then inquired, "Is that all it says?"

Jack, Bette, and Lev all leaned toward the speaker. "It says others were injured. That's all."

"No mention that it was a terrorist attack? No word about an Israeli policewoman being killed—knifed to death?" Jack demanded.

"No. But. . ."

"No hint it was a coordinated attack by ambush?"

"Jack," the words from 2,000 miles distant were clipped and brisk. "Are you all right?"

"Physically, yes," Jack retorted. "But no, I'm not all right. Look, I need to go. I'll call you later." And he rang off without waiting for Lord Halvorsham's goodbye.

Jack sat silently again, rolling the tall, chilled glass between his palms. Finally: "What label is this?" he asked Lev. When Lev replied, Jack set the glass down and pushed it away. He suddenly had no stomach for British gin.

◆◆◆

After the murder of the policewoman, and hearing that some Palestinian leaders approved of the deed as "resistance," Jack had to steel himself for the next round of meetings. He told himself his job required him to be thorough and impartial—but when he closed his eyes he still saw the face of that dying girl.

The local Gaza office of Rights for Palestine was in a concrete-walled structure on the bottom floor of what had once been a two-story building. The three-room space was entered through a flimsy wall of plywood patching where the concrete had been sheared off. Though the RFP had lavish offices in the West Bank city of Ramallah, the executive director, Rafa Husseini, insisted on meeting Jack here.

He'd motored to the checkpoint with Ghassan and Bette, but they did not cross the border with him. A pair of dark-green uniformed Gaza security police escorted Jack from the Erez Crossing on Gaza's northern border. On the drive Jack witnessed school-age children gleaning scrap metal from heaps of concrete rubble.

It was only about a mile to the RFP location, where the patrolmen waited outside for Jack's meeting to conclude. "How do you do, Ms. Husseini?" Jack said. "I understand this is a relatively new appointment for you. You were previously the head of communications for the Palestinian ambassador to Germany and also employed by the PLO's negotiations team."

"For whom I still consult, yes," the thin, middle-aged woman wearing a navy blue hijab acknowledged. "Please, sit." The two sat across a flimsy table in mismatched chairs. "I offer my expertise to the unity government established between the Palestinian Authority and Hamas. But my official duties are with the RFP, which as you know is a nonpartisan organization that only works to bring about better treatment for oppressed people everywhere. Thank you for coming here. It is crucial that you understand the oppression under which my people live their daily lives. The border crossing you used? It once allowed 800,000 Palestinians to find work in Israel every month. Now fewer than 15,000 can cross there in the same monthly span."

"As you know," Jack acknowledged, "the European Committee for Mid-East Policy has a task force dedicated to Gaza. This particular visit requires me to look into Jewish settlements and certain activity in East Jerusalem as barriers to peace." Jack purposely refrained from naming any rumor of a rebuilt Jewish temple. He feared the tirade such a topic would generate would destroy any meaningful conversation.

"The settlements are a crime and a violation of every previous attempt by the Palestinian people to achieve peace and security," Rafa said. "But you cannot understand the depths of Israeli oppression without witnessing occupied Gaza."

"Forgive me," Jack returned, "but I understand Gaza has been self-governing since 2005. There are no Israeli military forces on this side of the border, are there?"

"You see," Rafa said forcefully, "how you have been deceived by the Jewish-controlled media? The Jewish air force routinely violates Gazan air space. The Jewish military patrols the sea coast. How is that acceptable to any truly sovereign state? Did you know there is 40 percent unemployment here? How is Gaza to thrive without access to jobs and a working sea port?"

"Israel cites security concerns for needing to keep tight control on the border, and arms smuggling as the reason behind the naval patrols."

Rafa folded her hands and placed them on the desk in front of her. Her knuckles turned white and so did a line around her tightly clamped mouth. "Dr. Garrison," she said. "Israel spews hateful propaganda for Western—primarily American—consumption. This is apartheid, pure and simple. As heinous as ever existed in South Africa."

"And terrorist attacks from inside Gaza?" Jack queried.

"Greatly exaggerated!" Rafa stressed. "Pinpricks in the hide of a military giant! Israel's disproportionate responses have killed more than 2,000 innocent Palestinians since 2008. They are guilty of war crimes!"

"And the reports of mortars and rockets being fired from school grounds and hospital compounds?" Jack asked. "Also exaggerations?"

Rafa nodded fiercely. "Or the tragic actions of a handful of teenagers driven to despair."

Jack thought for a moment, but did not ask where despairing teenagers received their weapons or the training in how to use them. "I see," he said. "Will you be able to meet with me in Ramallah? I'd like to expand our discussion to include the West Bank settlement issue."

"Of course. The purposes of our two organizations are very parallel, aren't they? My work is much narrower in focus, but we both want a just and lasting peace with prosperity for all peoples, do we not?"

"Indeed we do," Jack agreed, thanking her yet again.

Once back in the auto driven by Ghassan, Bette handed Jack a folded newspaper and showed him the latest front page. The headline read: *Hamas Terror Tunnel Found Beneath Two UN-Run Schools in Gaza* .

Hamas maintained that such passageways were for legitimate military operations against Israeli military targets. A survey of such tunnels discovered in 2014 revealed their exit points were only 1,000 yards from Jewish civilian structures. When destroying the passages, Israel also asserted it disrupted a plot for 200 Hamas terrorists to simultaneously emerge by night and carry out widespread acts of murder and hostage-taking.

Now there were more such clandestine terror-highways.

The newspaper story detailed the discovery of a Hamas-backed infiltration passage running beneath two schools built by the United Nations Relief and Works Administration. The report pointed out the schools were still under construction, leading to the question: How much did UNRWA officials know about the tunnels directly beneath playgrounds and classrooms?

"How did your meeting with RFP go?" Bette asked politely.

Jack did not reply. Gripping the paper in one hand, he cupped his chin in the other and stared out the window.

Chapter Eleven

The breeze was fragrant and soft. It carried the scent of pine forest mingled with ocean air. *Reminds me of the Carmel Highlands above Pacific Grove, California,* Jack thought. He wondered about that association for just a moment before being glad he had not expressed it aloud. *No kidding,* he chided himself. *Guess I might be the last person to make that connection.* The place where he stood was on a slope of the Israeli National Park known as God's Vineyard—Har ha Karm-el—Mount Carmel. Like its namesake halfway around the world, the original Carmel was also the rocky headland of a peninsula thrust into the sea. Here it marked the southern barrier to the Jezreel Valley and guarded the left flank of Haifa, just as the Carmel Highlands loomed above Monterrey Bay.

They came here at Ghassan's suggestion. One day earlier Jack felt so battered and weary and hopeless about his mission he was ready to give up and go home. "I need a quiet place to sit and think things through," he said.

"Mount Carmel," Ghassan suggested at once.

Bette and Lev concurred. "Nothing better," Bette said. "You need to get out of the city again."

"The tension here can get oppressive," Lev agreed. "And I've only been up there once. I'm eager to go again—if you want my company."

"I may not be much for sparkling conversation," Jack admitted. "But yes, I'd like the company, please."

"Good call," Lev praised Ghassan. "What made you think of it?"

The Druze grinned sheepishly. "It's my home village," he admitted. "Daliyat al-Karmel on the east side of the park."

So while Ghassan spent the afternoon visiting his widowed mother, the remaining trio climbed the slopes. From the lowest levels, dotted with olive groves, they ascended through laurel and oak growth, until finally breaking into the pines.

A pair of trees, blown down in some Mediterranean storm, fell across each other beside a limestone ledge, forming a sheltered nook and some ready-made seating. "What do you think?" Jack asked.

"Perfect," the other two agreed.

While Lev and Bette sat some distance away, talking quietly, Jack wedged himself between a pair of lopped off branches. Lifting his face to the warm sun, he closed his eyes and felt his shoulders droop.

What was it about this land that created so much conflict? What drove people to such hatred and despair they'd go to certain death to kill someone else? A suicide bomber in Manchester—a bus shot to pieces in Egypt—a young woman slaughtered in Jerusalem—what did all these events have in common, and what could be done about it?

The Palestinians longed for a homeland. But hadn't it been the Jewish longing for their ancestral home that brought them here over the last one hundred years or so? If there was space and water and air enough for all, where did the unending hatred come from?

It was like there was an unseen war greater than the visible outbursts of violence that shattered lives and caused such grief. How could Jack explain this to anyone else if he couldn't wrap his head around it himself?

Suddenly the pastoral, tranquil beauty of the place was muted. The colors seemed dimmed, somehow. The air was less refreshing. An undercurrent of something—what was the word?—sinister—leapt into Jack's consciousness.

He looked around. There was no threat. There was no danger, but the suspicion of something unpleasant took away from the joy.

Jack suddenly had the sense of something being wrong—some reason for him to be depressed, quite apart from what he experienced in Jerusalem. What changed?

Or what was about to change?

♦♦♦

The air was full of voices. Some were human. Others were—something else.

A ring of boulders surrounded an oblong space of crushed, yellow grass. The encircling trees were dead or dying. Fallen leaves had long since been ground to powder underfoot. The leafless corpses of the oaks begged for rain from a sky so clear it seemed to never have seen a cloud.

In the center of the lifeless pasture was an ornate stone altar. It was built of blocks decorated with the wavy lines of storm clouds. Into some of its panels were carved a bearded figure wearing a cone-shaped crown, who strode about carrying a lightning bolt in his hand.

Ashes and dried blood and bits of bone littered the blocks.

Throngs—thousands of people—crowded around the oval clearing. They jostled each other. Some were angry. Some appeared nervous. Some laughed and made mocking sounds.

Some held infant children in their arms, or led toddlers by the hand.

Jack knew he was having another vision, but for the first time he was also frightened. He was not just a distant observer. He seemed to be in the middle of whatever was taking place. He was truly glad Eliyahu was beside him.

"Is this still Mount Carmel?" he asked.

"Oh yes," Eliyahu confirmed. "There has been no rain for three years. There is no grain. All the crops have failed. Even King Ahab cannot find grass to feed his horses. Instead of repenting of their sins and returning to Jehovah God, the people have intensified their worship of Ba'al Addu—the Lord of the Thunder. They think if they worship him hard enough he will bring back the rain. Look."

A double file of men dressed in ornate robes embroidered with stars and lightning bolts and crescent moons parted the sea of onlookers and walked toward the altar.

"Priests of Ba'al," Eliyahu commented.

The priests presented obvious contrasts to the common worshippers. Where the villagers' clothing was tattered and their faces gaunt and pinched, the priests seemed well fed and prosperous. Their shaved heads gleamed with oil in the morning sun and they appeared haughty and proud.

"Queen Jezebel promotes adoration of Ba'al and the fertility goddess Ashtoreh," Eliyahu said. "Ba'al and Ashtoreh demand all manner of sexual perversion as worship—and they get it. But the queen wants no opposition. She has had most of the prophets of Jehovah God killed. In fact, only one is left who is not in hiding. That one has sent out a challenge to the priests of Ba'al, to settle once and for all who is really God."

"How will they do that?"

"The lone, remaining prophet has challenged the 450 priests of Ba'al and the 400 priests of Ashtoreh to meet him here. This was once a place for worship of Jehovah God." Eliyahu extended a long, bony finger and pointed to where the stones of an abandoned second altar lay tumbled and scattered.

"It was a place for victories to be celebrated," Jack offered. "I heard that from here you could see where Gideon defeated the Midianites with just 300 men."

"But no longer," Eliyahu returned. Jack's guide nodded toward where a shifty-eyed figure wearing royal robes and a circlet of gold walked forward and rested a dismissive sandaled foot on one of the discarded boulders. "After his priests win today," Eliyahu said, "King Ahab will slaughter the prophet of God and claim total victory. The challenge is this: the priests and the prophet of God will each kill a bullock and lay it on the wood of an altar, but not set fire to it. The god who answers by sending fire is the only true God."

So Ba'al the Thunderer—the god of storms and lightning—was supposed to send down fire? No wonder mocking voices swirled through the crowd and on the air. It seemed Ba'al already had the upper hand.

"But I already know how this turns out," Jack remarked to Eliyahu, only to find his guide was no longer by his side.

A tall, long-bearded man, robed in a mantle of dark red, walked through the jeering mob until he stood a few paces from the king. Even though the newcomer leaned on a wooden staff, he stood more erect than Ahab, who shrunk from the prophet's gaze. The king hastily removed his foot from the altar stone and shuffled awkwardly in place.

The prophet was Eliyahu. He revolved slowly, letting his penetrating gaze rest on each face in the front rank of the crowd. The murmuring fell off in waves, from the front to the back, until all was still—except for what continued to sound like hisses, and whispered curses, and low growls.

Raising his voice so all the thousands gathered around the clearing could hear, Eliyahu demanded, "How long will you waver between two opinions? If the Lord is God, follow him; but if Ba'al is God, follow him."

The thousands of on-lookers remained almost completely silent. Here and there an infant whimpered or a small, fussy child was quickly hushed

The priests of Ba'al were first to offer their sacrifice. The most junior novices placed the wood on the imposing altar. The next more senior acolytes led out a bawling ox and slaughtered it. Knives flashed in the morning sun. Hot blood poured out on the thirsty ground.

The most senior of the priests arranged the meat on top of the wood.

The highest priest of Ba'al, an ancient figure of wizened face and peering eyes, advanced with an ivory staff. The head of the staff represented two curving horns. He extended his staff toward the altar, and in a high-pitched whine, called on Ba'al to send fire.

The growl on the wind increased.

Nothing followed.

The priest called again, and this time he added additional enticement: "As soon as you accept this sacrifice, O great Ba'al Addu," he said, "we will also give you the blood of this troubler of Israel—this Elijah." He pointed his staff at Eliyahu.

Still nothing happened.

"O Wondrous Ba'al," the high priest intoned. "Give us the fire from heaven and we will give you a hundred oxen—two hundred—a thousand. We will revel in the acts that please you, and you will reward us with rain."

A phalanx of priests took up the supplication as a chant: "O Ba'al, hear us," they sang—for an hour—without result.

Time for Jack sped up. The sun moved upward from just over the eastern hills until it stood directly overhead.

"Ba'al, answer us!" the priests shouted, and they danced around the altar.

"Perhaps," Eliyahu drawled, "Perhaps you need to shout louder."

An uproar of screaming followed the suggestion, but no fire from the sky.

"Maybe he's deep in thought, or busy, or traveling."

Gesturing for silence, the high priest of Ba'al offered, "We will give you the babies. We will bring our children to the fire for you, Ba'al. Give us your sign and the rain that follows. We will not withhold any sacrifice because we know you will reward us with crops and riches."

Jack saw a mother cover her sleeping child's face with the corner of her shawl and back away from the spectacle.

"Maybe he is sleeping and must be awakened," Eliyahu taunted.

Now the priests seized the knives with which they had killed and butchered the bullock and slashed themselves. They capered and danced in a frenzy, all the while scouring their arms and faces and each other with their blades.

The corresponding screeches on the wind increased, keeping tempo with the pace of the frantic movements.

The priests stabbed with swords and spears until every one of them bled from a dozen cuts or more. Some of them drooped and stumbled, weak from the effort and loss of blood. Their voices were hoarse and their songs croaked.

The sun sprinted across the sky. It was the time of the evening sacrifice. Jack was uncertain how he knew that fact, but he was sure of it.

And when the last of the priests was exhausted, Eliyahu called the people to gather around. Alone and unaided, the prophet of the Most High collected the tumbled rocks of the ruined altar. Selecting twelve he said, "One for each tribe. Your name shall be Israel—so says the Lord your God."

Even when the altar was built, Eliyahu did not cease from labor. He dug a trench around the base of the sacrificial space. After arranging the wood on top of the altar, killing and cutting up the bull, he made this demand of the people: "Fill four jars with water and pour them over the offering."

It was done.

"Again," he said.

"A third time," he required. The water ran off the sacrifice, over the wood, through gaps in the stones, and filled the trench.

Then Eliyahu lifted his eyes and his voice toward heaven. In that instant, all the growling, hissing, animal noises stopped. "Lord, the God of Abraham, Isaac, and Israel," he prayed. "Let it be known today You are God in Israel and I am Your servant and have done all these things at Your command. Answer me, Lord. Answer me, so these people will know You, Lord, are God, and You are turning their hearts back again."

King Ahab, under his awning of gold and blue, four hundred fifty priests of Ba'al, and the first five hundred of the onlookers tumbled over each other to get out of the way.

At the moment of Eliyahu's final syllable, not a lightning bolt but a massive tongue of fire appeared out of the clear sky. While the back ranks tried to see and the front of the audience tried to escape harm, the flame from heaven devoured sacrifice, wood, stones, soil beneath—and lapped up the water out of the trench. It then folded in on itself, rolling up like a scroll, and vanishing back into the sky.

King Ahab and the high priest of Ba'al backed into each other in their retreat. Wide-eyed, the priests of Ba'al picked their way through the crowd. Some abandoned all pretense of dignity and sprinted away.

The people of Israel prostrated themselves and buried their faces in the earth of Mt. Carmel. "The Lord—He is God!" they cried. Then repeating with one swelling voice: "The Lord—He is God!"

The hillside was empty. There was no longer the coppery smell of blood or the tang of smoke. There was no crowd of onlookers. No king. No prophet.

Eliyahu stood once more beside Jack. "What? What?" he demanded.

"The people of Israel not only realized the promises of Ba'al were false—they bitterly repented of ever worshipping him. In the name of saving their prosperity, they abandoned the One True God and offered him even their babies, thinking to preserve their wealth. They convinced themselves murdering babies was their right and privilege."

"And when they learned they had been deceived?" Jack asked, though he thought he already knew the answer.

"The false priests of sexual perversion and child murder were hunted down and killed—and then God released the rain upon the land."

Eliyahu's form began to shimmer and Jack realized the vision was drawing to a close. "Wait, please," he asked, respectfully. "What were those hideous voices?"

"The sound of the demons," Eliyahu replied. "At first they were trying to drown out the words of the prophet of God with their mockery. Later, they were afraid, because they knew the time of their power to influence the people with greed and lust was ending."

"And were they destroyed like the priests of Ba'al?" Jack inquired.

"No," was the response. "Sadly, no. They went away until a more convenient season, to infect another set of receptive, easily deceived people. No, their malevolent hatred knows no end until the end of time—they merely choose other vessels to do their bidding. Mark my words," Eliyahu urged as his form faded, "Wherever you find malevolent hatred and unquenchable rage against the God of Abraham, Isaac, and Jacob—wherever infants are murdered without qualm or hesitation—there are demons working the will of the Evil One in back of it all."

Eliyahu faded. The sun dropped below the western brow of the hill. Though he couldn't see it happen, Jack guessed it plunged into the sea, turning the waves crimson as it did the sky.

◆◆◆

A week after the murder of the policewoman and two days after Jack's experience on Mount Carmel, at his request, the second meeting with Rafa Husseini took place at the headquarters of the Palestinian Authority in Ramallah. The West Bank town was the de facto capital of the Palestinian state, but Jack knew better than to refer to it that way. The Palestinians maintained that Jerusalem was their capital.

Rafa Husseini's office was at the Mukataa, the same set of buildings where Mahmoud Abbas had his presidential palace and where Yassir Arafat's mausoleum was located. "Also, only temporarily," Rafa insisted. "He will be buried near the Dome of the Rock as befits the honor due such a leader of our people."

That comment already appeared to answer any question Jack might ask about rebuilding a Jewish Temple on that site. Instead he said, "I would like to get a better understanding of the settlement issue."

"You mean the illegal occupation issue. Planting Jewish towns on Palestinian land. What's more, the Israeli Occupation Forces patrol their illegal West Bank barrier and make travel for our citizens extremely difficult, if not impossible."

"Is it not true that because of the fence suicide bombings have been reduced to zero?"

"But not by the illegal apartheid wall! It is a deliberate attempt by Israel to damage the Palestine economy."

"So the shift by radical forces. . ."

"Legitimate resistance forces."

"So the shift in tactics to tunnels, knife-attacks like Damascus Gate, and mortar shells fired from Gaza was not due to the barrier?"

"Have you seen this?" she demanded, ignoring Jack's last comment and waving a press release from the Palestinian Office of Foreign Affairs. "Netanyahu," she pronounced the Israeli Prime Minister's name with obvious distaste. "Netanyahu has gone back to that illegal settlement called Ariel—on stolen Palestinian land—and declared it will 'always be part of Israel.' Is this fair? Is this the path of peace?"

"Israel says the settlements are necessary for security."

"Enslavement!" Rafa declared. "Illegal seizure and economic strangulation. The UN has repeatedly declared the settlements to be unlawful under international statutes."

"This would be the same United Nations that voted to partition the British Mandate of Palestine into Jewish and Arab states? Is it not true this area was already called 'The West Bank' when it was ruled by Jordan? And for nineteen years from 1948 to 1967 it was Jordan—not Israel—which prevented the formation of a Palestinian state?"

Rafa looked as though she might froth at the mouth. With recognizable effort she regained her composure. "I thank you for coming, Dr. Garrison," she said. "Unfortunately, I have another pressing appointment. Good day."

♦♦♦

It was while standing once again in the plaza before the Western Wall that Jack abruptly remarked to Lev, "I have to see for myself."

"What?"

"Up there," Jack insisted, thrusting an emphatic hand toward the Golden Dome atop the Temple Mount. "I have to see for myself what all the fuss is about." Turning toward Bette he demanded, "How can that be arranged? Do I have to go over to Ramallah again and come back with a Palestinian guide?"

Bette shook her head. "Nothing so complicated as that. Non-Muslims are permitted to visit the top from Saturday to Thursday between the hours of 7:30 and 11:00 in the morning, and in the afternoons from 1:30 to 2:30."

Jack flicked a glance at his heavy, silver Swiss military wristwatch. "It's only 1:00 p.m. now. Let's go."

"Hold it," Lev said. "Tomorrow morning, unless you want to go by yourself."

"Not happening," Bette returned.

Lev continued, "Gentiles have no special requirements, but I need to go to a mikvah first."

"A ritual bath? But why? Okay, ritual purity and all that, but you're a Christian."

"I also regard myself as a Jew, and as a Jew I respect the customs of my people," Lev corrected.

"Okay, tomorrow then. Will you join us?" Jack suggested to Bette.

She shook her head. "I can't miss reporting in. Go without me. Ghassan will be nearby if you need him."

So it was that at 7:30 the following morning the two men climbed the wooden structure leading upward to the Mughrabi Gate, the only portal allowed to non-Muslims. "Surrounded by all these ancient stones is this thing that looks more like a covered bridge from backwoods Vermont. And kind of an unloved bridge at that. Seems so—impermanent."

Lev agreed. "It was meant to be," he explained. "A dirt ramp leading up partly collapsed after a hard winter, so this was built. It was supposed to be replaced with a permanent bridge, but when the foundation work started in 2007 the Waqf protested. Said the Jews were trying to undermine the Temple Mount and collapse the Dome of the Rock."

Jack patted one of the slats of the bridge. Through the gaps he stared down at the throngs gathered for prayer in the plaza below. "Nonsense."

"Yeah? Well, there were even calls for a renewed Palestinian intifada."

Jack frowned. "Seriously?"

"Some of Israel's Arab neighbors got involved. They said proceeding with anything more permanent would make things tougher for them at home."

A man dressed in the uniform of a Waqf guard overheard this comment and scowled, but said nothing.

Lev shrugged and concluded, "That's Jerusalem for you, Jack."

They emerged from the wooden ramp facing a stone archway—the actual Mughrabi Gate—and passed through it to the Temple Mount plaza. To the south was the al-Aqsa Mosque. To the north was the Dome of the Rock.

"Now that you're here," Lev asked. "What do you want to do?"

"I think—I think I don't want a tour. I want to watch and think. Where would Solomon's Portico have been?"

Glancing at his friend curiously, Lev queried, "You want to see where Jesus did some teaching?"

"Something like that," Jack agreed.

The traditional route taken by observant Jews who wanted to avoid profaning the Temple was to walk around the plaza counter-clockwise, staying as close to the outside edges as possible. Following that same route, Lev escorted Jack to a spot about two-thirds of the way up the eastern side. "I'll leave you here, but I won't be far," Lev said. "I'll just stand over there in the shade and pray a little."

"I thought Jews weren't allowed to pray here?"

"Yeah, well," Lev replied. "So I won't be obvious about it." Smiling, he added, "Take all the time you want."

What did I want to see here? Jack mused. American tourists, their tour badges prominently hanging around their necks, were accompanied by incessantly droning guides offering "Kodak opportunities" and urging their charges to "Not miss this shot."

Elderly Muslim men sat on benches, talking.

Guards with walkie-talkies hanging from their belts patrolled up and down.

Jack closed his eyes and attempted to close his ears to everything but the softly sighing breeze.

♦♦♦

The Brits were here, Jack thought, staring around at the Temple Mount. *Before them the Turks, the Arabs, the Crusaders, the Romans, the Greeks, and the Babylonians all coveted and temporarily possessed this place. But it was the Jews who called it home.*

He wondered again why anyone cared so much about a couple square miles of earth. What made this limestone ridge surrounded by deep ravines important enough to die for?

What would all those conquerors have thought if they saw it today? The rich, bustling city beyond the ancient stone walls was infinitely preferable for modern, convenient living; yet it was this mountaintop acreage that remained a flashpoint.

It was amusing to think the thousands of pilgrims milling about here and in the city below might be descended from the earlier warriors. The

Jews, of course, and the Arabs. But what about the offspring of Crusader families, or the many-great grandsons of Babylon or Rome?

As if to confirm his premise, Jack's ears rang with the babble of voices. Arabic predominated, but he also heard English with American accents, with British accents, with Irish accents. French was succeeded by German, Italian by Polish, Spanish by Russian.

He closed his eyes, hoping to concentrate his thoughts.

Somehow, it worked. The cacophony of languages died away, leaving only the sound of the wind. How was that possible? Had Jack been struck deaf? But no, he heard the breeze sighing in the trees in the canyons, and the crunch of gravel under sandaled feet.

The wind blew from the southeast, out of the desert. It was a hot wind, full of dust and weariness.

The hilltop was deserted. Not just deserted but barren; swept clean. No golden dome surmounted the summit. No archways existed either, open or blocked.

No people.

Except for Jack and Eliyahu. "Where am I?" Jack fretted. "How'd I get here?"

Eliyahu laid a reassuring hand on Jack's arm. "You haven't moved." The cloaked figure tapped the tip of his wooden staff on the stone underfoot. "These stones have born witness to all the ages past," he said. "Have you not heard it was said, 'Teacher, rebuke your disciples?' And the response was, 'I tell you, if they keep quiet, the stones will cry out.'"

"But there's no mosque, no temple, no city!" Jack's cry was almost one of anguish.

"But there is that," Eliyahu said, lifting the tip of his staff and pointing it toward a rock ledge, weathered-looking, that protruded above the other stones. "Nor are we alone. See?"

Trudging into view, puffing with the exertion of the steep climb, came an old man with a long beard, leaning heavily on a staff like Eliyahu's, and a young man with no beard at all. They were dressed alike:

long robes of identically striped cloth; head coverings wrapped to shade their eyes from the glare and their mouths from the grit.

They stopped beside the stony outcropping.

On the younger man's back was a heap of wood. The cords tying the bundle lying across his shoulders had loosened, allowing some of the sticks to sag along his spine.

The elderly man had a knife tucked in the knotted cord that served him as a belt. From one hand swung a clay pot in a sling made of woven cords. The pot trailed a thin curl of smoke.

With the older man's assistance the younger eased the burden from his back and dropped the wood with a resounding crash. "This is where we will build the altar, my son," said the elder.

"My son!" Jack remarked to Eliyahu. "Is that Abraham and—and Isaac?"

"Yes," Eliyahu confirmed. "Let's get closer."

"Can't they see us?" Jack worried aloud.

"The stones here long ago took special notice of them," Eliyahu said cryptically. "As yet they have taken very little notice of us. No, they can neither see nor hear us."

Eliyahu and Jack approached the protruding ledge that lay atop its surroundings like a stone table.

"Help me gather what we need to build the altar," Abraham addressed Isaac.

While Abraham rested on the ledge, Isaac, his son, busied himself, locating and transporting large chunks of limestone from the ravines that slashed the hilltop.

Jack tried to interpret what was on the old man's face. What expression did Abraham carry? Was it fear? Grief? Determination?

When a dozen pillow-shaped boulders were heaped beside the wood, Abraham instructed, "Rest now, my son, while I build the altar." Carefully forming the structure side-by-side, row upon row, Abraham built his place of worship. While he labored, he remarked to Isaac, "This is the fourth altar I have constructed in this land. The first was at Shechem, beside the great tree there, when the Almighty promised me I would possess the land. That promise is made to you as well, my son.

"The second altar was at Beth-el—the House of God. And the third was beside the terebinth trees at Mamre. You have heard me tell that story many times before, my son."

Isaac nodded vigorously, but Abraham continued with wonder and delight as if this were his first recollection of that day. "There the Lord and two angels came to me, and He promised me—you, my son." Abraham bowed his head while he was still speaking. Involuntarily, Jack drew closer so as not to miss a single word. "He has promised me numberless descendants," Abraham said. "But the truth is: all I care about—is you."

With infinite care Abraham selected pieces of wood to build a combustible frame above the level of the altar, until it formed a bed of timbers above pillows of stone.

"All is ready," Isaac noted. "But, Father, as I asked you before: where is the lamb for the burnt offering?"

"And I told you, God will provide Himself the Lamb," Abraham said.

Jack wondered if he understood correctly. It sounded as if God promised to provide Himself as the sacrificial lamb.

There was no time to ponder further, because Abraham continued, "Now bring the cords which bound the wood. Come up here on the ledge and stand beside me."

The young man made no protest when his father looped and knotted the rope about Isaac's limbs and frame. Tenderly, gently, Abraham lowered Isaac so he rested on the wooden bed. With that done, Jack saw Abraham raise his eyes to heaven. He drew the short, curved blade from the belt about his waist and raised it high above his head.

The gleaming sunlight flashing from the knife pierced Jack's eye. Despite knowing the story—despite Eliyahu's words—Jack cried out, "No! Stop!"

The warning was unneeded. At the same moment as Jack's anguished shout a voice from the sky thundered, "Abraham! Abraham!"

The knife-wielding hand stayed aloft while Abraham replied, "Here I am."

It was not until the thunder boomed, "Do not lay a hand on the boy. Do not do anything to him," that Abraham allowed the blade to fall from his hand to the ground. "Now I know you fear God because you have not withheld from me your son, your only son."

A sharp bleating noise filled the silence when the words from heaven ceased.

Abraham freed his son from the bonds of death and together the two moved past Jack and Eliyahu toward the sound; toward the edge of a precipice.

There, in a clump of brush growing out from a rock fall, was a ram, caught by its horns in a tangle of brambles.

The scene to which Jack was witness sped up then. The ram slaughtered and placed atop the altar. The fire kindled from the coals in the fire pot. The fragrant smoke spiraling to heaven.

Abraham whispered, "The Lord will provide." Then he shouted to the heavens: "The Lord will provide!"

And once more the voice from above split the sky: "I swear by Myself, because you have done this and not withheld your son, your only son, I will surely bless you and make your descendants as numerous as the stars in the sky and the sand on the seashore. Your descendants will take possession of the cities of their enemies, and through your offspring all nations on earth will be blessed—because you obeyed Me."

A gust of wind tossed a handful of dust into Jack's eyes. Blinking furiously, he wiped them clear—but Abraham, Isaac, and Eliyahu were gone. Jack found himself on the edge of the precipice above the Western Wall, staring down at thousands of Abraham's—and Isaac's—descendants.

"On the mountain of the Lord it will be provided," he muttered.

♦♦♦

Instead of being fearful about what they would think, Jack was so ready to discuss his vision of Abraham and Isaac on Mount Moriah he could hardly wait. Lev would help him understand what he saw. So would Amir.

He had some reservations about telling Bette.

As always, Jack wished he still had Debbie. She would have listened. She would not have concluded he needed to see a shrink. She would not have said anything about him succumbing to Jerusalem Syndrome.

Then again—what if he was? Could he be going crazy?

It was not a dream. Jack was not awakened from sleep, realizing past experiences were recreated in his imagination.

This was different. He was fully awake, taking in the sights and sounds of Jerusalem's Temple Mount, and then he was—somewhere else. *Some* when *else, too*. And he returned from that journey—whatever that word meant in this context—to find he was in the same locale, only not exactly.

In the vision, he crossed the limestone ridge to look down the far side. Looking down at the Western Wall plaza meant he really *had* walked from the eastern rim to the west. Was it possible it was some kind of waking dream? Jack could think of no way to resolve the question, but there were parts of the encounter he could explore.

Did anyone see him cross the mountaintop? Did he appear to be in a trance—and did he seem to be talking to himself?

All of this was was why he asked Lev to see if Amir was available.

Jack and Lev, together with Bette, met Amir guiding a group of American pastors beside the ruins of the Pool of Siloam. "The pool was first built during the reign of King Hezekiah," Amir said. "It was needed to store the water brought by tunnel from the Gihon Spring in the Kidron Valley; the main source of water for Jerusalem.

"The spring arises at the foot of the Mount of Olives but finds its way here to the foot of the Temple Mount, after watering gardens and orchards along the way."

Mountains and trees again, Jack thought. *Am I hearing a pattern or just inventing one?*

"The pool was rebuilt during the time of the Maccabees," Amir continued, indicating the excavated stone steps leading downward.

"Then destroyed by the Romans in 70 AD and eventually lost from view beneath four meters—thirteen feet—of mud. It was only rediscovered in 2004. As you know," he said, acknowledging Jack with a wave, "it was here the man born blind received his sight. Jesus daubed mud on his eyes and then sent him here to wash—Siloam means 'sent.' Since we think their encounter was somewhere near the Temple, it was surely a test of the blind man's faith to find his way from there to here—more than a mile down what was a steep descent. Please take all the pictures you wish."

Leaving his charges happily snapping photos for future sermon illustrations, Amir joined Jack and the others. "Welcome!" he said, hugging each of them in turn. "How is your pilgrimage?" he asked, addressing Jack.

"I didn't know I was on one."

Smiling but half serious Amir replied, "Everyone who comes to Jerusalem is on a pilgrimage. Some of them know it before they come, some learn it while they're here. And some figure it out later."

"If people go on pilgrimages to get answers to their questions," Jack said, "then count me in."

"Just give me a moment," Amir said. He spoke to an assistant, then returned. "The group is going to tour the archaeology tunnel near the Western Wall," he said. "They'll be busy for at least an hour. Let's find a place to sit."

Not far from the ruined pool was a small park. Ringed with trees, a pair of benches gave the quartet a place to chat in comfort.

"What's up?" Lev said when Jack seemed hesitant to begin.

"Okay, here goes: Tell me about Shechem."

Lev and Amir exchanged curious looks. "As in today's location?" Amir inquired.

"Or in Bible times?" Lev added.

"Abraham's day."

"All right, Shechem," Amir said. "Thought to be near Nablus in the West Bank."

"Jacob's Well, where Jesus met the Samaritan Woman," Lev added.

Jack frowned as if not hearing what he expected. "And Bethel?"

"Not far from Shechem," Amir said. "Jacob dreams of a ladder to heaven."

"And Hebron?" Jack inserted abruptly.

"Jack," Lev said slowly. "You want to tell us what this is all about?"

"Not yet. Hebron?"

"The other direction," Bette contributed. "Thirty kilometers south of Jerusalem. But still also part of the West Bank."

"Abraham is buried there," Lev said.

"Ahh—Abraham," Jack repeated with a nod. He felt as if he'd finally received the response he'd been awaiting.

"Wait," Amir said, tapping his nose with his finger. "You just came down from the Temple Mount, yes?"

Jack and Lev concurred.

"So," Amir said, ticking off locations on his slender fingers. "Shechem, Bethel, Hebron—and Mount Moriah. The four places Abraham built altars to the Almighty."

Even though he was seated Jack felt the earth spinning. There was no way he knew that information previously, but he heard Abraham *say* it to Isaac. "Abraham really is connected with all of them?"

"And all are related to two promises the Almighty made to Abraham," Lev said. "One about how numberless Abraham's descendants would be. The second about him possessing all this land."

"But right now, *none* of those spots are in Israel?"

"That's what the Palestinians say," Bette responded. "All in the West Bank, but all connected to Abraham. Jack, what is this about?"

Swallowing hard, Jack resolved to discuss his vision, even if he sounded crazy. "Up there," he said, gesturing toward the Temple Mount, "I saw Abraham about to sacrifice Isaac. I don't mean 'saw,' like in my imagination. I mean 'saw,' like I was there in person."

Lev and Amir exchanged a glance. Bette's face was expressionless, impossible to read.

"I'm not crazy."

"Go on," Lev encouraged.

"I was there with Eliyahu—Elijah when we were on Mount Carmel. And, you remember, the man I met my first night in Jerusalem. The one who said, 'On the mountain of the Lord it will be provided.'"

"Same words used by Abraham," Amir noted, lifting his sunglasses to study Jack more carefully.

Jack nodded. "I heard about the altars from Abraham too. Anyway, when I—came back—I saw all of Abraham's descendants. I mean, Jews really are everywhere in the world now, right? Too many to count; like the stars?"

The trio of listeners agreed.

"But those promises to Abraham are only half fulfilled," Jack said. "Millions of descendants, but not in possession of the whole Promised Land. The locations of his altars. The West Bank is the heart and soul of the Promised Land."

"Jack," Lev cautioned. "Be careful, you're starting to sound like me."

"No, it's just. . ." How to explain when he didn't really understand himself? "I've been thinking about mountains and trees," he said, as if that clarified anything. "Is there more in prophecy about mountains and trees or planting on mountains—something like that?"

"How about Jeremiah?" Amir suggested. "Chapter thirty-one: I have loved you with an everlasting love. . .you shall plant vines on the mountains of Samaria."

"Like where, for instance?"

"I'm going to the Jewish settlement of Ariel tomorrow," Lev said. "It's in the mountains of Samaria. I'd love for you to join me and meet Lon Silver, the founder."

"Is it near anything we've been talking about?"

"Maybe midway between Shechem and Bethel," Amir said after consulting Bette.

"Perfect!" Jack said. "I need to see it."

"By the way, Jack," Lev said, laying his hand on his friend's arm. "No, I don't think you're crazy." He looked to Amir for agreement and got it. "I really believe what the prophet Joel says. . ."

"Old men will dream dreams and young men will see visions?" Jack quoted.

"That's the one."

"One word of caution," Amir added. "John says in his first letter: 'Do not believe every spirit, but test the spirits to see whether they are from God, because many false prophets have gone out into the world.'"

"Not sure how equipped I am to do that," Jack countered.

"Whatever you see or hear or experience, tell us about it," Lev offered. "It has to match the rest of Scripture, or something is off."

"Got it," Jack said.

◆◆◆

The little café in the West Bank city of Nablus was on a narrow street lined with pottery shops, fruit stalls, and vendors in soccer balls and plastic toys. T-shirts, printed in black Arabic lettering on Hamas green, proclaimed: *Nablus—City of Martyrs*. At the far end of the shopping area a green-domed mosque loomed overhead, but the mosque was dwarfed in its turn by a hillside crammed with ten-story apartment blocks.

Inside the café, the air was layered with blue tobacco smoke and lazy conversation. The tables near the entry were more desirable and were in use, but the restaurant was mostly empty. In a back corner a couple shared a table with plates of roast chicken, rice, pita, and hummus.

"So, brother," Rafa Husseini said. "Are you having trouble keeping track of your Dr. Garrison?"

"Not at all," Faisal said, pushing back from the table. "How did your meetings with him go?"

Rafa shrugged. "Stupid of those Hamas oafs to let their tunnel be discovered. But Garrison is a typical, western unbeliever. He is ready to blame Israel for everything."

"That attack near Damascus Gate was even worse than the tunnel," Faisal complained. "Young, stupid hotheads! At least they directed their assaults against the police and not tourists. But it is unfortunate Garrison witnessed it." He picked up the rubber tube of an argileh resting on the floor and took a long drag of smoke.

"Not necessarily," Rafa argued. "Our goal here is to convince him to report that the Jewish settlements need to be abandoned and Palestinian sovereignty enacted. He must believe that nothing short of granting all our territorial demands will bring peace. To that end, all unrest is good. Take the Noble Sanctuary for example—nobody with any brains thinks the Jews would be stupid enough to rebuild their Temple. But just the rumor that they might sends thousands of rioters into the streets and millions of dollars of donations into our treasury."

"Too many of our people want to live in peace with Israel," Faisal complained. "They see the prosperity of the cursed Jews and wish to share it, instead of working toward taking it all."

"What if Dr. Garrison experienced violent unrest even more closely?"

Faisal rubbed the amber-colored mouthpiece of the hookah on the sleeve of his jacket. "You don't mean kill him?"

"Certainly not!" Rafa exclaimed. "That would be a disaster! He is, after all, an American, and we dare not risk angering their government—not the one in power now. But if Garrison experienced the seething anger of Palestinian unrest—if the random but unquenchable resentment against the Jewish treatment of Palestine were, shall we say, emphasized?"

"I think I know exactly how and when," Faisal returned, nodding. He drew in, then aimed a precise arrow of smoke at the ceiling. "Leave it to me."

"Be careful," Rafa urged. "He must not be seriously injured."

"Leave it to me," Faisal repeated.

Chapter Twelve

"I met Lon Silver years ago," Lev said, leaning forward from the backseat of Bette's Corolla. "He's one of the original founders of Ariel and has been its mayor—I don't know—four times?"

"Five," Amir corrected. "I looked it up. And an MK with Likud," he added, naming the conservative political party with whom Silver had been in the Israeli parliament.

Just south of Route 5, Ariel sprawled across the Samaritan hills. "Elevation here?" Jack inquired.

"Six hundred meters," Bette said. "About 2,000 feet." Guessing Jack wanted more information she continued, "Part of the territory captured by Israel in the Six Day War, but there was no village here then. Ariel was built on barren land."

The directions Amir provided took them southeast into the hills and away from Ariel University and the city center. The dirt road that curved away from the highway was lined by olive trees, with vineyards just beyond them.

Wheeling the Corolla next to a parked tractor, Bette shut off the engine. A man in a blue work shirt and blue Levis with a wrench in his hand arose from kneeling beside the tractor. As soon as Lev emerged from the back seat the mechanic shouted, "Lev! So good to see you, my friend!"

Lev and Lon exchanged hugs. Amir got thumped on the back, while Jack also received an unexpected bear hug. "Welcome!" Lon said.

Instead of a hug, Lon extended a cordial handshake to Bette, accompanied by what almost appeared to be a bow. "Shalom, Officer Deekmann," Lon said. "And well done for what you did at Huwara. Come! Come with me."

What was that about? Jack wondered. The three males got big, jovial hellos, but Bette got—what was it? Respect? Admiration?

"So, Dr. Garrison," Lon said, his strong grip on Jack's shoulder propelling him toward a terraced hillside. "You are with the ECMP, eh? Perhaps you have questions for me about Ariel?"

"Yes," Jack said, surprised at the warmth of Mayor Silver's welcome. The ECMP was widely known to disapprove of Israeli settlements on West Bank land and Ariel was its fourth largest.

"In 1978," Silver explained, "I asked the military for West Bank sites that could be developed as defensible positions—as well as population centers. Of the three they offered, I chose this one. Why? I don't know! Truly crazy! Twelve miles inside the Green Line and only twenty miles from Jordan and on a likely Jordanian invasion route in case of another war. 'Give it to me,' I said, 'and I'll use it to defend Tel Aviv.' How could they say no?"

"Tell him about the hill," Lev urged.

"So who's telling this story? I'm coming to that. So this place, this hill..." Silver waved toward the northwest. "The Arabs called it Jabel Mawet—the Hill of Death."

Silver laughed at Jack's stricken face. "Arab exaggeration. No battles except against too little water and too much rock. We pitched two tents on top. That was the beginning of Ariel. Lion of God, eh? Some lion. That year forty families came. It was a hard winter. Water came by tanker truck. Only generators for electricity for four years. But now. . ."

Lon Silver paused and with manifest pride remarked, "Now 18,000 people call Ariel home. Ten thousand students—Jews AND Arabs—attend university here."

They reached the terraced hill where there was a flatbed wagon bearing a load of grapevines in plastic pots, and a heap of shovels. "So what are we doing here today, Lon?" Lev asked.

"I needed labor and look what I got," Lon said, picking up a shovel and extending the handle toward Jack.

Jack was amused but also impressed. What was the quote from the Prophet Jeremiah? Something about planting vineyards on the hills of Samaria? Was it not only one day earlier he asked that question?

Placing the blade of the tool on the first marked spot, Jack drove it into the earth. What was that unfamiliar sensation? Jack felt as if he were planting his heart in the soil of God's word. Jack made quick work of creating the hole for planting the baby vine. Kneeling beside the space, he shucked off the plastic shell, lowered the plant into its new home and patted the soil around it with a wish—a prayer?—it would prosper.

"So, we dig, we plant," Lon said. "And maybe we live long enough to taste the wine, eh?"

♦♦♦

On the other side of an equipment shed was a travel trailer; what the Brits call a 'caravan,' Jack thought. A wooden porch was added to the front and it was overhung with a canvas awning. A cheerful, gray-haired woman with attentive, sparkling eyes waved to the vine planters from the deck.

"My wife," Lon Silver said, waving back. "That caravan is like the one we lived in when we first came to Ariel. She put up with a lot, eh?" He laughed. "She puts up with *me*! Why? I don't know!"

After urging all her guests to a seat on the porch, Dorith Silver offered the choice of wine or pomegranate juice. Lon distributed cigars to the men. He offered one to Bette, but she declined. "Ha! Cuban," Lon said. He lit up, puffed the tobacco alight, and exhaled a fragrant, bluish cloud.

"So, Jack Garrison," Lon said. "How does it feel to be part of fulfilling prophecy?" Without waiting for Jack's response, Lon continued, "Also from Jeremiah: 'The watchmen will cry from Mount Ephraim, "Arise and let us go up to Zion to the Lord our God."' Do you know what is this 'Watchmen'? It is the Hebrew word, 'natzar.' It is the root word of 'Notzrim'; what we modern Jews call Christians."

"Like 'Nazarenes?'" Jack ventured.

Waving his cigar in agreement, Lon said, "Exactly! Why? I don't know. Perhaps our friend Lev can tell us."

"It also means, 'to keep safe,' or 'hidden until revealed later,'" Lev explained. "The connection makes sense: Jesus was 'hidden' in Nazareth until it was time for Him to be revealed."

Bette took a sip of chilled juice and asked Lon, "Are you saying Christians are the Watchmen who have finally come to plant vines in Samaria?"

Jack looked at Bette with renewed appreciation. This was exactly his query.

Pushing his wire-framed glasses back up on his stubby nose, Lon next ran his free hand over his short-cropped, sandy hair. "Am I a scholar? Am I a rabbi? But Jeremiah wrote his message what, 2,500 years ago? And aren't a couple Notzrim..." he jabbed his cigar at Amir and Lev, "planting vines on the mountains of Samaria?"

Jack thought about the odd sensation of connecting to the land and to the prophecies he experienced in the planting. Did he wish Lon Silver also included him in the recognition of the Watchmen? He still could not bring himself to share what he felt. Nobody sensible really believed 2,500-year-old prophecies were being fulfilled today—did they?

"You don't think of yourself as religious, do you, Lon?" Amir asked.

Lon shrugged. "But how can anyone live in such a place, at such a time, and not think about how we got here, eh? I am a fourth-generation Sabra. I was born before the State. I was a little boy during the War of Independence. A miracle, some say. A whole lot of miracles, I say! And 1967? More miracles. And I watched it happen."

Laughing, Dorith challenged him. "What did Golda say? 'Don't be so humble—You're not *that* great.'"

"Golda—as in, Prime Minister Golda Meir?" Jack asked.

Dorith nodded vigorously. "A big part of all those miracles, Lon is."

"Most, not all." Lon beamed. "My number one fan," he added, waving at his wife.

Amir resumed, "Do you know this prophecy from Isaiah? 'There shall come a rod from the stem of Judah. And a branch shall grow from his roots.'"

"Of course," Lon acknowledged. "Branch: 'netzer.' Like 'natzar,' eh? Branches that grow from underground—from the roots—are hidden until they aren't hidden anymore."

Lev added, "And many of us Notzrim—many around the world now—feel the need to better connect with our Jewish roots."

"And what better way to reconnect than helping plant vines in Samaria!" Lon declared. "So what say you, Dr. Garrison?"

"I say—you have given me much to think about," Jack admitted. Without speaking it aloud, he wondered if he had just seen—no, "participated in," another proof the prophecies of Scripture were real. *Millions of descendants of Abraham*, he thought, *returning to worship beside their ancient temple. And Christians planting vines on land that wasn't owned by Jews—or anyone else—for 2,000 years.* "Thanks," he said to Lon and Dorith.

"You must come again," Lon said.

♦♦♦

On the return trip from Ariel to Jerusalem Bette allowed Amir to drive. She sat beside him while Jack and Lev discussed the meeting with Lon Silver. "So, what do you think of our friend, Lon?" Lev asked.

"Is he always that energetic?"

"Oh, no. This was one of his quiet days. You should see him when he gets wound up. But seriously," Lev continued after the laughter in the car died down, "His grandfather and father were both mayors before him. His insistence and persistence and powers of persuasion are what brought the city to birth—and the university too."

"And that business about planting the vines on the mountains of Samaria being a fulfillment of prophecy—you set me up for that, right?"

"If you mean, did I know we would be working in the vineyard—honestly, no. It was not a total surprise. Since being semi-retired Lon often works in the orchards or with the vines or on some irrigation project or other. I've seen him with three cell phones dangling from his belt, along with a holstered pistol, and still hoeing a furrow, like something straight out of a hundred—or a couple thousand—years ago. But let me ask you a couple things."

"Go ahead," Jack said, staring out the window at a hilltop synagogue directly opposite a mosque on the other side of the highway.

"Even if Lon and I do read the same book, meaning Jeremiah, and both of us choose to believe it was prophesied 2,500 years ago that Christians would someday plant grapes in Samaria—even if I planned our visit that way, would that make it less true it's really happening?"

Jack thought a moment. "No," he grudgingly admitted.

"Then here's my second question: When you were digging and planting, did you—feel anything?"

Jack was suddenly alarmed. If he said yes, would it suddenly validate this whole prophecy thing? He hedged. "Like what?" he said. Amir and Bette paused their conversation and were listening.

Lev elaborated: "I can't answer for anyone else. All I know is the first time I planted a tree in Israel I instantly and powerfully felt connected to the land. Like I was rooted here myself, you know?"

Shrugging, Jack said, "Maybe that works for you because you're Jewish."

When Jack did not say more, Lev chose to let the topic drop.

They were driving through a range of low, brown hills devoid of human habitation or agriculture. "My turn," Jack said to Lev. "Suppose—just suppose, because I'm not suggesting I really think this—but if I did believe Bible prophecy had some degree of validity, and if I wanted to find some examples to share with a skeptic—what would you pick?"

Without hesitation Lev said, "That's easy. Top of the list is the return of Jews to this land."

"Gimme a break," Jack complained. "That is a political hot potato, not a prophetic fulfillment. If the UN hadn't voted in 1947 to partition Palestine into two states there wouldn't be an Israel, and we wouldn't be in this car having this discussion. No offense," he said to Amir and Bette. "But that is true, isn't it?"

Amir contributed, "I see it the other way around. Since God said Israel *would* be reborn, then the only things left undecided were the *how* and the *when*."

"You're not asking a big enough question," Lev offered. "Here's the larger context. Has any nation in the whole history of the world ever gone out of existence for 200 years—let alone 2,000—and then been reborn?"

"Not that I know of," Jack admitted.

"Especially a people who have never been in authority in any culture in which they've ever lived? Who have always been the ones being persecuted down through the ages? And how?" Lev said rhetorically. "Isaiah chapter sixty-six: 'Who has ever heard of such things? Who has ever seen things like this? Can a country be born in a day, or a nation be brought forth in a moment? Yet no sooner is Zion in labor than she gives birth to her children.'"

"My father is not religious," Bette said. "But even he taught me that to call Israel a miracle is about one million times too small an expression."

They came to a construction zone where the entire westbound traffic stopped. Amir pulled up behind a large, boxy van, with no way to see how far ahead the disruption extended.

"And there's this," Amir added. "God promised Abraham a multitude of descendants, yes? No one doubts the truth of that accomplishment, but how has He chosen to do it? Not from one other country where a sizable Jewish population preserved their faith and heritage—not from a half dozen nations—not from a single continent—but from tiny pockets all around the globe where Jews were scattered and from where they escaped persecution to come home to Eretz Israel."

Bette, who had worked with immigration, added, "Russia and Yemen, Poland and Hungary, out of the Holocaust. . ."

All in the car were silent for a moment. Jack remembered one of the greatest tragedies of human history was that had legal immigration into British-held Palestine been possible in the 1930s, then millions of lives might have been spared from the Nazis.

"Iran, Iraq, and Ethiopia," Bette resumed.

Lev thumped his chest. "And America!"

"Okay, okay," Jack said, raising both hands in a gesture of surrender, but Lev was not entirely finished yet.

"And don't think planting vines in Samaria is the only connection," he stressed. "Listen to this: 'See, I will bring them from the land of the north and gather them from the ends of the earth.' Jeremiah 31:8. And this has all happened within the last 100 years or so, and mostly within the last seventy."

Jack pondered what he'd heard and seen and experienced himself in the vineyard. To Lev he said, "So you include yourself as a fulfilled prophecy? Then let's talk about you. You're a Jew but you're also a believer in Jesus. How's that supposed to work and how's it fit in with what we're discussing?"

Something struck the door panel of the car like a hammer blow. Then came the report of a gun. Bette shouted to Amir: "Drive! Pull up beside the lorry! Go!" And to Lev and Jack: "Get down!" She flung herself over the seatback and on top of the two men just as a second round shattered the car window where Jack's head had been.

The engine roared as Amir piloted the Toyota onto the shoulder and behind the shelter of the truck.

"Keep down!" Bette urged.

"How about you?" Jack asked as Bette struggled to draw both her weapon and a phone. Ignoring him she thumbed a call while scanning out through the shattered pane of glass. "Dispatch!" she shouted. "Shots fired! Westbound Highway Five. Five klicks from the Sha'ar Shomeron interchange. Wait. I'll check. Is anyone hurt?"

Lev and Amir replied in the negative. Jack agreed, then added, "You are." He pointed at a streak of blood sliding downward from a crease on Bette's forehead.

"All okay," Bette reported. She rang off, then said again, "Stay down. Help is on the way."

No more shots were fired and in less than five minutes two police helicopters arrived. While one buzzed the hills alongside the highway, the other landed near the road.

As the quartet received an "All Clear" and uncurled from the Toyota, Jack remarked to Lev, "Ancient Scriptures are one thing—but they don't address modern realities, do they? Settlements build resentment and resentment causes violence." He felt angry at himself for having almost bought into a religious deception.

♦♦♦

It was like a council of war gathered in Jack's hotel suite at the King David. Bette and Lev sat across a round mahogany table from where Jack paced up and down the carpeted floor. "Just look at that," Jack insisted, pointing at the bandage on Bette's forehead. "You could've been killed!"

"It's a scratch. Nothing," Bette insisted.

"You could have been killed!" Jack repeated. "Like that police-woman I saw stabbed right in front of me." He shuddered at the memory. "Right in front of me."

"Protecting you is my job," Bette said.

"Well, I don't like it! Besides, okay, your job. So I could've been killed, or Lev here, or Amir." Pausing in his third circuit he faced Bette with his hands on his hips. "Unless you think I was specifically the target. Is that it?"

"There's no evidence to suggest that," Bette admitted. "The Highway Five corridor has been a place of random shootings at vehicles before."

"Jack," Lev said firmly, "We weren't even in an official car. Do you think you're being tracked by an assassin? Why?"

Remembering the creepy evening paranoia back in London, Jack rejected the idea as sounding too melodramatic. "Okay, so not me," he said. "But nobody should live like that." Another thought struck him. "Will there be reprisals? Burn down a village or something?"

"Jack!" Lev retorted sharply. "You don't mean that!"

"Well?" Jack demanded of Bette as he started treading over to the door and back again.

"Since no perp has been caught," the officer said. "No, there won't be any reprisals. When we can identify a bomber, yes, we do raid his home and sometimes we destroy it as a warning—a deterrent measure."

"There, you see?" Jack said.

"Be reasonable, Jack," Lev implored. "It almost sounds like you're blaming us instead of the one who pulled the trigger."

"I—no—I—" he ran his hand over his hair, but his eyes were fixed on Bette's wound. "I'm blaming this whole bloody mess…" he said. "The settlements are an obstacle to peace. That means a rebuilt Temple would be an even bigger problem."

"So taking barren land and making it bloom—creating a city in the desert—providing advanced education to young people without regard to their nationality or religion—vines and orchards and jobs—we should tear all that down?" Bette asked quietly.

"Israel gave up the Sinai, and we have peace with Egypt," Lev reminded Jack. "And Gaza is Palestinian, right? But it seems no offer for a Palestinian state is ever enough. And anyway, how'd 'land-for-peace' turn out for Prime Minister Chamberlain? Gave away Czechoslovakia, and it delayed the Second World War for—I dunno—one year?"

Jack threw up his hands. "So I give up, go home, and tell the committee there is no answer?"

"Just don't give up, Jack," Lev encouraged. "Travel more with me. Give it another week and then see. I think you owe it to Lon Silver."

Jack frowned.

"Sorry," Lev said, smiling. "My joke. Maybe you owe it to me—or to Bette here?"

Jack thought that through. It had been Bette Deekmann's life on the line. "Another week," he agreed, grudgingly. "If I'm not convinced there's some Israeli claim that can't be set aside, then I'm done here."

◆◆◆

The daytime temperatures were noticeably warmer as Israel headed into spring. The first wild flowers—pinks and yellows—dotted the hillsides of Galilee. "Welcome to Magdala," Amir said, beckoning his charges to come closer. "Yes, this village, discovered less than ten years ago, was the home of Mary of Magdala. She is mentioned in the Gospel of Luke, chapter eight, as having been freed by Jesus of seven demons.

She was in the group of women who helped support Jesus and His followers. And most famously, she was the first person to meet and speak with the Risen Lord."

Only three days after the shooting on the highway Bette's forehead displayed a barely noticeable adhesive bandage. She took no notice of it, but Jack scowled whenever he saw it. Jack, Lev, and Bette formed a tight semi-circle off to the side of the group of pastors and their wives Amir addressed. The pilgrims were inside a structure housing the recently excavated Magdala synagogue. They stood in front of the ancient carved block known as the Magdala Stone.

"Now this," Amir said, "is a reproduction of the artifact actually found on this site in 2009. The original is stored for safe-keeping and for further study by archaeologists. I have seen the original and I can vouch for the accuracy of the carvings."

While Amir continued lecturing and answering questions from the group, Lev quietly explained to Jack and Bette. "This was made to resemble an altar, but probably was a table or a lectern. You see the arches carved there, and the seven-branched menorah? Experts believe this is an accurate depiction of the Temple in Jerusalem—the way it would be made by someone who had been there in person."

"Is that why you wanted me to see it?" Jack asked.

"You're not one who ever doubted the Temple existed," Lev laughed. "It's the fate of the next Temple you have questions about. No, I just wanted…wait," he said, interrupting himself. "Let's just listen."

A rail thin member of the group waved to get Amir's attention. In a voice so hoarse as to be almost inaudible, he croaked, "Jesus? Was…?" The man paused to gulp a breath.

"Reverend Art Stuart. Retired pastor from Phoenix," Lev whispered. "Heart failure—beyond any medication. He always wanted to come to the Holy Land, so his friends sent him."

Everyone else in the cluster of listeners got quiet so the gaunt, gray-complexioned figure could be more easily heard. "Was Jesus—here?"

"We cannot say for certain," Amir replied. "We know this synagogue dates to before 70 AD. Scripture tells us that during Jesus' ministry in Galilee He taught in all their synagogues, so yes, it's a fair conclusion."

His head shaking and his body trembling, the terminally-ill man allowed himself to be assisted to a bench. Jack saw that the elderly minister had used up all his reserves of strength just getting the question out.

Lev stepped away from Bette and Jack and approached Amir. "Why don't we take a moment and pray for our friend, Art?" he said.

The group closed in around the seated man. Amir and Lev laid their hands on Art's head while all the others touched his shoulders or held onto his arms. "Lord," Lev said. "We ask for your healing touch for Art. Here we are, agreeing in prayer as You have said we should. Holy Spirit, please touch Art. Heal him."

Jack could hardly bear to watch. The old man was shaking from head to toe, and visibly distressed. It seemed wrong to keep him sitting hunched over on a cold, stone bench. He probably needed to lie down, maybe even be taken to the hospital.

"Lord," Amir continued the prayer, "Your word says You went throughout Galilee, teaching in their synagogues, proclaiming the Good News of the Kingdom, and healing every disease and sickness among the people. Here we are, in one of those synagogues, and every means every. We bring you our dear brother, Art, and ask You to do again what You did in this place before. Heal him. Heal him, Lord."

This was awful. Jack wasn't sure he could watch anymore. Besides being deathly ill, now Art would be an object of pity, and probably worse off for all the emotion.

There was complete silence for the space of six heartbeats. One of the women in the group gasped and Jack turned.

Art took a deep breath and then exhaled. His shoulders squared, his body grew erect. The trembling in his limbs ceased. He lifted his head and looked around, making eye contact first with Lev, and then with Amir, and then with each of his comrades. Another deep breath and then, "I—feel different," Art said in a firm, baritone. "Something's happened. I can breathe. That flutter in my chest—is gone."

Not possible, Jack thought. *Things like this don't really happen. Not in the twenty-first century.*

Even though hands still grasped and patted him on every side, Art stood upright under his own power. To Jack's utter consternation, the elderly pastor laughed. Laughed! "He healed them all!" Art said. "He healed them all! He's still healing, praise God! It's still true today!"

When the beaming pilgrims had their fill of taking pictures beside Art and the Magdala Stone, Amir led them back to the tour bus. On the way they continued laughing and praising and exclaiming, with Art's voice the loudest of any.

"What just happened here?" Jack directed to Lev.

"Yes," Bette agreed, wide-eyed. "What was that?"

"I have to say it this way," Lev explained. "I'm amazed—but not surprised. God still works miracles. Now you've seen one with your own eyes. You and Bette."

"Before that—before what just happened, happened—I asked why you brought me here. You couldn't have planned this?"

"Not in a million years," Lev agreed. "No, I brought you here because of the same reason thousands of visitors come to Israel every year. Jesus was really here, Jack. He really taught—*here.* He really performed miracles—*here.* And He said He was the Son of God—*here.* Now. What are you going to do about it? This is bigger than land or politics or even prophecy, Jack," Lev said seriously. "This is about eternity."

◆◆◆

Back in Jerusalem again after the miracle in Magdala, the air was very still. The morning sun warmed the pale, honey-colored walls. Shadows taller than their owners gestured and pointed, raised cameras or waved.

The broad expanse of steps leading up to the southern wall of the Temple Mount was formed of wide but shallow treads. Jack imagined the design caused the flood of pilgrims arriving for the feasts to make slow, dignified progress upward. The staircase ended in a pair of sealed archways, which were once the portals for worshippers to reach their holy destination.

Closing his eyes, Jack saw it as it was 2,000 years before: a Passover throng, their songs being echoed by those already there.

I rejoice with those who said to me, "Let us go to the house of the Lord." Our feet are standing in your gates, Jerusalem—pray for the peace of Jerusalem: "May those who love you be secure. May there be peace within your walls..."

Where did that quotation come from? Jack remembered reading the Psalms of Ascent, but he had no recollection of memorizing that one. Was this another vision?

His eyes flicked open, but did not see Jesus climbing the steps surrounded by pious, bearded worshippers in prayer shawls and phylacteries. Instead he witnessed a tight knot of modern believers in jeans and hiking boots gathered around Amir and Lev. *Pray for the peace of Jerusalem*, he thought.

Amir instructed his charges, "As large as this set of steps appears, it was much greater before the Romans and the devastation of 70 AD. As you can see, there were actually five gates at the head of the stairs, but the stairs below the Triple Gate are in ruins. This was the main entrance to the Temple area for the masses of pilgrims who came on Passover and Pentecost and Tabernacles. Jesus entered here with his parents as a child. He came here when He expelled the moneychangers. Perhaps He walked here during the days before His last Passover meal, just before His Passion."

Jack saw Art's lips moving but no sound came out. Had he lost his breath again? Had the healing in Magdala been temporary? But no, the man's color was ruddy, like a youthful King David, and he clambered up the steps ahead of the others.

"But it's not Passover I want to focus on just now," Amir said. "Let's talk about Pentecost instead. Jews came here to celebrate fifty days after Passover. If Passover recounts the escape from Egypt, then Pentecost recalls the giving of the Law on Mount Sinai. And you remember the riot in the camp while Moses was up on the mountain? Charlton Heston in *The Ten Commandments*, eh? Book of Exodus says 3,000 people died.

"But you've heard me say, 'Everything means something?' After Resurrection Sunday—after Jesus freed us all from the bondage of sin on that best of all Passovers, what came next?"

"The Holy Spirit," Art called out. "The sound of rushing wind and tongues of flame!"

"Just so," Amir agreed. "If these steps were where the pilgrims were, each hearing in his own language—Parthians, Medes, Egyptians, and Romans and Arabs—then doesn't it make sense this is where Peter preached?

"'Fellow Jews,' Peter said, 'and all you who live in Jerusalem…. these men are not drunk as you suppose. It's only nine in the morning!' Just like now."

The pastors and spouses chuckled appreciatively. Amir said, "No! But they *were* drunk! They were drunk on the new wine of the Spirit of God!"

Now the vision came.

Jack stood exactly where he was, but a feeling like wind where there was no wind swept him across centuries. Where he heard only English, now he heard a babble of voices: Greek and Aramaic and others he did not recognize. Yet the thundering voice of the broad-shouldered, barrel-chested man who was speaking came through clearly to Jack's ears. "This is what was spoken by the prophet Joel: 'In the last days, God says, I will pour out my spirit on all people. Your sons and daughters will prophesy, your young men will see visions, your old men will dream dreams.'"

That's me! Jack thought. *Visions and dreams. And we're much closer to the Last Days—whatever that means—than when Peter first preached here.*

"You're right," Eliyahu agreed, standing beside Jack on the third step up from the pavement. "Listen."

Together they heard the Apostle Peter remind his listeners that King David prophesied about the coming Messiah. Jack heard Peter confidently assert that Jesus of Nazareth was the embodiment of David's prophecy. That Jesus, though put to death on a cross, was raised to life again.

Peter swept his arms to encompass the group of Jesus' followers standing alongside him. "And we are all witnesses of it—God has made this Jesus, whom you crucified, both Lord and Messiah."

Jack heard shouts of "I believe it. What do I do? What?" then recognized it was his own voice mingling with a thousand more who heard Peter's words.

"Repent and be baptized," Peter said, "every one of you, in the Name of Jesus Christ for the forgiveness of your sins. And you will receive the gift of the Holy Spirit."

"Me!" Jack called. "I want that for me."

Peter and Eliyahu and the world of the first century disappeared.

Bette looked at him curiously while Lev nodded understanding and approval.

"And know this," Amir said. "When the law came on Pentecost at Sinai, 3,000 died for their sins. When the Pentecost of the Spirit came right here, 3,000 entered new life in the Kingdom of God."

"Help me, Lev," Jack said. "You've got to help me. I never understood what this was all about. Now I know Jesus is real and He is Lord. What do I do now?"

◆◆◆

Just east of the Temple Mount, across the Kidron Valley at the foot of the Mount of Olives, was a small olive grove. The evening breeze sighed through the silver-green leaves and whistled around the gnarled trunks of the venerable, thick-waisted trees. "This space has been known since Jesus' day as the Garden of Gethsemane—the garden of the oil press," Amir said to his pilgrims.

"Jesus came here after his last supper with his disciples," Lev added. "I want to take you back to that night. Remember, the story concludes with, 'after they sang a hymn, they went out...' What were they singing—the disciples, still blissfully confused, and Jesus, knowing full well what He was facing? What was it?"

Amir took up the story. "In Jesus' day, and continuing down to today, at Passover Jews sing Psalms 113 to 118, called the Hallel—like Hallelujah.

"Since the meal was ended, they must have been singing 118. Listen to some of the words."

Jack closed his eyes, expecting to be transported to another evening in another century. No vision came this time, but from somewhere a chorus sang along as Lev recited, "Out of my distress I called on the Lord; the Lord answered me and set me free. . ."

How had he never known that before? Jesus went straight from singing these very words to praying in the garden for release—but His release did not come until after His torture and death.

"The stone the builders rejected has become the cornerstone," Lev continued quoting. "This is the Lord's doing; it is marvelous in our eyes."

Where were all those other voices coming from, Jack wondered? Everyone in the travel group was quietly listening. No one was singing aloud.

Lev offered, "This is the place where the Lord felt the rejection, not only of the Jewish leaders, but of His sleepy friends; where He suffered the agony of bearing the burden of His mission all alone. Where He prayed, 'Not my will, but thine be done.'"

Jack felt the wind caress his face and a shiver prickled the back of his neck. The vision he saw of the tragic end to the Garden of Eden returned, crashing into his thoughts. A grieving departure from contentment and joy—the path of return barred. Now another garden of suffering provided the way back to paradise reopened.

He shivered again.

Amir said, "The burden Jesus carried—the cup from which He had to drink—could not be taken away, even though He sweat drops of blood with the agony of it. But He went through it all—for us."

"Some of you are bearing burdens here tonight," Lev said. "The Lord has shown me someone is weary from that load. You have been asking the Lord to let you put it down, amen?"

A young woman named Ann who came on the tour with her friend, Vicki, timidly raised her hand. "I was raised in a cult. My mom and dad are still caught in it. My heart breaks for them! I can't be with them and I can't help them get free. It's crushing me. I need Jesus to be real for me!"

Vicki put her arms around Ann and hugged her. Two more women stepped up to enclose Ann in an embrace of love and prayer.

Ann wept, then sobbed. "Let it go," Vicki urged. "It's not yours to carry anymore. Give it to Jesus."

It was as if years of pent-up stress and fear came out with each tear; nightmares of hurt and rejection fell away with each gasping cry.

Heaving a great sigh, Ann's eyes brightened. "Something's happened," she said at last. "I haven't felt this free in—forever!"

To Jack's surprise, his own hand was aloft. "My wife. . ." he said. "My son—I still miss them so much. . ." Tears overflowed from his eyes and scored furrows on his cheeks. "I've been so angry at God. I can't stop blaming Him. Even though I know it's killing me, I haven't been able to set it down."

Amir on one side and Lev on the other, surrounded him. But it was Art who laid his hand on Jack's forehead. "A man of sorrows, acquainted with grief," he quoted about Jesus. "He already knows everything you're feeling. God's not shocked that you're angry and hurting and grieving and bitter. He's not mad at you or trying to teach you a lesson. But He doesn't want you to hurt anymore, either. Can you put it down, Jack? Wouldn't you like to give it to Jesus now, tonight?"

"Yes. I've had enough. Enough bitterness. Enough anger. I want it all out of my life. God help me. Jesus, I trust in You. Be real for me."

Closing his eyes, Jack recognized the triumphant chorus of an invisible choir proclaiming: "I will not die but live, and proclaim what the Lord has done—This is the day that the Lord has made; let us rejoice and be glad in it—Give thanks to the Lord, for He is good. His love endures forever."

♦♦♦

Jack slid open the desk drawer and gazed at the crisp sheets of hotel stationery. The heading was embossed with gold lettering: "The King David."

On his iPhone, James Taylor sang, "You Are My Only One."

Striving to make his handwriting legible, Jack crafted two notes to slip into the stones of the Western Wall. The first was to God, and the second was a message to Debbie. His tears dropped onto the paper, blurring the ink.

Jack decided maybe his handwriting didn't matter. God already knew what Jack's note said: an apology for blaming God for everything gone wrong in his life. He was angry at God—for losing Debbie, mostly—but there were other things as well.

And as for his message to Debbie, though she was in heaven, she was among the few who could decipher his scrawl. His note to her was also a confession. How he wished he had been better to her. She knew so much more about life than he ever knew. And also she knew about death. And grief. How often had he quoted the lines from *As You Like It*?

All the world's a stage

and all the men and women merely players...

they have their entrances and their exits...

Jack did not expect her to make her final exit so early in the play. How could he survive life on his own? If he tried to play his part as a solo act, his heart would break and he would die.

As she lay broken, suffering, and fighting to survive in the ICU, Jack played her the James Taylor song flowing now from his phone.

In conflict with the plea from Taylor's voice. She left him.

All of it was in Debbie's letter. He folded the sheets, which contained his heart, down to tiny rectangles. He caught the early morning bus and carried the weight of all his grief to the Western Wall. Donning a kippa and a borrowed prayer shawl, he strode across the stone plaza like a small, broken-hearted boy coming home to tell his daddy he was beat up pretty bad by the school bully.

Jack found a crevice between the ancient stones and placed his deepest longings there. Pressing his cheek against the rough, tear-stained surface, he wept hard on his daddy's shoulder. He moaned and no one around him seemed to notice. Deep sobs wracked him. "Oh, God! Oh, Deb!"

He couldn't tell how long he leaned against God. Had he been there an hour? A day? Forever? After a time the trembling ceased. His tears ran out. For the first time he felt peace; an embrace of comfort for what was inconsolable loss, and forgiveness for a thousand failures.

Jack wiped his eyes with the back of his hand and took a step away from the stones. So many scraps of paper there—so many prayers.

The sun was rising. He smiled faintly, and said, "Thank you."

Chapter Thirteen

Once again in the official black limo, the drive from the King David Hotel to the Prime Minister's Office at 3 Kaplan street took just eight minutes. Ghassan expertly wheeled his way through light traffic to the parking area for the Israeli government offices. Because of security, Bette, Amir, Lev, and Jack walked the remaining distance.

"Dr. Mawire will be meeting us here," Lev said as Bette displayed her credentials at a third checkpoint. "This timing is perfect. I wanted you to meet Bibi, of course, and you have to meet Robert Mawire. Catching them both together is phenomenal. Fact is, you have no idea how important today is."

"You and Amir have both been hinting that this Mawire character is something special," Jack said, "but you haven't given me details. So? How about now?"

They were soon seated in a medium-sized conference room around an oval, dark oak table. A map of the eastern hemisphere of the world, centered on Jerusalem, occupied most of one wall. It was flanked by two flags. One was the national banner: blue Star of David on a white field. The other was a blue flag with its upper corner displaying a copy of the Israeli flag, while in the opposite bottom corner was a golden menorah.

"Now, about Mawire," Jack said impatiently.

Lev and Amir exchanged grins. "Dr. Robert Mawire," Lev explained, "is pastor of Good News World Outreach church in Texas. He's an

African, born in what was then Rhodesia, but educated in New Zealand and America."

Jack looked confused. "And his connection to Israel is. . ."

Ignoring the question, Lev continued, "He worked with presidents Reagan and Bush, (senior) on humanitarian aid projects for Africa. He's also chairman and CEO of WRNO Worldwide Shortwave Radio."

"And he connects to Israel. . .?"

"Jack," Amir said, signaling it was his turn to speak. "He's a prophet."

"Sorry?" Jack said.

"Robert contacted Prime Minister Netanyahu in '98. Told him he had a prophecy for him; God had a warning for Robert to deliver."

Suddenly Jack was eager to hear what followed. Bette was also leaning forward in her chair.

Lev continued the tale. "Robert said God told him there should be no land-for-peace deal. That Netanyahu would lose his place in office if he made such an agreement."

Racking his brain, Jack tried to recall the history of Israel back twenty years or so. "And?" he asked.

"The deal was made anyway. Netanyahu lost the next election, and, like Winston Churchill, spent some years wandering in the political wilderness before coming back into power."

"This is real?" Jack inquired.

"As real as what you've experienced in Israel," Amir said, smiling.

"And why is he here today?"

"That's the best part," Lev returned. "He contacted Bibi's office and said he had another word from God for him. The prime minister cleared his schedule for Robert to come—and we get to be here to hear the prophecy delivered."

A door opened and a slightly built black man with close-cropped silver hair entered the room. He beamed at everyone present, while grasping Lev by both hands. "Lev, my dear, dear friend," Robert said. "It's so good to see you. It's been too long; so very long."

Robert spoke with precision, but his smile never wavered. He greeted Amir and then he was introduced to Bette and Jack. "Dr. Garrison," he said warmly. "It is so good to meet you. I know of your work with the Committee, and I have heard from my friend Lon Silver you have seen Ariel. I had some small part to play in its growth. Magnificent achievement, is it not?"

While Jack was still trying to piece the puzzle together, the door opened again and Prime Minister Benjamin Netanyahu entered.

In an exact duplication of what happened a moment earlier, Netanyahu grasped both of Robert Mawire's hands and welcomed the black pastor as an old and valued friend.

"Your excellency," Lev said. "You know Amir, of course. This is Dr. Jack Garrison of the European Committee for Mid-East Policy. And this is your own Officer Bette Deekmann who has been doing such an excellent job accompanying us."

"Please, sit," Netanyahu urged.

Everyone did so, except the prime minister and Bette, who stiffened to attention and stood against a wall. "Officer Deekmann," Netanyahu addressed Bette. "You, also. Thank you for your service and your courage. Please have a seat."

Netanyahu remained standing. "So, Robert," he said. "You have another prophetic word for me?"

"I most certainly do," Robert agreed.

"And do you remember what I said to you when we met the first time?"

"You reminded me that in this country the fate of prophets who prove false is not pleasant. Stoning is the penalty."

Everyone laughed, including the prime minister, who then said seriously, "But you weren't wrong, were you? I have not forgotten. What do you have for me—this time?"

"It is just as clear," Robert said. "It is time—for the Temple to be rebuilt. You are to take the lead in seeing that it happens."

Jack felt as if he might choke and he reached for one of the bottles of Ein Gedi water standing at each place around the table. What did Mawire say? Just like that? Rebuild the Temple? Cut through Middle Eastern politics and worldwide opinion and rebuild the Jewish Temple? Prime Minister Netanyahu constantly walked a tightrope between negotiations with the Palestinians, the fragile peace with Muslim neighbors, the support of the U.S., and even differing challenges within Israeli politics.

And Robert Mawire just said it straight out? As if to confirm Jack's unspoken questions, the smiling prophet emphasized to the prime minister: "You are the Father to your people. You are to restore the Tabernacle of David."

The prime minister rested his chin on his palm for a moment, then went out of the conference room without speaking. What just happened? And what was going to happen now?

Netanyahu was back less than a minute later, carrying a framed print. Holding it so the image could not yet be seen he said, "This is in my office. I look at it and think about it every single day. This is what it's all about." The prime minister of Israel revealed the drawing.

It was a detailed artist's rendition of what the Jewish Temple looked like before its destruction by the Romans. "I look at it every day," Netanyahu repeated. "You know, it is in partnership with good friends of Israel—Christians and Jews from America, and from around the world—that the reality of the holiness of this place lives and will always live.

"We Jews lost our land and were flung to the far corners of the earth. For thousands of years we have been trying to do just one thing: rebuild our lives as a free, proud, independent people, capable of defending ourselves," Netanyahu said.

Robert Mawire's chocolate-brown face glowed.

"Jerusalem," the prime minister continued, "is where King David walked—where the great prophets walked—where the Maccabbees fought. Mentioned 700 times in the Bible, this is our land, our city; it is ours by rights. This is the site of the holy Temple Mount. . ."

♦♦♦

When the gathering with Benjamin Netanyahu concluded, and the prime minister excused himself to attend another meeting, the remaining participants adjourned to Amir's office at Partners with Zion. Over glasses of iced pomegranate juice they continued their conversation.

"Dr. Mawire," Jack began. "You obviously really believe what you said to the prime minister about Jerusalem and the Temple. And it seems he agrees with you. What gives you so much confidence? I mean, most of the rest of the world disapproves."

"Well," Mawire responded, adjusting his glasses by one earpiece. "The one thing you have to realize is God is still the Holy One of Israel. This is an eternal covenant. He still blesses Israel; protects Israel. He neither slumbers nor sleeps. Other nations may prepare for a coming confrontation, but God is going to watch over Israel."

"You are not very—shy—when it comes to expressing yourself," Jack observed.

Robert laughed, and so did Lev, who added, "Let me tell you how 'not shy' this man is: He told me modern Israel is a fulfilled prophecy, so I and my congregation had to stand with them. Told me to stand with Israel was an honor; to share in that prophetic journey. I said, 'what's that mean?' Robert said we needed to give money to support the development of Ariel; to give to a secular Israeli cause. I said, 'How much?'"

Pausing for dramatic effect, Lev continued, "Fifty thousand. Just like that: $50,000. How do I get my congregation to agree to that? Robert assured me if we wrote the check and set it aside, the following Sunday the church offering would be double the usual; that it would be more than we'd ever received."

"I get it," Jack said. "And then shortly after that Sunday, Lon Silver cashed a $50,000 check to buy grapevines."

"Computers, actually," Lev said. "Vines are prophecy fulfilled, but here's what you didn't see: Ariel is one of the most advanced 'smart' cities in the world."

Amir arrived with lunch for everyone: sabich sandwiches.

"Benjamin Netanyahu is a man of wisdom," Robert said. "He is humble. He is an anointed man like David; like Solomon."

"But what about the rights of the Palestinians?" Jack challenged, around a mouthful of pita stuffed with fried eggplant.

"You aren't the first person to ask that," Robert pointed out. "Abraham said to God, 'What about my son, Ishmael?' And didn't God say, 'I'll give him twelve nations'? All that oil! But the land—this land," he repeated with emphasis, "belongs to Isaac. So has God cheated the Arab peoples? No, God answered Abraham's prayer."

Watching Amir drip Amba sauce onto his sandwich, Jack repeated the action, then savored the sweet mango and tart vinegar seasoning.

Dabbing his face with a paper napkin, Jack asked, "How do you explain that to the Palestinians?"

Spreading his hands wide to embrace all those seated around the room Robert said, "Who were the first Christians? Not Gentiles. No, no—Jews." He pointed at Lev. "Jesus was a Jew. He lived in a Hebrew family. He's still coming back as the Son of David. After them, Samaritans and Africans." Robert patted his chest. "And Arabs," he noted, waving to Amir, who returned the salute. "This is the pattern of the biblical church. This is the will of God—Jews and Gentiles working together. There is a biblical way of embracing everyone, right, Lev? Right, Amir?" He got vigorous nods of agreement in return.

"So," Robert concluded. "We have been seeing great miracles as we work with the Palestinian people and with the Jewish people, because God does not discriminate. God has called Jew and Gentile to come together in Him; to become One New Man. The Roadmap to Peace," Robert said with pointed emphasis, staring at Jack, "is the Bible."

♦♦♦

Jack and Lev walked alone in the Garden of Gethsemane. "Do you remember the Far Side cartoon with the little boy raising his hand in class and saying, 'May I please be excused? My brain is full?' Well, that's how I feel."

Lev laughed. "Not surprising. I know I've said this too many times already, but Israel—Jerusalem especially—has that effect on lots of people. That is, it has that result if they really come seeking God in their lives."

"Is that what I came for?" Jack asked.

"Yes," Lev returned. "You just didn't know it. But God did, and He was here, ready for you to realize it."

"You and Amir," Jack recounted. "Bette and Lon Silver. Robert and Bibi Netanyahu. All the pieces were here all along, but I couldn't see the image 'til it was assembled."

"And Eliyahu," Lev added. "Don't forget him."

Jack plucked an olive leaf and stared at it. "How could I? I've seen mankind kicked out of the perfect garden. I heard the demons shriek and the angels sing. I saw Abraham ready to slaughter his beloved son. Did I tell you I tried to shout for him to stop? I couldn't help myself."

Lev smiled gently and laid his hand on Jack's shoulder. "That one must have been especially difficult for you to watch."

Nodding slowly, Jack said, "And I heard the voice of God say He would provide Himself as the Lamb of Sacrifice. I already knew Abraham and Isaac foreshadowed Jesus on the cross, but I never really thought about what it cost the Father to let Jesus go through with that."

Jack shuddered. "When I heard Peter preach, his words went right into me. I was there, helping crucify Jesus." Jack shook his head. "Do you know how much pain that realization cost me? I don't want to be the one to ever put another lash on Jesus' back. I don't want to be the one to drive another spike into His hands!"

"I understand, my brother," Lev agreed.

They walked for a time in silence interrupted by gravel crunching under their feet.

Taking a deep breath, then slowly releasing it as if checking for pain in his chest before speaking again, Jack continued. "I saw a real healing take place—Art, of course. And then Art, living proof miracles still happen, was part of my own healing—part of bringing me back from despair."

"So—what will you do now?"

"You mean, about my assignment? For the Committee? I'll go back and tell them Israel and Jerusalem irrevocably belong to the Jews."

"You know," Lev said softly. "That's not what they want to hear."

"No," Jack agreed. "And they won't understand if I say God told me and that settles it, so I have to think of what else to say. Of course, there's this: Trading land for peace never works. The militant Islamists don't want land. They don't even want a state of Palestine. What they really want, at bottom, is for there to be no Israel. That's the only thing that will satisfy them."

There was silence. Jack guessed he and Lev were thinking the same thing: maybe many of the ECMP members would actually agree with the radical Islamists about eliminating Israel.

"And the question of rebuilding the Temple?" Lev added.

"And why shouldn't the Jews have a holy place to worship?" Jack demanded. "Even leaving out ancient promises—leaving out future prophecies—why should the Jews be the only people on earth not allowed to worship in their ancestral homeland in the way they choose?"

"You're talking like a Zionist," Lev teased.

"Yes, and a Christian Zionist at that."

"Shall I tell you what Bibi told Robert the first time they met?"

They found a bench and sat down together.

"He said, 'You Christians. You love dead Jews. You don't like us living Jews. You tour the ancient places because you're in love with dead Jews—how about loving the children's children of those dead Jews?"

"Ouch!" Jack said.

Lev clasped his hands. "That one got me too. That's what Amir and Robert and I are all about here: We want to bring people over to see the ancient rocks—but to also meet the living stones. We want them to do both—meet the secular and sacred."

"That's powerful."

Lev laughed. "Thanks, but it's not original. Robert taught me that."

Jack said eagerly, "So now I'm a Christian again—or maybe I wasn't before but now I am. And I have so much to learn and I can't wait. How is it you call Jesus, you Jewish Christians?"

"Yeshua ha-Mashiach," Lev answered. "Jesus, the Messiah."

♦♦♦

"He has had a meeting with Netanyahu," Brahim Rahman said to Lord Halvorsham. His tone dripped disapproval.

The British peer stood in front of Rahman's desk like an errant school boy in his headmaster's office. His hands were clasped behind his back and his head was bowed. "Ah—yes?" Halvorsham returned. "A courtesy meeting, no doubt?"

"I think not. The plan to alarm Garrison, to convince him peace could not be achieved alongside Israeli settlements, has failed. He was in Netanyahu's office with people known to unconditionally support Israel—even a Jewish temple! He now has a positive view of the Jewish state."

"Surely he was. . ."

"Be silent!" Rahman commanded.

". . .just being polite."

"You assured me," Rahman continued, "that Garrison was completely supportive of the Palestinian cause. You told me since he was an American he would be a valuable voice in front of world opinion."

"I—I don't know what to say."

"Recall him at once! Tell him we need his report immediately. Tell him in the light of the attack on the vehicle in which he was riding, he must terminate his visit at once. It doesn't matter what excuse you use. Order him back here!"

"Immediately."

♦♦♦

"I can't understand it," Jack complained to Lev and Bette as they sat in the Presidents' Hall at the King David. "I only just emailed to say I needed more time to continue my research in order to give them a comprehensive report."

"Do they know about your—change of heart?" Lev inquired.

"Not unless they can read my mind," Jack retorted. "Or they have been listening to our conversations."

The humorous remark landed with a thud beside the coffee and croissants as the trio considered the implications.

Bette asked, "When do you have to return to London?"

"That's just it," Jack complained. "Immediately. They say. . ." He gave
Bette an apologetic, guilty look. "They say since Israel can't guarantee my
safety I have to go back at once. The Committee is lodging a formal com-
plaint with the Israeli government about the—the failure of security. They
even mention you by name, Bette." He added, "I'm sorry. They completely
misunderstood."

"Or deliberately recast events to suit their agenda," Lev remarked.

"Don't worry about me," Bette said brightly. "If we Israelis worried
about our reputations every time we were accused of something, we would
have shrunk to nothing long ago. But I am sorry you have to leave so suddenly." Her tone conveyed a personal disappointment.

The words made Jack's heart give an odd blip.

It made Lev study her with curiosity.

"Before you've completed your research," Bette added hastily. "But
listen: I have an idea. Have you replied to that email yet?"

"No," Jack admitted. "I wanted to talk with you. . ." He looked back
and forth to make it clear he meant both of them. "Discuss it before I
answered. What's your idea?"

"Let's go north again," Bette said. "Mount Hermon."

"All the way up there? Why?" Jack asked.

"Because it shows Israel on the front lines against terrorism," Bette said.

"And it's hugely significant in prophecy," Lev noted, expressing warm
approval.

"And because wireless communication is notoriously unreliable up
there," Bette said. "You may not even receive the recall notice for—a couple
days?"

♦♦♦

"I hope you brought your overcoat," Bette remarked as the road
wound higher and higher into the mountains. Up ahead loomed the
snow-capped peak of Mount Hermon, the highest elevation in Israel.

"So I see," Jack remarked. "Where are we headed, exactly?"

"Neve Ativ. It's where the ski resort employees stay."

Jack took his eyes off the summit to glance at her. "Seriously?"

"Israel is full of surprises," she teased. "We are over 2,000 meters and the summit is close to 3,000 meters—9,000 feet."

"I live in England," Jack joked in return. "I can do metric." Jack pulled his cell phone out of his pocket. "Yeah," he added happily. "No coverage."

Amir leaned forward from the backseat where he and Lev sat. "Just east of us is the UN Disengagement Observer Force Zone. You have no idea how long it took me to learn to say that!"

"No Man's Land is easier and just as correct," Lev observed. "Have you seen it on a map?"

"Not a detailed map," Jack admitted. "Why?"

"The UN zone looks like a crumpled bit of spaghetti," Lev said. "Stretches from the northern border of Jordan, up past the Golan Heights, 'til it separates Israel and Lebanon and Syria."

Bette agreed. "Nowhere wider than thirty kilometers," she said. "Some places as narrow as three. And guess where the UN peacekeepers sleep?"

"On the Israeli side?" Jack guessed.

"It's that or risk a Syrian mortar round or ISIS grenade landing on their cots," Bette noted. "We call this area, 'the eyes of the nation.'"

Wheeling into the parking area beside the Hotel Rimonim made Jack laugh again. Clustered around them were A-frame cabins the same as Jack saw in the Swiss Alps or at Lake Tahoe in the states, pretending to be those in the Swiss Alps. "No skiing now, of course," Bette added. "The season is only a month long; sometimes less. We missed it this year."

"I'll have to come back," Jack announced.

Bette said, "Three bedrooms in our chalet. I'll let you gentlemen arm wrestle to figure out who shares with whom. What do you say to dinner in an hour?"

"Perfect," Jack replied. "This mountain air gives me an appetite."

♦♦♦

The buffet at the Hotel Rimonim, Mt. Hermon was not lavish but the salad bar was European-style (or American, Jack thought) and presented lots of options. It was easy to make a meal out of the offerings Jack found there, together with fresh-baked yeast rolls and lentil soup. The quartet ate without a lot of conversation.

Maybe they're deferring to me, since I'm the one playing hooky, Jack thought. *Or maybe I'm not the only one altitude and the air up here makes really hungry.*

Dessert was more interesting: two dozen substantial-sized cups of crème brûlée waited on a tray for the handful of diners to discover.

Tapping the caramelized sugar topping with a spoon just like gently cracking a boiled egg, Jack remarked to Lev, "So you said there are prophetic details connected with Mount Hermon too. Like what?"

Lev gestured for Amir to take the lead. "This mountain has been treated as a sacred place since time too far back to count," Amir said. "We Arabs give it the title Sheikh—like a chief among mountains—and also it is called *al-haram.*"

"Just like the Temple Mount," Jack noted.

Lev took over. "It's mentioned several times in Scripture as an exotic or distant location, like the verse that talks about 'the dew on Mount Hermon,' but it hasn't always had pleasant associations."

"Oh? Meaning what?"

"There have been lots of pagan temples on the mountain," Bette said, "including one dedicated to the god Pan—you know, the cloven-hoofed one. A temple and a town and a whole religious industry grew up around a grotto and a spring of water. Place was even called 'Panias,' because of Pan."

Jack took a bite of custard. "You are a constant surprise, Officer Deekmann," he teased.

"When I was in the military I did Alpine here," she explained.

"Some scholars say," Lev took over again, "This is the Mount of Transfiguration; the place where Jesus temporarily revealed His divinity to a few close friends—and talked with Elijah and Moses about the end of His earthly life. That makes all kinds of sense. The headwaters of the Jordan needed to be cleansed of two thousand years of pagan worship. Jesus came to redeem the whole earth from the curse of the Fall, true? Jesus staking a claim on Mount Hermon was like taking on Satan right on his home turf."

The stone pillars and wooden beams supporting the roof of the dining room wavered oddly, and Jack's eyes blurred a bit. Was he about to have a vision right here and now?

The moment passed and Jack's sight cleared. He looked down at the custard cup and saw it was empty. He could not remember finishing it. The other three studied him, waiting for him to comment. *Too strange. Better to leave it for now*, Jack thought. "Anybody besides me want another one?" he said.

♦♦♦

The air smelled like wood smoke and cedar trees. The stars of the Milky Way cut a jeweled path across the night sky. The late-arriving moon broke the horizon with a glow like a forest fire.

"I don't think I've seen this many stars since I was a kid." Jack stretched his hands toward the campfire. He and Bette were alone outside the cabin on a rustic wooden bench.

Bette was golden in the light. She lifted her face toward the sky. "The moon shines bright, on such a night as this, when the sweet wind did gently kiss the trees, and they did make no noise, on such a night. . ."

"Shakespeare."

"*Merchant of Venice*."

"How do you know Shakespeare?"

"The love scene between Jessica and Lorenzo. When Jessica, daughter of Shylock the Jew, elopes with the Gentile Lorenzo. *Merchant of Venice* is Shakespeare's most anti-Semitic play. After it was performed in London, gangs of thugs roamed the streets, beating up Jews."

"Well, that just takes the romance right out of it," Jack said, flipping up the collar of his overcoat.

"Truth—it was required reading in a Hebrew University class. Anti-Semitism in Literature. How do you know it?"

The breeze sighed through the tops of the cedars. "My wife was a professor of English literature. The Romance of Shakespeare was one of her most well-attended courses."

Bette hugged her knees and recited in a whisper, "In such a night did Jessica steal from the wealthy Jew, and with an unthrift love did run from Venice. In such a night did young Lorenzo swear he loved her well, stealing her soul with many vows of faith, and ne'er a true one. . ."

Jack poked the dying embers with a stick. "You have out-nighted me. I concede. Can we start over? Please?"

"Your turn." The flickering light danced on her face.

He paused a moment and looked up. "On such a night as this Jacob slept beneath the stars and dreamed of angels and a ladder to heaven."

She replied, "On such a night as this Jacob wrestled the Angel of the Lord and received a blessing as the sun rose."

"Just one more truth, Bette?"

"Alright, then."

He moved closer to her, putting his arm around her. Her breath was on his cheek. "On such a night as this—I think—I mean, I know I could—fall in love again." He kissed her hesitantly. The embers sparked and flared as she fiercely returned his kiss.

♦♦♦

Jack stood on the highest peak of Mt. Hermon, yet he was not cold. A patchwork blanket of snow littered the ground and lay heaped in crevices. The rocky outcropping on which he stood was just below the summit. A confused wind whistled around stone pylons, tossing handfuls of frost crystals toward pinpricks of stars.

Jack was now so familiar with experiencing visions he turned expectantly to locate Eliyahu. His guide nodded toward him, leaning into the wind, propped against his staff.

"If this is what I think," Jack said, "You should be in this vision—like at Mount Carmel—and not just here with me. You are Elijah. And this is about the Transfiguration of Jesus, isn't it?"

Eliyahu did not reply. His left hand, which was grasping his beard to keep it from billowing around his face, gestured toward the peak.

On the height, which had been vacant a moment before, stood two robed men. The wind ceased and the light brightened so Jack could both see and hear clearly. One of the figures was tall, handsome, regal of bearing and proud of face. His clothing was rich with brightly colored silk. His eyes were a penetrating sapphire.

The other man was shabby. His garment was frayed and faded. His face was gaunt and pinched. His cheeks were sunken, and the bones of his face were prominent beside weary eyes.

But the tired eyes caught Jack's attention. They were brown, flecked with gold. Sorrowful, but kind. . .a deep, embracing kindness quite the opposite of the haughty superiority in the gaze of the other.

"All these things will I give you, if you will fall down and worship me," the regal man said.

Satan! This was not the moment of Jesus' transfiguration but the time when the devil took Jesus to a high mountain to test Him. So if the handsome, proud one was the devil, then the frayed and tired figure was—Jesus.

"Look!" Satan demanded, sweeping his arm up and pointing toward the glimmering gray in the east. "Look at all the kingdoms of the world!" As if projected against the sky, the image of a peacock throne appeared. On the seat of absolute authority sat an imperial sovereign, crowned with gold, while two dozen courtiers lay prostrate on their faces. A palace appeared, reaching up to the heavens, all of its terraced balconies lined with flowers. Jack caught the scent of jasmine and sandalwood.

"Look!" Satan demanded again, pointing south down the length of the Jordan and across the Dead Sea and over the desert.

There the pyramids loomed, challenging eternity, cloaked in gleaming limestone. A hundred slaves pulled an ivory chariot. In the royal cart rode a haughty Pharaoh, gilded rod and flail across his chest.

"Look!" Westward now. Marble columns, arches, aqueducts. Caesar, his brow encircled with a gem-encrusted laurel wreath, accepted the cheers of thousands in a stadium the size of a small city.

The vision of the world spun. Great cities sprang up. Sprawling metropolises pushed out from coastlines and riverbanks. Skyscrapers erupted, reaching proudly upward like Babylon, like Egypt, like Rome.

Jack recognized familiar scenes: the London Eye placidly revolving beside the Thames—the Eiffel Tower, shadowing the Seine—the Transamerica spire, pinning the head of San Francisco to the cobalt waters of the bay.

Washington, Moscow, Beijing, Tokyo—Jerusalem.

"All these things will I give you," Satan repeated. "If you will fall down and worship me. They are mine to give, you know. The man and the woman surrendered their deed to me—willingly, I might add. I did not force them."

Why doesn't Jesus speak? Jack fretted. *Why doesn't He reply?*

Shadows fell across the scenes. The lights on the great wheel beside the Thames flickered and died.

Two hundred-story towers erupted in flames and collapsed in on themselves.

The shining coating on the pyramids sloughed off like a snake shedding its skin—and sand buried what remained.

The vision spun back toward Babylon; zoomed in past the royal assembly. In a side chamber, a steward added poison to a cup of wine. In another, a pair of viceroys stabbed a rival to death. A throng of common people scattered before two advancing armies. The sky was darkened with a hail of arrows and a shower of spears.

Slaves toiled around the pyramids. Overseers whipped those carrying stones until the sandaled feet of the bearers following slipped in the blood.

The arena was filled with the sound of shrieking. Gladiators slashed and stabbed and bled and died, while the onlookers cheered.

Children, emaciated and dying, lay in the arms of mothers too weak to beg.

Lepers were hounded out of cities and into desolate wilderness.

People were forced out of their homes to trudge through heaps of snow, keeping only what they could carry.

Men in brown or black uniforms herded hollow-eyed, frightened families into dark enclosures, beyond which furnaces loomed.

"Do you think that changes anything?" Satan demanded. "Yes, most will be abandoned or destroyed. But if you serve me, then those you favor will be rewarded. Isn't the most important thing to be on the winning side? Do you think you can follow the path the prophets have set out without pain and misery and death for you? Do you think the ages to come will honor and respect you? Don't you know you will be deserted and betrayed by your closest friends? And in ages to come, that will be the pattern of your followers: choose death and destruction, or denial and betrayal. Which do you think they will choose? What do you care if some are crushed? That is nothing compared to ruling! Bow down and worship me. Call me El, and all the kingdoms are yours."

In a voice that surprised Jack in its intensity and authority, Jesus spoke: "Get away from me, Satan! For it is written: 'You shall worship the Lord your God, and Him only shall you serve.'"

Like a candle, when it is blown out, leaves a trace of smoke to mark its end—as when a green spot hovers in sight after an incautious view of the sun—Satan disappeared, but a look of malevolent hatred lingered on Jack's view of the scene.

Jesus, now alone on the summit, was surrounded by other beings—respectful, helpful creatures, offering bread, a thick robe, a cup of scented wine, and a bowl of warm water for washing.

"Time for us to go," Eliyahu said, pointing Jack toward a path descending between two boulders.

"Wait," Jack insisted. "One question first. Satan—the Accuser—he wanted to be called El. He wants to be acknowledged as the god of this world? Is that it?"

"You know what he said: 'I will ascend to the heavens. I will raise my throne above the stars of God.'"

♦♦♦

Jack woke up in his bed on the second floor of the cabin. The snow and the stars and the cities and the conflicts all receded, replaced by plastered walls, a framed print of an Alpine skier, and a three-drawer dresser. He was wide awake and full of questions about what he saw. Why was he ever reluctant to talk with Lev about his visions? Now he could hardly wait to bring up the most recent—to get Lev's take on what it meant and why Jack experienced it.

But what about Bette? She was another matter altogether, especially after last night at the campfire. Last night? Jack glanced at his watch. Three hours ago.

Their relationship was definitely headed somewhere beyond friend-ship—if both of them wanted it to. What would Jack's visions mean to her? She said she wasn't religious; certainly wasn't Christian. *I need to sort this out before I share it with her.*

Would she think Jack was crazy?

Okay, and what if Iran dropped a nuclear weapon on Israel tomor-row?

Right. Enough worry for now. Nothing else, except—Jack really needed to talk to Lev.

Even though it was two in the morning, Jack tapped on Lev and Amir's door. Bette was safely tucked in the single, tiny chamber at the very peak of the A-frame, so if the men spoke quietly she would not be bothered.

That was the way Jack reasoned with himself: not that he was keep-ing something from her, he was being courteous. He didn't want her to be disturbed. "Lev," he called softly.

"Hmmm? Jack? What?"

"Got questions. Need to talk to you."

"Yeah, okay. Come on in."

The bedside lamp between two narrow twin beds clicked on and Jack swung the door silently open. Jack stood in the entry. "Got some questions for you," he repeated.

"Yeah," Lev said, sitting up in bed. Amir blinked at the light and fumbled with his glasses. "Yeah. I saw you and Bette beside the campfire. I figured you'd need a little man-to-man."

"What? No, not that. I mean, yes, but not now. Something else. Listen, let's go downstairs so Amir can sleep."

Seated beside the fireplace in the living room, Lev pulled two armchairs closer together and said, "So what is this about?"

"I had another vision tonight. A dream, I guess, since I was asleep. I was here—I mean, not here, here, but here on Mt. Hermon, and I saw Jesus."

"Transfigured?"

"No, that's what I was expecting, but it was His temptation. I saw Satan tempt Jesus with all the kingdoms of the world."

"Okay, you got my attention," Lev said. "Now slow down and tell me every detail."

Jack's retelling took less time than his memory suggested the actual event lasted. The vision seemed to go on for hours. He recalled for Lev every detail he recognized, then mentioned the ones he guessed at. "I've never been to Japan," he admitted, "but I'm pretty sure that was Tokyo. Beijing too. London, Paris, D.C.—those could be images from my memories. But the Orient—I've never been there. And scenes out of ancient Egypt or Rome? And something like Babylon? I mean, if my imagination was really that good I should be a writer."

"So a true picture of something that actually happened here on this mountain 2,000 years ago, combined with visions of past and future kingdoms," Lev agreed. "London was just a Celtic village when Jesus was on earth."

"But, see, I don't know why," Jack complained. "I know what I saw, but *why* did I see it? Why *me*?"

"It seems to me," Lev said, scrubbing the bristles on his chin, "every vision you've had has been of a mountain. Moriah, Eden, now Mount Hermon. You know, many times—maybe more than any other way—when God wants to impart something important to humans, He chooses a mountain peak to do it. Sinai. Mount Carmel—Calvary."

"But why me? Why now?"

"Listen, Jack, you already know I believe the Temple is going to be rebuilt? Just like the rebirth of Israel in 1948, and us recapturing the

Temple Mount in 1967, the Temple itself—on a mountain again, right? The Temple will be an important milestone toward the End of Days."

"You don't have to explain that one. End of the world stuff. I get it," Jack agreed. "So how's that all tie into tonight?"

Lev spread his hands. "I think you just got us an update. All the civilizations of the world are coming to a conclusion. The devil offered Jesus a short cut to establish His kingship and Jesus showed him all the anger and greed and bloodshed. Here's the thing: Satan never actually held the deed to this place. He had a mortgage, but the debt's been paid in full. For the past couple thousand years the Accuser's still been collecting interest, but his clock is about to run out."

The two men sat silent, staring into the future. Lev rubbed his eyes and yawned. Another thought struck Jack, and he asked, "So my vision tonight was another—sign?"

"Bingo!" Lev said. "And here's the rest: you asked me why you were the one getting the visions? Did you ever stop to think maybe that's the wrong question?"

"What do you mean?" Jack flipped the collar of his robe up against a sudden draft.

"Maybe the question should be: Since you *are* the one receiving the messages, what are you supposed to *do* with them?"

Jack gnawed his lip. "How do I figure that one? If I'm the only one getting these messages as you call them. . ."

"But you're not," Lev corrected. "There's somebody else I want you to meet who'll help you sort this out."

"What, tonight?"

"Not tonight. Get some sleep—if you can. I'll tell you more tomorrow. Oh, and Jack—go ahead and tell Bette about your dream. If you think you might be falling in love with her you need to trust her."

◆◆◆

Perched atop a boulder on the slopes of Hermon, Jack watched the pre-dawn sky ripen into scarlet over Syria and Lebanon. Stars faded. He considered the night's grim and violent vision of the decaying world.

Bette's voice interrupted his reverie. "Red sky at morning, sailor take warning, eh?"

"So they say." His breath steamed in the frigid air.

"Well, look. I brought us coffee. American-style. There's a Keurig in the kitchen. Dunkin Donuts brand. Black. I couldn't find the sugar or the cream." She sat beside him, passing him a mug. "You're up early."

"I hardly slept." He warmed his hands on the cup.

"I know you were restless. It's my job to know. You know?"

"Standing guard over the American professor?"

"Something like that." She sipped her brew.

"What is it about this place?" Jack whispered. "I dreamed last night. I dreamed that in this place Satan offered Jesus all the kingdoms of the world if He would bow down and worship him. You know the story? The temptation of Christ?"

Bette nodded.

Silence. Wind stirred the trees. Bette looked across the lands beneath them. "Everyone knows it. I also listened to what Lev said yesterday, that this mountain is where Jesus was transfigured. Moses and Elijah appeared to Him here—it was the Messiah reclaiming the fallen world. Does it surprise you if I say the temptation and the transfiguration both happening on this mountain makes sense to me—if it really happened that way?"

"Go on."

"The rest of the puzzle…So let me tell you what I knew of this place when I was a kid. When I was a kid I was afraid of this mountain. We—my family—would come here and camp, you know. My father told us the legends around the campfire. Like ghost stories. In the book of Enoch, Mount Hermon is the place where the Watchers, the Fallen Angels, descended to earth. They swore they would take the daughters of men as their wives. The Watchers bound themselves under a curse that they would serve Lucifer and defy God. So this was called the Mountain of the Oath. The temples of the pagan god Ba'al were here. It is the place where Lucifer surveyed the world he stole. The headwaters of the Jordan River are here, formed by the snow and dew of Hermon. And this is the point of my father's story." She held up her two index fingers. "Two drops of dew, like brothers, begin their journey here in the same place. One dewdrop flows into the Jordan to give life to the vineyards of Israel. The other dewdrop forsakes Israel and flows down and down from these heights to end in death, stagnant in the Dead Sea. As Moses challenged the children of Israel, 'I have set before you life and death, blessing and curse.' Choose life. Or choose death."

The defiant words Jesus spoke to Satan were clear in Jack's mind. He whispered, "And Jesus answered Satan, 'It is written, you shall worship the Lord your God and Him only shall you serve...'"

The corners of Bette's mouth formed a slight smile. "Yes. As a Jew, my father taught us this. Choose life. So, each human is like a single dewdrop of Hermon; choosing life or choosing death. Who we follow: God or Satan. Living water—or stagnant water, stinking and dead. My father told us kids the Mountain of the Oath symbolizes man's eternal destiny; the unseen battle of Light and Darkness for men's souls."

Jack studied her profile a moment. There was so much more to this woman than he imagined. "We'll need more than one cup of coffee to finish this discussion, I think." A blast of light exploded on the horizon. "The sun is rising."

"Yes. Light strikes the mountain peak first." Bette nudged him. "Come on, then. Our coffee is getting cold out here."

Chapter Fourteen

Having dropped Lev and Amir at the Partners with Zion office, Bette returned Jack to the King David. "I've got to go report in," she said.

"Come and have lunch with me first. Besides, we have to make plans for dinner tonight."

"Really?" Bette said with an arched eyebrow. "Lunch *and* dinner. Giving me orders, Dr. Garrison?"

"Nobody bosses Wonder Woman's cousin around. But lunch and dinner are both needed for me to learn more about your own super hero powers." Jack extended playfully hesitant fingers toward her hand.

Bette laughed and grasped his arm eagerly. "Actually, I wanted to take you to a concert tonight, but Lev has someone he wants you to meet, remember?"

"Whoever it is can't be as interesting as you!"

The desk clerk spotted them arriving and called out, "Dr. Garrison! A message for you. It's marked urgent."

Jack frowned as he accepted the envelope. He and Bette stepped into an alcove flanked by potted palms.

"Knew it was too good to last," he said, ripping open and scanning the note, then handing it to Bette. "I've been ordered back to London." Bette read the communication while Jack continued fuming. "Not asked when I was returning. Not requested to come back. Ordered!" Jack's finger stabbed the page with such force he almost knocked it out of her hand. "'Flight tonight,' it says. 'Ticket waiting at El Al counter,' it says. I've got a good mind to. . ."

Bette got his attention by looking directly into his eyes. "Are you ready to quit your job? Because that's how you sound. There must be some important reason for them to be so abrupt."

Jack grinned sheepishly. "It's just that I'm not ready to leave—you," he concluded.

"I don't want you to go either. But if your Committee hadn't sent you here, we wouldn't have met in the first place, right?"

"But I don't like this. It stinks. I think. . ."

Planting a kiss that rendered Jack first mute and then incapable of speech, Bette silenced his tirade. When she finally broke off the embrace she said, "Go and convince them your work here isn't done. Then come back as soon as you can."

♦♦♦

Jack called Lev to tell him the news that he was called back to London.

"You've got time for dinner. You can't go until you meet my friend Daoud," Lev insisted.

In the evening, the shops and restaurants of Jerusalem were open and bustling with shoppers.

Jack made his way to meet Lev at Between the Arches Café just outside the security checkpoint near the exit of the Western Wall. There was a long line of people waiting for tables. Lev sent Jack a text telling him he and his friend were already seated downstairs.

Jack descended the steps. The cavernous restaurant was surprisingly cool. Voices echoed against the walls and resounded in a deafening cacophony, apparently the norm of Jewish nightlife.

Spotting Lev and Daoud at a too-small table on the opposite side of the packed room, Jack waved.

"Shalom! Shalom!" Lev pushed out a chair. "Jack, you're late. This is my friend Daoud Farouk. Daoud—this is Jack Garrison. An American by way of London."

Jack shook hands with Daoud, who looked remarkably like a young version of the actor Omar Sharif.

"Pleased to meet you." Jack's stomach rumbled at the exquisite aromas of Israeli food drifting from the kitchen.

Lev slapped him on the back. "I hope you're hungry. Daoud already ordered for all of us."

Wine was poured and in the center of the table was crushed olive dip with a basket of Focaccia bread; hot, flaky, fluffy, and perfectly seasoned.

"What are we having?" Jack asked.

Daoud replied, "Shakshuka—the apex of eggs for dinner! Pile of pita. Eggs poached in spicy tomato sauce. Crumbled feta cheese."

Lev added, "You only get it here, Jack. This is the place. Someday I promise you'll be somewhere—I don't know—somewhere in the world and you'll wake up in the middle of the night and remember your shakshuka dinner with Lev and Daoud. And the next thing you know you'll be craving it and on a plane. . ."

"Right back in Yerushalayim!" Daoud finished.

Cheerful conversation went with the meal, and Jack's irritation at being ordered back to London diminished somewhat. Only after the shakshuka was consumed and coffee ordered did Lev and Daoud come to the point of their meeting.

"I was born and raised a Muslim," Daoud began his story. "My father was a high official in our mosque and fully committed to the ideology of Yassar Arafat and of Mohammed. Me and my brothers and sisters were schooled in a radical madrassa. Our religion taught us to hate the Jews. If a Jew hid behind a stone, the stone would cry out, 'here is a Jew, come kill him.' This is also true about Christians, we were taught. Christians are just as bad as Jews."

"Tell Jack about your sister."

"Yes. My sister. She was two years younger than me. She was sixteen at the time when she met a Christian boy quite by accident at the library. She was forbidden to go to the library, so she told my parents she was visiting a friend. Anyway, so she meets this Christian boy several times and they talk—only talk—they become friends and they talk about how

Jews and Christians and Muslims should not hate—just the talk of teenagers dreaming. Then this Christian boy tells her about Jesus, who is all about love. And my sister became a secret believer. She kept a little New Testament hidden under her pillow and read it. Somehow my older brother discovered her deception—that she had a Christian boy as a friend. This was very bad. My brother and his friends confronted her. They beat her until she was almost dead. They left her in a park, bleeding, almost dead. Then they went to find the Christian boy to kill him too."

Daoud's coffee grew cold and his face clouded with the memory. "So someone finds my sister. She is taken to the hospital here. Hadassah Hospital. In Intensive Care. Almost dead. We get a call to come because she may not survive the night. And as we go to the hospital her Christian friend is being hunted so he can be beaten to death that very night."

Lev frowned, and urged Daoud to continue. "Go on—tell him the miracle."

"I did not recognize my sister when I saw her. Broken. Her face so battered—my mother and father wept bitter tears. How could this happen? My mother asked. What animal would do this? Then my other brother tells her it was for the honor of the family. And he tells my father that our eldest brother has done this and will do more to the Christian who dared to defile her. I ran from the hospital in the night, certain she would die. I ran all the way to the top of the Mount of Olives. And I was crying out with all my heart to this Jesus whom my sister came to love. I told Jesus that if He would save her from death that I would turn my heart to Him. And then—in the olive grove there I fall asleep as I weep. Suddenly I see a very bright light and a golden man with light beaming from his hands and his feet and from a place in his side—and I know it is Jesus."

A wave of chills swept over Jack as he listened. "Were you dreaming? Was it a vision?"

Daoud considered the question carefully. "It was real. It could only be real. So—Jesus asks me what I want. I tell Him—I want my sister to live. And I want to truly know God. Not a god who fills us with hate, but the God who loves. The God who brings peace for us all—salaam—shalom. And then Jesus says to me, 'Daoud, go back to your family. Your sister will live.' I knew it was Jesus. He heard my prayer and answered. The light from His wounds bathed me in warmth and peace. And that has never left me."

"And the miracle," Lev urged.

"My sister lived. Against all odds. She recovered and within days was well. She and I were given sanctuary with the family of the Christian boy. Others in my family have become Christians. My oldest brother who tried to kill her. She has forgiven him. She married the Christian boy and they have two beautiful children. They are in America now."

Daoud spread his hands. "And so that is my story. There is no peace between Arabs and Jews and Christians without the love of Jesus. His light will quench the fires of hate between the sons of Isaac and of Ishmael. So Lev wanted you to hear this. Put this in your report. Jesus will come soon to Jerusalem. His Holy Temple will once again stand on this mountain. Then every knee shall bow and every tongue confess that He is Lord. And I am not afraid to tell the whole world. Pray for the peace of Jerusalem."

It was still early when the three men parted.

Jack stood at the window of his hotel room and gazed toward the Temple Mount. Something big was coming. Jack felt it. A miracle was coming soon which would crack hearts of stone and bring peace to Jerusalem.

◆◆◆

In the distance, projected lights of a classical concert reflected on the Western Wall like flames. Jack propped his feet on the railing of his balcony as the universal language of music drifted on the breeze.

His suitcase was packed for his flight to London. The limo would pick him up soon, yet he clung to these last moments, determined to drink in every detail.

His room service meal was mostly untouched and the hotel room was dark behind him.

Debbie would have loved Jerusalem and this night, he thought, sipping his wine. His life would have been so different had she lived.

And now? There was Bette. Fierce and brilliant. Angry and gentle. Wise, yet quiet in her wisdom.

Debbie and Bette. There never were two women more opposite. One loved the romance of *The Merchant of Venice*. The other saw a threat against her people within the plot. They could have played the lead roles: Portia and Jessica.

Jack wondered if perhaps both women viewed the world rightly. Romance and bitterness were inseparable truths for the descendants of Abraham.

There was no time to sleep, though Jack longed to dream again. The stars blended with the twinkling lights of Jerusalem until there was no distinct line between heaven and earth.

"On such a night as this..." he whispered.

Thousands of years of history overlapped and melded into one eternal moment: "What was, what is, and what shall be."

Past, present, and future flowed like a deep river from this holy mountain.

On such a night as this—Abraham. Isaac. David the Shepherd. David the King. King Solomon the Wise, builder of the First Temple. Conquering armies. Dissolute kings and holy prophets. Wise men. Shepherds. Jesus of Nazareth. Judas. The cross and an empty tomb. The Mount of Olives where Jesus ascended and where angels promised He would return again.

All history remained active and alive, embedded in the stones.

In the distance, the orchestra played the final song: the national anthem of Israel. Hatikvah, The Hope. Jack stood at attention and sang quietly.

The phone rang and broke the spell. Jack did not turn on the light before answering.

"Your airport limo is here, sir," the voice said in perfect American English. "Shall I send the bellman to help with your luggage?"

"No, thanks. I can manage. I'll be down in a minute. Have my bill ready for me, please."

Chapter Fifteen

Jack stood in Lord Halvorsham's office in the Gherkin. He had been standing for several minutes already, not having been invited to sit since he arrived. The flow of criticism aimed at him gave no sign of stopping.

"And where did you disappear to?" Halvorsham demanded. "Sent no word of your travels. Ignored all attempts to reach you, delayed your return for several days. . ."

"May I speak now?" Jack inquired. Taking the pause in his boss's tirade for consent, Jack said, "I have never been required to give daily reports on previous missions for the Committee and I certainly wasn't told to do so this time. I traveled to an area where no cell phone use was possible and as soon as I received the message back at my hotel I returned to London as—ordered."

Jack deliberately leaned on his last word in the hopes of provoking an apology or at least a partial retraction, but neither appeared.

Instead, Halvorsham continued, "And what possessed you to be so insulting to the Islamic religious authorities? And to the Rights for Palestine group? Aren't you aware the RFP group is a valued ally of ours in the quest for peace? And having chummy conversations with enemies of peace like settlement mayors and Bibi Netanyahu?"

Why had he never noticed this bias before, Jack wondered? Since when did a supposedly impartial think tank label the Jewish prime minister "an enemy of peace"?

Stiffly Jack replied, "I'm not aware of insulting anyone."

"You most certainly did!" Halvorsham insisted. "It was only by much prolonged and abject apology for your behavior I was able to head off a report to the Foreign Office about you. Think how badly that would have reflected on the Committee!"

An apology for Jack's behavior? So far there was no mention of the stabbing death of the policewoman Jack witnessed, nor the shooting attack of which he was almost a victim.

"My instructions," Jack explained, "were to conduct interviews and record impressions about Jewish settlements in the West Bank, and attitudes toward the rumored construction of a Jewish Temple in Jerusalem. These things I have done. You will have the report in a week."

"Jack," Halvorsham said with a concocted half-smile. "We value your expertise and your candor. We know Palestine is the hottest stove in the world. It's no wonder you had such a struggle. Perhaps we should have sent several assistants with you to share the work. Maybe this was too much of a load for one man."

"I found it very—interesting," Jack said.

"Yes, well, take a few days to get your thoughts in order," Halvorsham said. "Before you commit anything to paper, think it through carefully."

If that was not a barely veiled threat, Jack was no student of human communication. "I certainly will," he said. "Indeed, I will."

♦♦♦

It rained earlier, but wasn't at the moment. There was no wind worth mentioning. The temp stood at 9C/48F degrees; pleasant enough for London in March.

Jack emerged from the Slug and Lettuce pub in County Hall. The historic building was once the seat of local government but was now a Marriott hotel. The pub was part of a chain and catered to tourists instead of locals. The fish-and-chips were good and not too pricy.

Jack was back in London. He always found the best way to reconnect with his adopted home city was to get out and walk in daylight. Since Lord Halvorsham "encouraged" him to recover from the trip to Israel, Jack took him at his word and opted for an hour stroll along the river followed by an hour lunch before taking the Tube back to work.

From where Jack stood, transportation was a coin toss: back east to Waterloo Station or across Westminster Bridge to Westminster Station. Since the rain stopped Jack decided in favor of the views crossing the Thames.

Strolling west along the bridge Jack faced the Houses of Parliament. On his right was the slowly revolving wheel of the London Eye. The chimes of Big Ben rang half past two.

It was more difficult coming back to London this time than it had ever been. Before a year ago, previous trips abroad meant coming home to Debbie—now she wasn't here. Walking around London during the last months was a way to grieve—to at least revisit places he and Deb had been together.

Now part of Jack's thoughts remained behind in Jerusalem. Jack didn't like the feeling of being in a place he knew better than any big city in the world, and yet no longer sure he felt a part of it. It was—weird.

He wondered again what Bette was doing. Given the time difference she was at work, he knew that. A couple recent phone calls were awkward. Bette was on another assignment; one she couldn't talk about. And Jack could not say for certain when he'd be returning to Israel.

Glancing at his watch, Jack decided he'd better pick up the pace. He wouldn't make it back to his office before 3:15 as it was. Business at ECMP usually wrapped up around four, so he'd better hustle.

A black, four-wheel-drive auto, traveling at a high rate of speed, barely made the corner onto the westbound side of the bridge, the side opposite Jack. "Too fast," Jack muttered aloud. "Stupid."

A moment later as the Hyundai started swerving Jack revised his estimate. "Must be drunk."

Then it happened: the vehicle mounted the curb, striking pedestrians like nine-pins. One woman was tossed into the path of an oncoming bus. Another was flung over the railing into the river.

As Jack watched in horror, the car jerked away from the sidewalk, then shot back into another knot of pedestrians, this time a group of school children.

"God! Dear God!" Jack prayed aloud, breaking free from his trance and sprinting across the roadway toward the injured.

There was a crash. The out-of-control car swerved yet again and collided with a barricade outside the Houses of Parliament.

It was a scene from a horror movie. Victims were sprawled on the road, on the walkway, up against the railing. A woman was tossed in the air and lay beside a revolving stand displaying postcards of London.

Jack knelt beside the first victim he came to. It was a schoolboy, thirteen or fourteen, Jack guessed. The boy moaned and clutched his arm. "*Ça fait mal!*" he said in French. "It hurts!" It was broken, but the only bleeding was from what appeared to be cuts and scratches. "It'll be okay," Jack said. "*Tout ira bien, oui?* Keep calm—uh, *l'aide arrive.*"

He moved on to the next injury, just as someone at the Parliament end of the bridge shouted, "Watch out! He's got a knife!"

Not again! Jack thought. *This can't be happening again—not here. Not in the heart of London.*

But he knew it was terrorism.

What could he do? There were victims everywhere! How could he protect any of them if a terrorist came back onto the bridge with a knife or gun—or another car?

Screams erupted from inside the fence surrounding the Parliament driveway. How big was this attack? Were terrorists inside Parliament?

Shots rang out—two, followed by one more, then momentary silence.

A pair of police cars screamed onto the bridge.

Jack went back to tending the wounded. There was a woman whose foot was crushed. She was shaking uncontrollably—going into shock. Stripping off his overcoat Jack tucked it around her. "Stay calm," he said again. "Help is on the way."

When he reached another female victim two other Good Samaritans already knelt beside her. She was lying in a pool of blood. One of the volunteers looked up at Jack's approach. "Can I help?" he asked.

The man shook his head. "She's gone."

Ambulances appeared, paramedic services, more police constables. A police helicopter arrived overhead. All of central London was awash in sirens.

Jack looked at his watch again. Five minutes passed since the attack started. It felt like five hours.

◆◆◆

A glance in the bathroom mirror explained why people stared at him in horror on the taxi ride home from the bridge. His face was smeared with blood, his shirt and trousers spattered with gore from the victims. Jack stuffed his blood-soaked clothes and shoes into a black plastic trash bag and sealed the top with a twist tie.

He turned the shower water on and stepped under the nozzle without waiting for it to warm. Red-dyed water flowed from his hair and swirled around his feet. A wave of nausea swept over him. His mouth was dry. He stepped out and retched into the toilet, rinsed his mouth, and resumed his shower. Scrubbing his hair twice, he squeezed his eyes shut, hoping the images of the day would disappear.

Dressing in sweats, he carried the garbage bag downstairs and walked barefoot over the cobbles to a large dumpster at the end of the street.

He shuddered, remembering again his vision of terror in London as he stood alone on Hungerford Bridge. Churches and synagogues in flames; tall buildings burning like torches. If the vision was true, there was much more violence yet to come upon the great city. The rise of anti-Semitism in Europe increased exponentially over the last year even as Christians were persecuted with a brutality unseen since the early Church. It was as though the demons of hell were loosed against Jews and Christians.

He glanced up to see Debbie's cat gazing serenely down at him from the neighbor's upper story window. He remembered the dream of Debbie wrapping the battered shoebox in gold foil. A strange present. As if his mom's old family photos were a gift for him.

Making a cup of tea, he pondered the visions which came to him unbidden. Deb beneath the Christmas tree was the first of many. Nothing surprised him anymore.

Was there something more to what he saw that night? He wondered where the shoebox was. His cousin sent it to him in London after his mother died. He scarcely looked at the old faded snapshots and placed it on the top shelf in the closet.

Suddenly he felt desperate to look into it. Leaving his tea on the desk he hurried to the cupboard. Throwing down stacks of linens, he grasped the treasure and returned to his chair and cup of tea.

Balancing the box on his knees, he lifted the lid. What was it Deb tried to tell him? There were neat stacks of pictures recording his childhood from infancy to college graduation. Photos of his parents' courtship and wedding. A 5x7 of Jack in his high school wrestling singlet with an inscription on the back in his mother's handwriting: "*Our Jacob, wrestler of angels. . .*"

Jack smiled slightly as he came to an envelope with a letter and photo of his mother at age seven and Jack's long dead grandmother, Rachael de Louzada. The little girl, clutching a teddy bear, squinted unhappily into the sun beside her dark-eyed, French mother. Something was scrawled in French on the back. "Reunis. 1946."

Reunited?

Jack removed the letter from its yellowed envelope and began to read:

> *My darling Jack. So many years have passed since the day this photograph was taken. My lifetime has passed. Since you are reading this, the cancer beat me, but I know you will feel my love for you. There is a story behind this picture which you have never known. I did not want you to grow up with the story of suffering. I thought until you were a man, the bitterness of life's cruelty would make a shadow on your heart. Both your dad and I wanted only happiness for you. Never bitterness.*

This was taken in 1946, the day I was reunited with my
mother after six years of separation because of the war. I have
not told you before now, my mother and father were Sephardic
Jews whose family escaped to France centuries before. When
the Nazis came I was smuggled out of France at the age of one
year and brought to America. My mother and father were left
behind, arrested by the Nazis and transported to a concentra-
tion camp. My father Jacob did not survive. My mother sur-
vived. After the war we were reunited in America. I was a
typical American child by then. I did not know my mother
and though she tried, I could not accept her as my mother. I
remained with my American family and was adopted. I told
you that my mother passed away before you were born. Here
is the truth: your grandmother immigrated to Israel in 1948.
She hoped I would come to her one day but I did not. After a
time, she gave up trying to contact me. This is my failure, not
hers. But long ago I had to forgive the little girl who was me.

Golden light from the afternoon fell on the photograph of Rachael
de Louzada. Jack's mom looked so much like her. Beautiful. Jack read
the pain in Rachael's eyes.

The hope of reunion with a precious daughter she gave to the care
of strangers.

The teddy bear clutched in the arms of the little girl—a gift chosen
in love and offered in hope.

But the little girl had no love or longing to give her mother in return.

So, in the end, Rachael de Louzada not only lost her husband, she
lost the little girl whose life she fought so hard to save.

"So," Jack murmured. "I am Jacob. And I am Israel."

🌢🌢🌢

The television set mounted in the corner of the Warwick Castle pub
replayed the attack over and over again. Local patrons watched the

coverage as if spellbound. At the bar, they brooded over their pints and murmured threats against the Muslim population of London.

Jack sat alone against the far wall beneath a framed etching of Warwick Castle. His supper of shepherd's pie, bread, and Branston pickle was half eaten. He sipped his dark brown Newcastle Ale slowly. He stubbornly refused to look up at Sky News. The carnage of a minute and a half could not be changed; the lives lost without warning could never return.

After the twentieth replay, he moved his meal to a picnic bench outside the pub to wait for Bette's call from Tel Aviv. Someone left a copy of the *Daily Mirror* on the table. Jack refolded it with the front page inside so he wouldn't have to see more gruesome images.

On page three was the photograph of a prosperous-looking Arab man in a western business suit. The caption said his name was Brahim Rahman. The headline over the brief article stated: "Levantine Shipping Investigated for Money Laundering."

I've seen that guy, Jack thought, just as the phone rang. He tossed the paper aside.

"This is Jack."

"Jack? Jack, your name came through headquarters as one of the people on the bridge." Bette's voice was shaken.

"Yeah. It was pretty bad."

"You're okay."

"I'm not hurt."

"Jack. . ." There was a long moment of silence. "When I saw your name. . ."

"I'm okay, Bette. I—it was terrible. A few seconds of madness. And the whole world is turned upside down for so many. When I saw the knife attack in Jerusalem. . ."

There was a pause while Jack recalled thinking how that victim could have been Bette. Shaking off the additional horror, Jack said, "I suddenly realized what Israel lives with—every day. Years on end. And now it's here too."

Bette cleared the emotion from her voice. "Nothing is certain in life. Ask a Jew in Jerusalem. We don't part from one another without saying, 'I love you.' When are you coming back?"

"Soon, I hope. Bette—so much I want to tell you. So much has happened. I need your help. I need to find someone in Israel—she would be very old now."

"Who is she?"

"She immigrated to Israel in 1948. She was a survivor of some Nazi extermination camp. I found a letter about her from my mother."

"Yes? Just a minute, let me write down her name."

"Rachael de Louzada. Transported from France early in the war. Her husband didn't survive. Jacob de Louzada. And she might be dead by now. But the last anyone heard of her she was in Israel."

Silence as Bette wrote down the names. "Sure. I'll pass it along. Who was she?"

Jack rubbed his forehead. He had not realized how badly his head ached until now. "She is my grandmother. . ."

♦♦♦

The staff room at ECMP headquarters was very utilitarian: plain tile counters, round tables with plastic chairs, refrigerator, and coffee maker—no windows. Therefore, it was not popular with the staff. Their offices were more comfortable. Group conversations were not encouraged at ECMP.

Today, however, the room was packed, because it did possess a television. Even though it was only a couple days later and there was hardly anything new to report, all the British and foreign news services were providing continuous updates on the Westminster Bridge attack.

"To recap: Five dead, including the killer," the broadcaster intoned. "Fifty people hurt, some of them seriously."

Amateur video and still shots of the tragedy surfaced: a woman being thrown under the wheels of a bus, another victim flung over the railing toward the river, the Hyundai diving in and out of the crowds on the bridge like an attacking wolf harrying a flock of sheep.

The form of the unarmed police constable who tried to intervene, stabbed to death, lying in a pool of blood.

Even though Jack tried to keep it secret, word somehow got out that he was a witness to the attack. Now every new horror—every additional gruesome detail—caused co-workers to ask: "Did you see that happen?"

Other than admitting he was on the bridge and tried to help some of the injured, Jack said nothing about what he witnessed. The visions were too real; too nauseating. The less time spent reliving them the better.

Jack filled his Ronald Reagan coffee mug—the one Debbie gave him; the one carrying the motto "Trust but Verify." He prepared to retreat to his office. Someone called out, "They're about to release the nationalities."

The murmured conversations ceased. Additional graphic bars of the sound control appeared on the screen as the volume was run up on the set.

"Besides three innocent British victims," the announcer's voice now boomed, reverberating throughout the lunch room and down the halls, "an American is also dead. Many victims remain in the hospital in critical condition. The injured include visitors from France, Romania, Korea, Germany, Greece, Poland, Ireland, Australia, Italy, and China. Still others remain unconfirmed."

"Like a roll call at the United Nations," someone said loudly.

"Shh!" another worker urged.

Just nations were named—as if the identities of those whose lives were disrupted or completely destroyed were only figureheads, standing in for their countries. What did family members think when they heard their loved ones rattled off like the verses of a Christmas carol: "Three French hens, two Italian children, and a dead Romanian"?

The specter of terrorism was worldwide, Jack acknowledged. If it could strike innocent civilians in the heart of London—and thereby maim or kill people from a dozen nations—nowhere was safe. Terrorism was now the whole world's problem, whether the world was ready to admit that fact or not.

"It is now known the attacker's name was Khalid Masood," the announcer boomed. "He was British, born Adrian Elms, but took the name Khalid when he converted to Islam in 2005. He has also gone by the name Khalid Choudry. Police sources say Masood was not previously being tracked as dangerous.

"A radio communiqué from a Middle Eastern terror group claims Masood was, 'a soldier for the Islamic State.' Authorities dispute this claim, suggesting instead Masood acted alone. We have received word that in a last text message before the attack Masood wrote he was acting for revenge against western militaries, for their actions against Muslims in the Middle East."

"Bloody Islamic terrorist! Like we need to have it analyzed before we name it," a mailroom clerk at Jack's elbow growled.

Lord Halvorsham popped his head into the break room. "Turn that down!" he demanded. "We can hear it out at the reception area. And get back to work. The best thing we can do to honor the victims is to prevent it from ever happening again—and that means finding a just and permanent peaceful solution to all the injustice in the Middle East."

Some of Jack's co-workers scowled at Halvorsham's words. A few others nodded approval, but without enthusiasm. All began to drift out.

"Jack," Halvorsham added as he turned to leave. "Finish your coffee and come see me, please."

♦♦♦

Jack sat in a mahogany armchair in Lord Halvorsham's comfortable office. Unlike his last experience in the chamber, Jack was made to feel much more welcome this time. "Terrible shock you had," Halvorsham said quietly. "Perhaps you'd like something better than coffee. Gin and tonic, perhaps? Or a glass of wine?"

Jack declined both. He stared blankly at a framed reproduction of Holbein's portrait of Sir Thomas More hanging on the wall to the right of Halvorsham's desk. *Saint Thomas More*, Jack thought. *More stood up against the most powerful men of his day and paid the ultimate price for staying firm in his Christian convictions.*

Halvorsham used a coaxing, entreating tone with Jack. "Now you know better than anyone in this organization—better than most people in the whole world, I daresay—how important our work here actually is. We must not just talk about peace, we have to do something—something real, rational, and concrete."

Jack turned his stare on his boss. Halvorsham backed up a step to sit down with the desk between himself and Jack. "What do you think would have prevented what happened Wednesday?" Jack asked. "Would pulling back on troops to allow ISIS to butcher more children be satisfactory? Would apologizing to the Palestinian thug who murdered a policewoman serve the cause of peace? How about allowing a caliphate to spread radical Islam all across Europe, let alone the Middle East and North Africa?"

"Jack, Jack," Halvorsham said, spreading his hands in supplication, "I don't say anything this bad can be remedied overnight, but the way you talked just now is a good example. Using inflammatory language as you just did hinders the cause of peace. Surely you must see that."

"I see the governments of Europe should be standing shoulder-to-shoulder with Israel," Jack said firmly. "It's the only democracy in the region; the only nation in the region that allows freedom of religion; the first place terror attacks are attempted—before they come here. They are the front lines. We should be learning from them."

"Our mission is not military or security," Halvorsham said sternly. "It's about getting justice for downtrodden people. It's about getting the Palestinians the land they deserve."

"You mean the land they could have had twenty years ago when Arafat was offered more than ninety-five percent of his demands and he turned it down? That land? The land that will never be enough? The concessions that will never be adequate?"

"You know we can't have that sort of talk around here." In total disregard of what Jack said, Halvorsham continued, "We are finally making some headway in pressuring Israel to be more reasonable and proper toward the Palestinians. UNESCO has put forth a resolution asserting that, as an occupying power, Israel has no legal or historical ties to Jerusalem.

"Our office developed some of the language used in the resolution and provided some of the support material," Halvorsham said proudly.

"No legal or historical ties," Jack said, laughing scornfully. "What amazing fiction! I'm a historian in case you've forgotten. I deal in facts— not political make-believe." He paused, but his anger continued to swell even as Halvorsham shrank back in his chair. "United Nations Educational, Scientific, and Cultural Organization? That would be the same United Nations whose relief and works agency runs the schools in Gaza? The same schools Hamas hides their terror tunnels under?"

Halvorsham stood up. "I'd hoped," he said, "you'd had time enough to recover from your trip. I'm very much afraid the events on the bridge have caused you to have a relapse. Your thinking is fuzzy. You need extended time off. A six month leave of absence seems called for and some medical intervention."

"The events on the bridge?" Jack repeated scornfully. "You mean the Islamic terror attack that killed or crippled dozens? No, but you're wrong. There's nothing wrong with my vision or my thinking. I see things more clearly now than ever before. You'll have my resignation in the morning."

"I believe that would be best," Halvorsham agreed. "Don't bother coming in. We'll box your things and have them sent round."

Turning at the door, Jack added one more thing. He pointed at the painting of St. Thomas More and said, "Why don't you send that portrait along too? It's obvious you have no idea who he was or what he was about."

♦♦♦

Sitting beneath the image of Salisbury cathedral in his living room, Jack lifted his cell phone from the end table, studied it, laid it down again, then retrieved it once more. The mantle clock—the anniversary clock Jack gave Debbie for their first anniversary—still ticked faithfully. The hands pointed to eleven o'clock—1:00 a.m. in Israel.

Deciding he couldn't delay any longer, Jack stabbed Lev's number and waited out five buzzes on the line. Lev and Jack had exchanged emails since the Westminster Bridge terrorist attack, but had not spoken. Now, after ending his time at the ECMP today, disappointment surged over Jack at not being able to reach his friend. He prepared to leave a voicemail message and sign off for the night.

At the last moment, Lev answered. "Hello, Jack! Everything okay?"

Taking a deep breath, Jack plunged in. "I'm sorry to call so late," he said. "Bet you were asleep."

"No, no. Big things happening here. I only just got in. What's up? I figured you'd call when you were ready to talk."

"I left the Committee today," Jack said. "I mean, for good." He took a few moments to briefly explain what happened and why he absolutely could not remain employed there. "The Committee isn't working for peace," he said, "unless it's a peace dictated by Palestinian terms. Now I understand why the Danish delegate left: in this upside-down view of who's causing the trouble, there can't be peace as long as there's an Israel. They wanted me to come up with a report blaming Israel for everything bad in the region for the last eighty years, and the Jews for most everything bad since—forever."

Lev laughed. "As my grandfather would say, 'So what's new, nu?' My people always get blamed. But seriously, Jack, what's this mean to you?"

"That's what I called about," Jack admitted. "London just doesn't— it doesn't feel like home anymore, you know?"

Lev's voice from Jerusalem sounded distant, but still conveyed concern. "Must be tough," he offered. "You've used work to get you through the last year, but now that isn't enough—isn't even possible."

Jack gazed again at the pictures Debbie selected and the furniture she directed Jack to arrange before replying. "Nailed it exactly," he said with a catch in his voice. "I dunno what to do with myself," he admitted.

"Back to America?"

"I could get a teaching job," Jack agreed. Then the real reason behind the late night call came with a rush. "And there's more. I just found out—I'm Jewish."

Jack explained about the box, the revelation of what his family connection was, and about searching for his grandmother.

"So. . ." Jack interrupted his tumbling flow of words. "What would you think about me coming back to Israel? I mean, I don't know what for yet, but. . ."

"Stop right there," Lev affirmed strongly. "I was just waiting to hear you say it. I want you to work with me. I've thought it ever since traveling with you. Since the conversation we had at Gethsemane. We need you, Jack. We need your communication skills. We need your help getting the truth out past a global media all too willing to, like we said, blame Israel—blame us," he emphasized, "for everything."

"But where would I stay?" Jack said. Even as he spoke he knew it was a feeble objection. "I paid a year's lease on this place so I can't afford much."

Lev swatted away the issue. "You'll stay with me at the Partners' Hotel. It ain't the King David, brother, but we'll make do. How soon can you get here? Like I said, we got big things happening."

"Would day after tomorrow be too soon?"

"Perfect. There's a group of UN delegates arriving for a tour of Israel. Amir and I have promised the PM's office to help show them around."

"Seriously?"

"They want to see a combination of the modern state and the ancient sites. Who better than us? Who better than you?" Lev stressed. "Academic credentials and diplomatic experience too."

Jack laughed as he protested, "Easy on that diplomacy stuff! Remember I just got canned for my inability to keep my mouth shut."

"Then come where you're appreciated!"

♦♦♦

How had Jack ever regarded ECMP as fair and unbiased? Thinking back over previous meetings and reports, he perceived blatant anti-Semitism—and he was part of it.

Now that Jack had resigned it was difficult for him to define exactly how he felt. He was relieved, certainly, to get away from the prejudice, but he also experienced some guilt for his previous involvement. Part of what he hoped to accomplish with Lev was—what was the word?—a form of restitution.

Then too, seeing Bette again soon was a positive electric charge—but there was a nagging negative in the sense of unfaithfulness to Deb's memory. He knew Deb would never accuse him of that, but he couldn't help it.

The idea that Israel might continue unfolding to him in dreams and visions was both humbling and exciting—but London had been home for so long. . .

It's a trial step, he told himself. *Nothing permanent yet. If things don't work out with Lev—or with Bette—I can always return here.* He could find a university position again somewhere—maybe. Many institutions of higher learning were even more openly anti-Israel than the ECMP.

Enough! Jack thought. *Bette is in Jerusalem. That's enough of a future for right now.*

There was just one thing he absolutely had to do before heading back to Israel.

When Jack resigned he thought there was nothing in his office he cared about. Books, papers, a couple inexpensive art prints of PRB scenes Deb picked out for him, but nothing with any real emotional investment—except the walking staff.

Jack was not about to leave it behind, nor trust someone else to ship him something so awkwardly shaped. It was the weekend and Jack had no idea if his keycard had already been deactivated, but he couldn't wait until Monday to call. He headed back to 30 St. Mary Ax to see if he could get in.

Both outer door and inner office opened with a swipe of Jack's card. He scanned the room once, felt no regrets, then grabbed the hiking stick and headed back to the elevator.

The lift dropped only a single floor and the door reopened to reveal two men. One had his back toward Jack. The other was an Arab male in a business suit. The expensively-dressed man looked Jack in the eye, put a hand on the other fellow's arm, and said tersely, "Sorry. Please go ahead. We're not quite ready after all."

Jack nodded and punched the "Close Door" button.

♦♦♦

Brahim Rahman did not release Faisal's arm for a full minute after encountering Jack at the elevator door.

"I saw something in his eyes," Rahman said. "Some recognition of either me or you."

"Not me," Faisal replied. "He's never really seen my face and he didn't get more than a glimpse right now."

"He's smart," Rahman said. "Who knows what he might put together if he has time to think it through. I thought getting him out of the Committee would be enough, but now I'm not sure."

"What would you like me to do?"

"Take care of him tonight," Rahman ordered as he punched the call button for the lift. "Can you get to his flat before he does?"

Faisal shrugged. "Motorcycle. Fifteen minutes—perhaps twenty. It will take him at least an hour."

"Do you have everything you need?"

"Always," Faisal Husseini confirmed.

♦♦♦

Out on the street, heading for the Tube while toting the walnut rod got Jack a few odd looks but no remarks.

It was only when back on the Bakerloo train he figured something out: the wealthy- looking figure was the man whose photo Jack had seen in the *Daily Mirror*—what was his name? Jack couldn't remember. The story had something to do with money laundering.

Was there anything familiar about the other man? It seemed so, but Jack didn't think there could be. After all, he only saw the man's build, his back, and a hint of his profile. It almost seemed like his arm was grasped to prevent him from turning to face Jack. *Pretty silly notion,* Jack thought.

A pair of German tourists with rucksacks and camping gear chose that moment to admire his hiking stick and Jack put the brief encounter out of his mind.

♦♦♦

The streetlight at the corner of Formosa and Elnathan Mews was out. There was another lamp, but it was at the far end of the cobblestone lane. Even though it was fully dark Jack wasn't bothered. Number four was only a few homes in from the cross street, and the bright yellow door was impossible to miss, even in the shadows.

Jack sniffed the air. Someone was cooking: cabbage. There were times when Jack thought he could identify London's neighborhoods by the prevailing aromas at meal times.

Leaning the hiking staff against his left shoulder, Jack fished in his pocket for the Yale latchkey. The door swung open into the hallway that ran straight toward the kitchen. He stepped in and kicked the door shut behind him. Jack fumbled for the light switch, found it, then flicked it up and down in frustration. Burnt out.

When Jack left home it was still day, so he did not leave any light on in the kitchen or on the lower stairs. The farther inside he went, the darker it became, except for the faint glow from a lamp at the very top of the stairs. It didn't matter. Jack and Deb shared this space so happily he knew it by heart; could probably climb all the way to the skylight without opening his eyes.

Jack hung his latchkey on the hook by the entry and headed for the stairs, passing the door out into the garage. The carpet underfoot muffled his steps.

From somewhere in the distance came the wail of a siren. Closer by, but in the other direction, loud rock music came from the barge converted into a pub down in the canal basin.

Grasping the hiking stick by the antler with his right hand, he let the tip trail behind him. After he passed the kitchen, over his right shoulder was the doorway leading into the dining room. Jack hadn't entertained any guests since Deb's death, so the room was left unused.

It was not until his left foot was on the first tread of the stairs that he heard a noise behind him in the dining room. He barely had time to turn his head before a masked assailant, dressed all in black, burst out from behind the dining room door, brandishing a knife.

Without turning to face the threat, and out of instinct rather than a plan, Jack pushed down on the antler. The butt end of the walking stick pivoted upward into the attacker's midsection.

The first stroke of the blade was downward, but it missed Jack's shoulder by half the length of the staff. The invader batted aside the stick and charged.

It was difficult to turn on the stairs. During Jack's pivot toward his opponent he let his right hand slide downward on the stick while his left grasped the antler. The hiking stick became a quarter-staff—and it worked. He managed to parry the second blow with the middle of the walnut rod.

"Help!" Jack yelled. "Help!"

The glow from the light at the top of the stairs illuminated the adversary's eyes—the only visible part of him because of the ski mask over his face and the gloves on his hands. The eyes were fiercely determined; not the look of a robber, but of a killer.

Jack's cell phone was in his inside coat pocket. No chance to reach it to dial 999. The only thing keeping him alive was the hiking stick.

The third frenzied slash was upward, aimed at Jack's belly.

Jack brought the staff down hard on the attacker's wrist, preventing the thrust from reaching him.

What happened next was faster than all the previous movements.

After the last blow the tine of the antler was facing the assailant's face. With every ounce of his strength, Jack thrust the walking stick forward and upward—directly into the opponent's right eye.

With a loud shriek, his adversary dropped the knife, clutched his face, and fled toward the front door, where he fumbled with the latch.

Jack took a step after him, then stopped. What if this guy had more than one weapon on him?

The moment's indecision was enough to allow the invader to fling open the door and rush out into the night.

Jack slammed the door and locked it, then quickly reopened it and stepped out into the lane. What if the invader had not been alone?

Moving to where his back was protected by the corner between two walls, Jack relinquished his grip on the staff long enough to thumb a call to the authorities. He stood brandishing the sharp end of the staff at every noise until the police arrived.

♦♦♦

PC Buttram was a five-year veteran of the Metropolitan Police. She was young enough to remain energetic; experienced enough to be skeptical.

"Not hurt?" she asked Jack for the third time.

"No," he repeated. "There's a drop of blood by the front door, but it must be his." Jack was seated in his living room, but the hiking stick was still in his hand. Every light in the flat was on and every room had been searched—inside the cupboards and under the beds, too.

"And nothing taken?"

"No."

"And nothing damaged except the latch on the skylight. The perp came up the fire escape, and over the roof, and got in that way. Now why do you say he was out to kill you?"

"You should have seen the look in his eyes," Jack said with a shudder.

"Uh-huh," PC Buttram said, making a note.

"And he wore gloves and a mask," Jack emphasized.

"Well," the officer said slowly. "These home break-ins—there's been a rash of them, you see? The perps aren't very smart but they know enough not to leave fingerprints, or let themselves be seen."

"But nothing was taken," Jack protested. "Sorry, I'm repeating myself."

"Here's the way I have it figured," Officer Buttram explained. "You surprised him, coming home like you did. He was startled. Probably on something too. Meth addicts sometimes exhibit psychotic behavior. You said he departed when you resisted."

"After I jabbed this in his eye," Jack said, showing the tine of the antler.

"Do you have any reason to think someone wants to kill you?" PC Buttram inquired. "Anyone ever try to kill you?"

"I've been shot at," Jack replied.

"Really? When was that?"

"In Israel. A car I was riding in was shot at."

"Oh." Officer Buttram snapped her notebook shut. "We'll put out the word to the hospitals for unexplained eye injuries."

"And you think it's safe for me to stay here tonight?"

The policewoman nodded and left.

Nevertheless, Jack dragged the stepladder from the garage all the way to the top of the topmost stairs, and nailed the skylight shut. Then he slept with the hiking staff beside his right hand.

Chapter Sixteen

T he throng at the airport contained Israeli cabinet ministers and diplomats, religious leaders, security personnel, television cameras—and Jack. "Why'm I here?" he whispered to Lev. "I just got back yesterday."

"Because today's a historic day," Lev shot back.

As the representative of Partners with Zion and a friend of Lon Silver, Lev was invited to attend the Ben Gurion Airport reception for Prime Minister Narendra Modi of India. A double file of IDF forces stood at attention, lining the carpet from the plane's boarding ramp to the awning under which the crowd stood.

This soon after arriving back in Israel, Jack expected a breaking-in period at least. He had no idea what Lev expected of him or what his duties were. "Roll with it," Lev added.

Prime Minister Netanyahu met his Indian counterpart at the bottom of the plane's steps. They exchanged an embrace and some whispered words of greeting. The two men stood at attention beside the Air India One Boeing 747 while the national anthems of both nations were played. Blue-and-white Israeli flags snapped in the stiff breeze beside the saffron-white-and-green banners of India.

"Twenty-five years since India formally recognized Israel," Lev said when the music ceased. "But this is the first time a sitting Indian PM has made a personal visit. India has a sizable Muslim minority and a minuscule Jewish population too. Do you get it? Up to today the only foreign leaders met at the airport have been the pope and the U.S. president. This is a big deal."

Jack realized if he was going to be of use he had a lot of catching up to do—and quickly.

Turning to the microphones, Benjamin Netanyahu's broad smile was beaming as he formally greeted Modi on behalf of the Jewish state. "Welcome, my friend," Netanyahu said in Hindi. Switching to English he went on to say it was altogether fitting for the leader of one democracy to greet the leader of the largest democracy in the world.

Lev turned toward Jack and raised his eyebrows. World opinion had long wavered to see if Israel was even going to survive. Now, it seemed, some countries decided that Israel—the most modern, most democratic state in the Middle East—was past due being embraced by the community of nations.

"We had something to do with this," Lev said. "America, I mean. And Christian Americans especially. New partnerships—India and Israel—Christians and Jews—lots of new ground being broken, faster than ever."

Jack nodded, but his head swiveled as he scanned the crowd for Bette. Where was she?

India's prime minster was a trim, distinguished figure whose silver hair gleamed from his head, his neatly trimmed beard, and even his eyebrows. When it was Modi's turn to speak he said, "It is my singular honor to be the first ever Indian PM to visit Israel. We have to secure our societies against the common thread of terrorism."

"That's as plain as it gets," Jack said. "Is it true there's no official visit to the Palestinians?"

"Nope," Lev confirmed as applause erupted all around them for the Indian prime minister's remarks. "This trip is all about better relations and more trade—technology and agriculture."

"Bet the Palestinian leadership is torqued," Jack observed, thinking about Rafa Husseini's open hostility toward all things Israeli. "Say, Bette should be here. I wonder where she is?"

"Don't know how to break this to you," Lev returned with a grin. "But she does have to work for a living and you're no longer her assignment."

"Yeah? Well, I may have to do something about that," Jack said. "Long term, I mean."

♦♦♦

At the moment the two heads of government were exchanging hugs and speeches in Tel Aviv, Bette was some fifty miles away. She was posted at the Mazmoria checkpoint south of Jerusalem, on the road to Gush Etzion.

The call on the restricted phone only used to connect her to Yamam headquarters came at five that morning. Without explanation Bette was told to be in uniform and report to the commander immediately.

Once more she stood at attention in front of Commander S.'s desk. "I need you to help out with security on highway 398," her boss ordered. "We have intel; an attack timed to embarrass Netanyahu on the day of PM Modi's arrival. I want you out there to assist. Uniformed show of force. Be alert."

Technically Bette was still part of Border Police operations, but checkpoint security was in the distant past on her résumé. Bette knew better than to ask why she was selected for the duty, but Commander S. volunteered an explanation anyway. "I need to get you back out in the field," he said. "I'm afraid you may have lost some of your edge doing convoy duty for the American. Now get going."

That was six hours earlier. Increased security meant slower travel through the checkpoint. Papers were examined, photographs compared to the occupants. Suspicious vehicles were pulled out of the line and thoroughly searched. So far the only contraband located was a half kilo of hashish and five kilos of dried parsley for sale to tourists as Arab marijuana.

The line of cars waiting to be checked so they could proceed north extended out of sight past a gas station and a tire store. Bette yawned and wondered what Jack must think about her absence. She shook her head and tried to regain her focus. It was dangerous to not pay attention. It could get you killed.

The car Bette walked alongside was a beat-up station wagon containing an Arab mother and father and six—no, seven—kids. Mom was gesturing with one arm out the window and yelling at nobody about being late for a dentist appointment. Dad looked stoic and grim and much like he'd rather be anywhere else.

The next car back was a small, white Mitsubishi. The subcompact-sized four-door vehicle was crammed full of six full-sized Arab men. The man in the front passenger seat looked out the window at Bette, gave a perfunctory wave of his hand, and looked away.

Despite what the commander implied, Bette's observational skills had not lost a beat. Without conscious thought she noted the front green-on-white West Bank plate: 4530943.

Bette stared into the interior of the car. None of the men looked at her.

Something wasn't right. Arab men, especially traveling in a pack, usually leered at Israeli women and often made rude commentary. These men did neither. Instead they seemed to be concentrating on the road ahead—even though the station wagon was no more than three feet in front.

The Mitsubishi edged forward, then stopped again. Bette stepped farther back along the line, then glanced over her shoulder—4003943 the rear plate read.

They didn't match. Bette's hand dropped to the butt of her sidearm. Mismatched plates meant a stolen car—at the very least. She whistled sharply to the border policemen walking the other side of the line of cars and gave a sharp jerk of her head toward the suspect vehicle.

Three other border police joined the confrontation. Five Israeli weapons covered the Mitsubishi. "Hands where we can see them," the ranking sergeant ordered in Arabic. "Pull it over there out of the line and get out—slowly!"

The six men emerged, hands in the air. Lined up alongside the vehicle, the driver was asked for his ID card. He claimed to have lost it.

None of the six occupants, who all appeared to be between the ages of eighteen and twenty-five, had any form of ID on them.

"Keep them over there," the sergeant directed.

More policemen converged on the car and proceeded to take apart the headliner, the door panels, and the trunk. Success was not long in coming. Underneath the spare tire was a bag containing glass bottles full of gasoline and stoppered with rags, two stun grenades—and five butcher knives.

After the car and the would-be terrorists were removed from the checkpoint the sergeant remarked to Bette, "Good call. Had they made it into Jerusalem we'd be looking at a major—bloody—incident. Well done."

♦♦♦

The professional barriers between Jack and Bette were now completely down. By candlelight on the terrace of the King David, he drank in her gold-flecked, brown eyes like rich, smooth Sabra liqueur.

"So I'm no longer your responsibility?"

"Not officially, no." She held up two wine glasses. "Here is the situation. Are they half full? Or half empty?" She poured the deep purple liquid into one glass, and the wine brimmed to the rim. "Very full I think." She winked.

"I get your point."

"I never told you before—I was warned by my superior before you left—I was not permitted to fall in love with you."

"After you were once again the hero—heroine—of the hour, that was extremely ungenerous of him."

"That's what I said. And you know what he told me? He said, 'This guy is not even Jewish.'" She sipped the wine and passed the glass to Jack. "So now you are fired from your official position and don't need a bodyguard. My falling in love with you is no longer an issue."

He took a drink and held the wine in his mouth for a moment. "I taste hints of chocolate and raspberries."

"And I simply taste wine. You see? I am not a woman of nuances. Straightforward. The wine is good. The wine is bad."

"And what was your first impression of me?"

"I did not like you at first. But what is that song? From *Phantom of the Opera*? 'I've grown accustomed to your taste?'"

Jack laughed. "I think it's, 'I've Grown Accustomed to Your Face...' And it's from *My Fair Lady*."

"Well—that too—your very nice face—so whatever. Anyway, my boss cannot tell me not to fall in love. It's too late anyway."

"And I didn't expect to fall in love with you, Bette. Life is filled with good surprises."

"Mostly good and we must do all we can to protect ourselves against the bad surprises. I've asked for time off. So I can spend time with you."

"That's the best news I've heard this week."

"I think you are being tailed, you see. I think you are not safe, Jack."

"Why? What?"

"A feeling mostly. Instinct—after so many years."

"So you are a woman of nuance after all."

"My mother calls it maternal instinct."

"A bear with her cubs." He took her hand and kissed her fingertips.

"And you are my cub, Jack."

♦♦♦

It was only two days after their candlelit dinner when Bette insisted she had somewhere to take Jack and it couldn't wait.

"Someone I want you to meet." Bette and Jack wound through market crowds in the busy Old City Souk. "He has lived here a very long time."

Off a narrow side street was a high wall and a scarred gate. Bette smiled over her shoulder, then touched the mezuzah on the doorpost with her fingertip, and kissed it. She punched a security code on a keypad. The lock clicked and the hinges of the entrance groaned as the door swung open, revealing a cool, walled garden. The space was twenty by thirty feet, bordered by a stone house on one end, and shaded by a huge purple Jacaranda tree and festooned thick with flowers.

A colorful ceramic plaque declared SHALOM; peace. Indeed the secret refuge lived up to its name. The gentle trickling of water and the soft music of wind chimes made the serene atmosphere seem almost timeless.

Bette inclined her head toward a bench, indicating Jack should sit. Jack had not suspected this place existed behind the high walls, but he had long since ceased to be surprised by anything in Jerusalem.

Minutes passed in silence. Bette did not attempt to explain and Jack instinctively knew he should not ask questions.

Jack heard the sound of a door open and close from within the shadowed alcove. A silver-haired man with a short, closely trimmed beard stepped into the sunlight. He wore pleated, linen trousers and a tan canvas jacket. His white shirt was open at the collar. An old black and white photograph was pinched between thumb and forefinger. He raised the picture, gazing at the image, and then studied Jack closely, almost with wonder, as he shuffled toward them.

Bette and Jack rose. She exchanged greetings with the stranger in Hebrew. Bette introduced Jack. "Sol Baruch, this is my friend, Jack Garrison. From America."

"Shalom," the old man clasped Jack's hand in a surprisingly strong handshake. "Sit. Sit, please." The old man moved a wrought iron chair directly opposite the bench and sat down. He smiled slightly and leaned closer. Searching Jack's face intently, it seemed as though he was trying to memorize every detail.

At last Sol spoke in heavily accented English. "So. You are Jacob de Louzada."

"He was my grandfather."

The old man held up the faded photo. It was as though Jack was looking at his own face in a mirror. "This is Jacob de Louzada. This is you." With a gnarled finger he pointed at two grinning, young men in berets and suits standing before the Eiffel Tower. "And this is me, with Jacob. We were Sol and Jacob, friends like brothers—from infancy, even. We attended the Sorbonne together. And this photograph was our last day together. Before the war, you see." Faded blue eyes brimmed. "When

I saw you enter through my window here, it was as though my dear friend Jacob had come into my garden. You are so much like the way I saw him the last time at the train station."

Emotion constricted Jack's throat as he gazed at his grandfather's image for the first time. "Yes. I see that. Our resemblance. We really are so very much. . ."

"I would have known you anywhere. You are taller than Jacob, I think. Or perhaps I am shorter. But you are indeed his grandson, without explanation or question."

Jack ducked his head slightly and searched for words. "I am looking for my grandmother. Jacob's wife." He briefly explained all he learned in his mother's note. Sol nodded again slowly, then shook his head in sorrow at the last revelation.

"I am sorry, Jacob—may I call you by his name?"

"Yes." Jack squeezed Bette's hand in gratitude. "Of course. You can call me Jacob."

"Well, then. My life is complete. I tell you, your face is a miracle to me now."

Bette interjected, "Sol, do you know anything about Jack's—I mean—about the wife of your old friend? It is believed she came here to Jerusalem in 1947. Maybe '48."

"Ah. War of Independence. Hard years—I never met her, you see. I only heard in a letter from my friend Jacob that he had met the love of his life. That they married. They had a child—a baby girl. And they wanted to make *Aliyah* but were denied visas by the British Mandatory Government. And then, of course, it is just as the story says. Their baby girl they put on a kinder transport. Giving your mother up was a terrible grief for your grandfather. His last letter told me he wished he had listened. He wrote me they should have left France. And by then it was too late. The Nazis conquered France. And I heard no more from Jacob. I thought Jacob and his wife both perished in the death camps." The old man relived it all. He wiped a tear with the back of his hand. "Never forget, we say. Never forget? But already the whole world has forgotten the Holocaust. And now—the young Jews in Europe—in France, are living through what we lived through. They should all come to Israel now before it is too late."

Bette tried again. "The Agency has reached out to you, the ones who came from France during the British Mandate. You are the only one who answered."

Sol placed his hand on Jack's hand. "I am sorry, my son. I would not know her. She would not have known me. Never met. And now—there are so few of us left."

Jack tried not to let his disappointment show. "I am grateful, Sol. Very grateful. I did not expect—after so many years—to learn what you shared in one afternoon. "

Sol nodded. "I believe everything means something. The day I heard your grandfather had not survived was June 14, 1946. That very night there was a Blood Moon over Jerusalem. I was gathered with a small band of Haganah resistance fighters. It seemed somehow to me this eclipse was a sign from heaven that one day we would be free—that Israel would truly be a Jewish homeland—that Jerusalem must be our capital city again after 2,000 years. I did not know what it meant until just recently. Now I have learned your American president was born on June 14, 1946—on that very night. As the Blood Moon appeared over Jerusalem the future president of America—who would one day declare Jerusalem as the eternal, undivided capital of Israel—was born. Yes. That fulfillment somehow softens the memory of the terrible night when I grieved your grandfather's death." Sol raised his finger with an idea. "I have kept a packet of your grandfather's letters. Give me a few days to search. You and beautiful Bette come for Shabbat dinner? Sunset this Friday. I will search for the letters. Somewhere in my treasure chest of memories. Perhaps you will like them?"

"You can't imagine how very much. . ." Jack paused. "And just one more question? You see, I know nothing about him. Only today I learned I am his double. So—if you could. . ."

Sol spread his hands wide. "Anything, my son. Anything for the grandson of my dearest friend."

"You say you and my grandfather were at the Sorbonne together. What did he study?"

"I will tell you! Jacob de Louzada was a musician. Yes. Extraordinaire. French horn. A talent unlike any other, it is said. First chair in the Paris symphony orchestra. And he was also an artist. His great love was the potter's wheel." Sol pointed to the ceramic sign on the garden wall. "That was his parting gift to me. SHALOM. Yes. Peace is what we have all longed for. He was a man of a great and beautiful soul. So: Shabbat dinner. We will talk all you want."

◆◆◆

The Old City walls surrounding the Temple Mount gleamed in the spotlights. The moon rose in the east, casting a golden glow on the sacred mountain of the Lord.

Jack thought through Sol's story about Jacob de Louzada's struggle to escape to British-ruled Palestine. Suddenly his grandfather was real in Jack's thoughts. Jacob was a man like any other who longed to live his life in peace and freedom. SHALOM. Mount Zion shone like Eden to centuries of exiled Jews.

Their deepest longing? To return home. That was God's promise planted deep in the heart of the remnant of Jews—Shearith Israel—to gather those who were scattered from the four corners of the world.

The return of Jack, grandson of a man killed in the Holocaust, was the fulfillment of biblical prophecy. As long as one Jew remained alive to experience the biblical promises of return and redemption, then Satan had lost his long battle to make God a liar.

Jack's mind was filled with questions about Jacob he wanted to ask Sol. Even small details seemed like lanterns placed along the dark path of Jack's personal journey. He knew now the visions Eliyahu showed him were links in a golden chain leading from God's promises to Abraham to the fulfillment of all prophecy in this present day.

Leaving the curtains open, Jack climbed into bed. So much more he wanted to know. He would count the hours until he and Bette could sit down at the Shabbat meal with his grandfather's dearest friend. He would count the minutes until he could read the letters and know the heart of Jacob de Louzada.

♦♦♦

"You speak their language. You have the credentials and the résumé," said Lev as he explained Jack's new role with Partners with Zion. "Amir and I know how to speak to pastors and ministry leaders, but we need to expand this program. Remember what was said about showing visitors both ancient rocks and living stones?"

The hands of the clock in the PWZ conference room indicated 6:30 in the morning, and the meeting was already a half hour old.

"I think Lon Silver said that," Jack suggested.

"That's where I first heard it," Lev agreed. "Anyway, when men and women from congress or parliament, or university professors, or investigative journalists, come to Israel, we need to connect them with the land, the history, the prophecy, *and* the people. Like we do the ministry folks. We need you to be part of the broader reach."

"But why do you need me?" Jack protested. "You can already call up Bibi and go see him. You know how to talk to politicians as well as me."

"Remember how you saw the handwriting on the wall, and cities and nations crumbling?" Lev said. "Don't you think those things mean time is short and we need all hands on deck? Besides," Lev added. "Now you're family. Can't refuse a family need, can you?"

Jack grinned. "Never thought about refusing. I just hope you like the results. After all, I got fired from my last job for my lack of diplomacy."

Amir leaned forward to offer: "What do you Americans say? No time for beating around the bush? Straight talk—plain talk—is what's needed. And more of it."

"Okay," Jack conceded. "You got me. Now, tell me about Hebron and why it's so important."

Waving a feta cheese-stuffed breakfast roll, Lev gestured toward the map of Israel hanging on the wall. The West Bank territory resembled a misshapen kidney bean curling around the eastern side of Jerusalem. In the southern lobe of the bean, in the Judean mountains, was the ancient settlement of Hebron.

"Arabs 200,000," Amir said. "One thousand Jews."

"Conquered by Joshua," Lev added. "Given to the Levites as one of their cities. King David ruled from there for seven years."

"And the Tomb of the Patriarchs," Jack said. "Abraham's buried there. That part I know."

"Next to the Temple Mount," Lev continued, "most important and most disputed place in Israel. Since both Jews and Muslims revere Abraham, it's significant to both—Christians too, of course. The Ibrihimi mosque on top is a repurposed Herodian building, dating to the time of Jesus."

"Over the Cave of Machpelah," Amir elaborated. "Abraham bought it when Sarah died. He and his wife are buried there, along with Jacob and Leah. . ."

"Not Rachel," Lev interrupted. "Her tomb's near Bethlehem."

"Isaac and Rebekah," Amir continued around a mouthful of sesame seed topped bagel. "And some say—Adam and Eve. Legend makes it the threshold of the Garden of Eden."

Jack saw again his vision of the garden being walled off and the tragic loss experienced by Adam and Eve. "We've been trying to get back there ever since," he murmured.

"But global anti-Semitism makes it a political football game too," Lev noted. "UNESCO just declared Hebron a 'Palestinian World Heritage Site in Danger.' Not Jewish. Not even Jewish *and* Palestinian—even though the patriarchs existed, what? Twenty-five hundred years before Muhammad was even born?"

"Bibi already responded," Amir said with a smile. "Took a million dollars from Israel's commitment to the UN and redirected it to the Jewish Historic Preservation Fund for Hebron. He said it was in response to, 'another delusional UNESCO decision.'"

Lev was more sober when he added, "What Bibi said next is also true: 'Israel will continue to guard the Cave of the Patriarchs, to ensure religious freedom for everybody—and to guard the truth.' He went on to say—and he's right—'Only where Israel is present—like in Hebron—is freedom of worship assured for everybody.' You know, in the rest of the Middle East, mosques, churches, ancient monuments, and synagogues are being blown up—all when Israel isn't there to protect them."

Jack let it all sink in for a moment. "I need to see it for myself," he said.

◆◆◆

Sabbath came at last. Jack's anticipation made the waiting hard. He adjusted his blue-and-silver-stripe patterned tie in the mirror, then hurried down to the lobby where Bette waited for him. She stood and grinned playfully at him. His breath caught at her beauty. Better than Wonder Woman, he thought, drinking her in. Her dress showed off her figure, but was long sleeved and modest, suitable for a Shabbat dinner. The material was made of gold and rust-colored autumn leaves that caught the flecks of gold in her eyes. Highlights of red shone in thick hair that tumbled over her shoulders. She wore large gold hoop earrings. Full, moist lips curved up at the corners and glistened with subtle red lipstick.

"I like the package. Where's the Glock?"

"In a convenient location."

"Where I come from, 'dressed to kill' has a different meaning."

"Where I come from a girl's ready for anything."

"Where have you been all my life?"

"That's a pretty tired line."

"Well, I'm wide awake now!"

She blushed. "I'm more comfortable in a uniform."

"The world's loss, if that's the case." He took her arm.

She playfully flipped his necktie. "This won't do."

"No? Not Shabbat wear?"

"No. Not safe. It makes a great handhold for a terrorist. To break your neck."

"I see." He removed the tie and shoved it into his sports coat pocket. "Working even on your day of rest?"

"Never stop." She held up a bottle of wine. "For our host."

Fifteen minutes later the playful banter vanished as Jack and Bette turned up the side street toward Sol's secret garden. The cramped alleyway was crowded with people milling outside the old man's house.

"Oh no." Bette shoved the wine bottle into Jack's hands. "I'll find out. . ."

An ambulance with flashing lights was parked against the high wall. The rear doors were thrown open.

The gate into the garden was wide open. Bette flashed her ID to an EMT and began to ask a string of questions in Hebrew. Her face clouded as the answers came back.

She turned to Jack. "They say—Sol is—Jack, Sol is dead. A heart attack, looks like. There's nothing we can do here. We should go."

At the entrance to Sol's house a stretcher appeared.

Jack felt like he had been kicked in the gut. He fixed his eyes on the place where the SHALOM plaque hung. It was no longer there. In the midst of the garden was a table set for Shabbat dinner; white linen table cloth, china, silver, candlesticks were all in place.

Bette tugged his arm, turning him from the sight. "Oh, Jack. Nothing we can do. I'm so very sorry, Jack. Come on. Come on, let's go."

♦♦♦

The apartment Faisal rented was in Ramallah, but he did not expect to carry out Rahman's orders there. After the failed Elnathan Mews attack, Faisal was hurriedly returned to the West Bank. The fact Allah practically delivered Garrison into Faisal's hands by the target's return to Israel was clear. Now it was merely a matter of picking the right place and time—and the cloned cell phone simplified that.

The two men Faisal recruited in Hebron were male, but that biological fact did not confirm they were adults. One was sixteen, the other fifteen. They were radicalized in their childhoods at their local mosque. Both listened to the radio broadcasts of ISIS leader Abu Bakr al-Baghdadi.

Both wanted to be suicide bombers.

Faisal's first task was to convince them otherwise.

"We want to strike a blow at the heart of the Jews!" Idris exclaimed. "We want to blow up a thousand Jews at the Buraq Wall."

Faisal slapped him on the back of the head. "Be silent! You would never get within a thousand yards before the police shot you dead! I thought you had a serious desire for *jihad*—for *istishhad*. Perhaps I was mistaken. Go home. Go back to your toys."

"No!" Omar protested. "We do want to be warriors. We do want to be martyrs! Truly! Tell us what to do."

"That's better!" Faisal said soothingly. "Here in your home city you will have the opportunity you seek and it will be glorious. You will not only find *istishhad*, you will be gaining revenge for your brother, Idris, and for your father, Omar."

Both older men were killed by an IDF missile strike in Gaza while attempting to launch a mortar round at a target in Israel.

"What do we do to prepare?" Omar asked.

"Nothing! And you will say nothing! You will wait until I say it's time to strike and then you will obey."

♦♦♦

Crowds of Israelis lined the road and raised their voices in song as the body of Sol Baruch was carried to the Jewish Cemetery. At least one hundred musicians playing "Im Eshkachech" followed the procession.

Bette translated the words from Psalm 137,

> If I do not raise you
> and if I do not raise you
> Jerusalem
> Above all my joy
> Above my highest joy. . .

"Who was this man? Who was Sol Baruch?" Jack asked in awe as he and Bette made their way through the packed street. "I didn't know I was meeting with an Israeli hero."

"You Americans have Ben Franklin and John Adams and your Declaration of Independence—so Israel has men like Sol who made *aliyah* when Eretz Israel was still occupied by the British. And he planted vineyards and also fought beside other Jewish refugees for our independence. He fought in Haganah. Risked his life every day for the restoration of the nation of Israel. A hero. But you know what Sol will be remembered for? Not that he could shoot a gun or that he was wounded defending the road to Jerusalem. Sol Baruch is beloved because he was a music teacher. A teacher of Jewish children who lost their parents and some who survived the Holocaust. Yes. All these people you see—secular and religious—all of them were touched by his kindness and by his music…"

They approached the gates where a group of two dozen elderly Jewish women were seated. Dressed in unadorned black dresses, the women looked on as Sephardim males in black prayer shawls processed past them.

Bette halted with Jack beside the old women and explained, "These won't enter the cemetery. An ancient custom with the Sephardic women. Customs are changing now, but these still follow the old ways. I'll wait outside with them."

Jack felt the unwavering gaze of one old woman fixed on him. Her glare reminded him he was hatless and dressed like an American businessman—out of place. And, after all, he only met Sol one time. Jack sensed the old woman's disapproval as he held Bette's hand.

"I'll meet you here afterwards." Jack joined the men in the procession to the grave.

Bette was right about Sol.

Psalms were read in Hebrew. An IDF soldier spotted Jack as a non-Hebrew speaker and summarized the eulogies into English. In the end, yes, the life of Sol Baruch was remembered best by former music students who were now old men themselves.

The service was short. Jack exited the ancient cemetery and found Bette waiting for him.

He was silent on the walk back to the car.

"God is good," Bette said as they buckled their seatbelts. "He let you meet this man who loved your grandfather like a brother. You took an hour to speak with him in his garden and you entered your family's past. It was important to you. I'm sorry it can't be more, Jack."

Jack wondered if he should admit how disappointed he was he did not receive the letters of Jacob de Louzada. In the end he decided it was best to keep quiet.

"Can I take you to dinner?" he asked.

"I'm sorry. Not tonight. I have a meeting. But tomorrow for breakfast? The hotel? Before we drive to Hebron?" She pulled up at the Partner's Hotel entrance.

"Listen." He took her hand. "Something you said about never parting without saying—I love you. . ."

Bette smiled. "It's true. You never know, do you?" She leaned close and lifted her face to his. Their lips met and lingered.

"This feels more like hello than goodbye." Jack kissed her again. She did not resist.

"Oh, Jack. I'm so happy—tomorrow then. We'll pick up where we've left off."

Chapter Seventeen

Bette piloted her new, late model, pewter-colored Suzuki SX4 down Highway 60 toward Hebron. It was roomier than the Toyota, "but no sexier," Jack declared. "I thought you'd go for a Mazda or something with some pizazz."

"Next time," Bette declared. "This is what I could afford right now."

Jack wondered if having the window shot out of the Toyota motivated her to get something of a different shape and color. He decided Bette Deekmann was made of tougher stuff than that.

Spring arrived like a green-and-flowered cloak. South of Jerusalem the roadsides displayed orange poppies that reminded Jack of the Sierra Nevada foothills. The Suzuki overtook and passed a tour bus. "Bullet proof glass on that van?" Jack noticed.

"Can't have anxious tourists," Bette declared. "This road used to have a lot of random shootings, but not so much anymore."

Jack opted against teasing Bette about the "not so much" comment.

She took his lack of response as a request for more information. "Hebron is like the mini-version of the whole issue," she said. "Two hundred thousand Palestinians—seven hundred Jews. Jews have lived there since—well, you know, since before King David. Through the Roman era, Byzantine, Arab, Turks—right up to the riots of 1929. About seventy Jews killed, the rest expelled. No Jews 'til 1967, when some came back."

"And now?"

"Jews and Palestinians share the city." She edged in past another tour bus to make the exit marked "Kiryat Arba," the Jewish town adjacent to Hebron. "And freely moved around in it until the mid-nineties. A wave of killings—both ways. Jewish teenagers murdered. A Jewish madman killed Muslim worshippers in the mosque. Then the Second Intifada happened." Bette shook her head. "Now it's divided, you know? Barbed wire. Security cameras. And the travel restrictions cut both ways. No Palestinians travel to the Jewish sector—even though some Palestinian families still live there. No Jews at all live on the Palestinian side. IDF soldiers patrol checkpoints."

"Why do they stay?" Jack asked. "The Jews in Hebron, I mean. It can't be easy for so few Jews."

"It is, what do you say? A Catch Twenty-Two. The Palestinians want a Hebron with no Jews at all. If the Jews living there now move away, they know they'll never come back."

Bette parked the Suzuki in a lot not far from the Tomb of the Patriarchs in the Jewish sector of Hebron known as H2.

"And that's how we get in? Right over there?" Jack asked, pointing to the fortress-like structure dominating the scenery.

"To half of it, anyway," Bette said. "To see the Muslim side of the building you have to go out and around and in a separate entrance."

"So we'll do that, right?"

"You can," Bette told him. "Jews—Israeli Jews anyway—are not permitted on the Muslim side."

Jack appreciatively scanned Bette's modestly stated beauty. "How they gonna tell?" he asked.

"Listen," she corrected sternly. "You may have a nice, secure new job, but I want to keep the one I have now, yes?"

"Okay, okay," Jack conceded. "I'll come back with Amir some other time." Giving her a big hug he said, "Today's really about being together. I'm so glad you were able—and wanted—to come."

She gave him a big kiss that sent a rush of chills up the back of his neck. She stood on tiptoe and tugged on his hair. "My pleasure," she breathed in his ear.

They joined the back of a group of Americans touring the synagogue. As custom dictated, all the males wore head coverings. Jack put on the kippah Bette gave him. Besides the traditional kippot Jack noticed three ball caps and a Texas cowboy hat.

The guide, a portly Israeli whose thinning hair barely provided an anchor for the hairpin holding his yarmulkah, said, "These are the monuments to Abraham, over here, and to his wife, Sarah, over there."

"Who'd you say?" cowboy hat inquired.

"Our patriarch, Father Abraham and our Matriarch Sarah," the guide patiently repeated.

"That's what I thought you said. Buried in the wall, are they?"

"No, no! In the cave below us. Cave of Machpelah. Cave and land was bought by Abraham when his wife died."

A teenage boy in a baseball cap waved his hand. "How far below?"

"Sixteen feet, yes?" The guide offered. "Five meters."

"We going down there?" the boy persisted.

"No. No one goes there. Respect for the dead, you see? But if you'll follow me across the hall we see the monuments. . ."

"Thought we were gonna see the cave," cowboy hat complained.

"No, no cave. But if you follow me we will see monuments to Jacob and Leah."

"Now you know why I sometimes pretend to be a Brit," Jack whispered.

Bette shushed him, but giggled.

Jack laid his hand on the wall. *My people are buried down there*, he thought. *No longer "their people." My people.*

Noticing his momentary inward gaze Bette leaned closer and said, "This would be a good place to have a vision, true? Abraham learning of the son of his old age. Grieving for Sarah. And perhaps it's true what they say about Adam and Eve being buried here too. If this is the gate to Eden, they wanted to get back as close as they could to what they had lost."

Jack nodded. "Mark Twain wrote—you know Twain?"

"Of course, silly!"

"Twain wrote his idea of Adam and Eve's story. Humorous, mostly. But when Eve died and Adam buried her, he wrote this epitaph: 'Where she was, there was Eden.'"

"Ah," Bette sighed. "Very romantic." Then straightening up she said, "But are you having a vision?"

Jack grabbed both her hands and stared into her eyes. "I sure am," he said.

Bette blushed and dropped her chin, but smiled. "Don't be sacrilegious. We're in a synagogue."

"Don't want to be sacrilegious," Jack returned. "Okay, let's go. We finish the tour, then lunch time. My treat."

"Perfect. I know a great falafel place just a block from here."

Even though they didn't need the car, their path to lunch took them back past where it was parked. A pair of Arab boys dressed in Levis and wearing matching ball caps looked up at their approach. "Hey, mister. We wash your windows, eh?" the taller of the two offered, while the shorter pantomimed scrubbing a windshield.

"You give us money. A dollar, U.S. dollar?" the shorter demanded.

"Sounds like a bargain," Jack said agreeably. "Oops, wait. No U.S. dollars."

"Jack," Bette said tersely. "Something's not right. Where's the bucket? Where's the water?"

Moving closer, the pair said, "It's okay, lady."

"Back behind your car, see?"

"How'd you know which one was mine?" Bette demanded.

The noise of running footsteps erupted from an alleyway behind them. A man wearing an eye patch and waving a knife with a jagged blade was only ten feet away. Shouting, "Allahu akbar," he flung himself toward Jack.

Bette drew the concealed pistol from her waistband, just as the taller of the two boys grabbed her arm. The first shot went wild, shattering an adjacent car's windshield.

This can't be happening again! Jack thought. *Not here! Not now!*

At the last second before the knife plunged into Jack's chest, Bette crashed into him, knocking him out of the way.

Bette triggered off another round, but Jack didn't see where it went because the other teenager tackled him. His assailant only captured one of Jack's legs. Kicking out hard with the free limb, Jack had the satisfaction of feeling the sole of his hiking boot crunch into the jaw of his opponent.

Jack heard Bette cry out, and another shot boomed. Then the second boy hit Jack from behind. His head bounced off a cement post and Jack fell to the ground, unconscious.

He didn't know how long he was out, but it couldn't have been long because when he looked up Bette was standing over him. "Are you okay?" she asked.

Both hands on his head, Jack peered past her to where the adult attacker lay on the ground. "So you got him? It's over then? What happened to the boys?"

"Ran off," Bette said. "Jack, I. . ."

What was wrong with her? Her color was funny and she stood with her left hand pressed awkwardly against her stomach.

"I—I love you, Jack," she said. The pistol dropped to the pavement. Then her knees buckled. Her hand fell away from her belly, revealing a bright splash of spreading crimson.

Then she collapsed.

♦♦♦

Jack sat on the curb, his head in his hands. He was holding an ice pack against a sizable knot on his skull. He was a little nauseated and his vision was blurry, but he was otherwise okay—physically.

"Please," he begged for the tenth time. "Let me go with her."

The paramedic treating Jack said patiently, "Officer Deekmann is being airlifted to the trauma center at Hadassah Hospital in Jerusalem. She'll be there in ten minutes. You have, at worst, a mild concussion. We will transport you to Beit Hadassah Clinic here in Hebron. It's a fine facility. They will take good care you."

Jack could not get past the vision of Bette being strapped onto the gurney. Her skin was the same color as the policewoman who was knifed at Damascus Gate; the one who died. When Jack called her name, Bette's eyelids fluttered—but that was all.

The helicopter landed at an open plaza near the car park. Bette, a flask of IV fluid already flowing into her arm, was whisked past Jack and loaded aboard the aircraft.

"I'll skip the treatment," Jack said. "Can't I just ride with her?"

Even as he asked again the rotors spun up and the helicopter lifted off. It banked overhead, then sped away toward the northeast. Jack's eyes followed the aircraft while it dwindled to a tiny speck and then disappeared. Jack felt his worst fears rising, like the helicopter soaring upward, and his hope diminishing, just as the craft diminished to a vanishing pinprick of light.

"I still refuse treatment here," Jack said, struggling to stand. Jack displayed a set of car keys in his hand. "I have her keys. I'll drive myself to. . ."

"You're in no shape to drive," the paramedic stated flatly. He called out in Hebrew to another of the medical personnel. There was a brief discussion, then the first attendant again addressed Jack. "I'm getting off duty right now and am going to take the bus back to Jerusalem. I'll drive you to Hadassah and then I can catch another bus home from there."

♦♦♦

"I lost my cell phone," Jack explained to the security officer in the main waiting room of Hadassah Hospital. "It's almost midnight. They were supposed to ring me with any news about Bette Deekman's surgery. It's been nearly seven hours. I'm Jack Garrison."

"Sure. I'll check." The officer nodded sympathetically and phoned the surgical floor.

A few words were exchanged on the phone in Hebrew. "Sorry, Mr. Garrison. She's still in surgery. Why don't you head back to your hotel? They'll ring you there if there's any news."

Jack shook his head and glanced around at the nearly empty room. "I'll stay. Thanks."

Only one family group remained. They were clustered around an old woman in a seating area in the far corner.

Adult children and grandchildren snoozed on couches and in chairs. The elderly woman gazed at Jack.

Jack met her gaze. The old woman crooked her finger, motioning for him to come over.

"Shalom." She lifted her chin and peered at him with weary blue eyes. Her wizened face betrayed years of hard work under harsh sun. Her words were heavily accented. "Young man. I have seen you sitting there alone."

"Yes. My—friend—was stabbed in Hebron today."

"It's all over the news. My grandson, Yosef, saw it on the Google." She inclined her head toward a sleeping young man of about twenty. "His cell phone tells him everything. The Hebron attack. I am so very sorry. You are American? Yes? Her American friend, Jack something— was not injured, the news said. And your photograph they showed."

"Yes. I'm Jack Garrison."

She extended her hand. "Jack, I am called Dodi. We—our family—are waiting for news about my sister-in-law. She had a heart attack today and is in surgery now."

"I'm so sorry," Jack sympathized. "It's a long night."

"Yes. Very long. Thank you—Jack. I thought I recognized you. And perhaps I recognize your friend—Bette—as well? Your pictures are both on the news, you see."

"Yes. . ."

She continued. "And when I saw the photographs I think I remember you were both at the funeral of Sol Baruch? Yes? I am correct?"

"Yes. We were."

She raised a finger to her temple. The blue number of a concentration camp tattoo was on her wrist. "I thought so. She is such a lovely girl."

"Thank you. Yes. Very. Saved my life. And other lives. "

"I thought it was her. And you—when I saw you at Sol's funeral. I thought to myself, you look familiar to me. So much like a young man I knew once. A very, very long time ago. And Jack, how did you know Sol?"

A doctor, still in scrubs, entered the room and made a beeline toward the family, interrupting the conversation. The physician's weary burst of Hebrew announced good news. Like a pile of puppies, family members roused themselves and smiled and hugged one another. No translation needed.

Jack backed away, unnoticed by the happy family. They exited, exultant.

Jack was left alone to wait.

Another hour passed. Returning to the desk, he asked again for news. Another call to the surgical floor.

News at last. Bette was out of surgery and just moved to recovery. She had survived thus far. It could be hours before they could move her into the ICU.

Jack was urged to go back to his hotel; he could see her in the morning. Again Jack insisted on waiting.

🌢🌢🌢

It was all too familiar.

Jack stood rooted in front of the entrance leading to the ICU ward of Hadassah Hospital. His arms hung limply at his side. He stared at the locked double doors.

Dread. Helplessness. How could this be happening a second time in his life? His thoughts took him back to St. Thomas Hospital in London; back to Debbie in the hospital bed. Her tangled blond hair was fanned out on her pillow. Machines and graphs, IV bags. Tubes and wires. The ventilator down her throat. Her eyes opened and filled with such love for him as he held her hand and told her everything for the last time. They both knew this was farewell. Her mother was flying in from the States. Would she make it in time? Jack thought he could not live through that day. Or the days to follow.

And now? Bette. Out of recovery after eight hours of surgery. Critical condition. Jack knew what he would see. He was afraid of what lay behind those doors.

The sign, in Hebrew, Arabic, and English, read: "ICU—3."

He glanced at the phone used to call the trauma ward nurses' station that would allow him admittance. Whispering almost inaudibly, he rasped, "Oh God, please..."

From behind, a hand touched his shoulder. A heavy-set nurse with warm brown eyes asked him gently, "May I help you?"

He managed to find his voice. "I'm here for Bette—Deekmann. I'm Jack Garrison."

"Oh, yes! Mr. Garrison. Yes. You are on the visitor's list." The nurse punched in the code and the doors clicked and swung open for him.

The ICU station was on the left overlooking a dozen curtained cubicles on the right. He waited as a dark-haired nurse finished entering data at a computer.

"I'm here for Bette Deekmann. Jack Garrison."

"Ah. Mr. Garrison. She has been asking for you."

"Yes. Please, how is she?"

"Still very critical. She needs to rest but has been trying very hard to stay awake. Asking for Jack. Only a few minutes please. Room 316."

Taking a deep breath to steady himself, Jack stepped through the curtain into his worst nightmare. The room was cool. Almost too cold. Bette's face and lips were pale, almost the color of the sheets. Machines and tubes were festooned around her head as he expected. He stood at the footboard and touched her exposed toes. Too cold. Most of the pink nail polish she wore was removed for surgery. All that remained was a daisy painted on her big toe. He imagined her choosing her flower. Sunny girl. Happy, smiling Bette. "I'll have that one..." A daisy suited her. Jack covered her foot with a blanket and moved to stand beside her.

Long dark hair was brushed back and neatly braided. He touched her forehead.

"Bette? It's Jack. I'm here, Bette."

Long thick lashes fluttered and her eyes opened. She almost smiled. He leaned close and kissed her cheek. Too cold.

She breathed his name. "Jack?"

"I'm here Bette. I'm okay. I'm okay."

She closed her eyes and nodded with relief. "Jack. . ."

Her flesh seemed too beautiful and fragile to hold such a bright and powerful soul.

"I know—I know, darling. You just need to get well. . ."

A single tear escaped from the corner of her eye. "I—don't—know—if..."

"Please, Bette. Please. You gotta fight. I need you to fight. For me."

She nodded.

The curtains stirred. The nurse entered. "Mr. Garrison? Time."

"Okay." Jack took Bette's hand. "I gotta go now. I'll be back, okay?"

Bette fixed her gaze on him, pleading. She squeezed his hand tightly and mouthed, "I love you."

"Yes. And I love you."

Important words, he thought as he made his way out of the trauma ward. Looking over his shoulder and up to where he guessed her room was, he caught a cab back to the hotel. He thought of the painted daisy.

Bette had warned him, "Never say goodbye without saying 'I love you.' Life is so uncertain. A person never knows when it might be the last goodbye."

♦♦♦

Sunlight streamed through the twelve Chagall stained glass windows in the synagogue at Hadassah Hospital. Bathed in light and color from the windows representing the twelve tribes of Israel, Jack, Lev, and Amir quietly prayed together. Jack's friends carried the promise that all Israel was praying for Bette. What better place to call upon the God of Abraham, Isaac, and Jacob for the miracle of Bette's healing? Jack took some comfort in that, but the attack replayed over and over in his mind. Had he done all he could do? Was there anything more he could have done?

Jack walked back from the sanctuary to the main lobby. He spotted Dodi, the old woman he met in the waiting room the night before. Today, she wore the blue uniform of a Hadassah volunteer. From her station behind the information desk she spotted him reading the grim headlines. "Shalom, Jack! Have you had any rest?"

"Not much. How is your sister-in-law?"

"She'll make it. She has another great-grandchild due in November, and she told us all she refuses to die. Life is the best motivation to keep living. True?"

He nodded. "True."

"So—Jack? Have you eaten? It's my job to make sure visitors know how to find the cafeteria." She took his arm and escorted him down the corridor. "You need to stay strong for her, young man." She preceded him through the cafeteria line and the salad bar. "Why is there no chicken soup in a Jewish hospital?" She scolded a cafeteria worker. She ordered Jack, "Sit here. Eat. Sometimes when things are very difficult a good meal is just the thing." She poked his newspaper as if it were a vile thing. "Never mind that. We all know the truth. If you need anything, I am here. And listen, tomorrow you and I are going to have lunch together. My shift is over at noon and I will expect you to pick me up at the information desk. Then I want to hear all the information about what a nice American boy like you is doing in a place like this."

She made Jack smile for the first time since Hebron. "It's a date," he agreed.

She scuttled away, leaving Jack to his meal.

He managed a few bites for the sake of obeying this typical Jewish grandmother. Grilled chicken and sautéed vegetables grew cold. Jack's appetite was gone. He scanned the article in The International New York Times: *Israeli Officer Kills Palestinian in Hebron.*

The story reported the confrontation was provoked by the American companion of IDF officer Bette Deekmann. The facts were so grossly distorted Jack could hardly believe it was the same incident.

A tall, gray-haired man in a plain, black uniform without insignia approached and sat down across from Jack. "Shalom, Dr. Garrison. I am Officer Deekmann's commander. May we speak a moment?"

Jack stared for a few seconds, wondering if this was a vision, and then wondering if he still possessed the ability to speak. "Some headline, huh?" he replied.

"So the whole world knows Officer Deekmann shot the attacker dead. But the facts appear to have been left out of the story."

"No choice. They're all nuts. The media, I mean."

"We apprehended one of the Palestinian teenagers," the commander reported. "We will soon have the other. He says all he knows of the man who recruited them is the name Faisal. Do you know that name?"

Jack shook his head. "Common enough."

"Did you recognize the man, or have any reason to think you were a specific target?"

"In Hebron?"

"We think he flew to Israel from London the same day you returned."

"London?" A realization leapt from Jack's muddled thoughts. "Just before I came back here from London," he recounted, "I was attacked in my home. The police said it was a burglar, that I surprised him—but it felt more—personal—than that. I think he was trying to kill me."

"Yes?" the commander encouraged. "Go on. What happened?"

"I defended myself with a—a walking stick. I jabbed it in his eye."

A soft bell pinged in the corridor and a voice speaking Hebrew made an announcement before falling silent again.

"Ah," the commander said. "And in Hebron the now dead terrorist wore an eye patch. So you think it might be the same man?"

Jack's momentary energy dissolved as quickly as it came. He pushed his tray back. "How could I know?" he said. "Just a thought. Doesn't really make sense, does it? Anyway, why does it matter?"

The officer pointed at the twisted headline. "This is why it matters. What is it your president calls it? Fake news."

"At the moment all I care about is Bette surviving."

"And it is our job to make certain Israel survives as well."

"She had no choice but to kill the guy. That's what I can tell you now. And if she doesn't make it…" His voice trailed away.

"You are a praying man, Dr. Garrison? She is getting the best care possible. She is much beloved, and all her friends—including myself—are bringing her to HaShem for His mercy."

Jack nodded his thanks.

"If I were you, I'd get some rest," the commander encouraged. "And hold to hope. Sometimes it is all we Jews can do—and it has never failed us yet."

We Jews, Jack thought. *Blessed are You, Lord God, King of the Universe—Who gives us reasons to hope.*

♦♦♦

Jack returned to his hotel, tired and lonely and fearful. Lev was away. The lobby was empty, except for a few jet-lagged pastors poring over texts and emails on their cell phones.

When Jack stopped by the front desk, the attendant greeted him with genuine concern. "Shalom, Dr. Garrison. It's so good to see you back. Are you well, sir?"

"Well—thank you. Bette Deekmann is still critical. But stable. It's a painful road, but we won't give up hope."

"Spoken like a true Israeli, Dr. Garrison. Pain is real but so is hope."

"True—yes—and—I'll remember that." Jack did not want to talk about hope. He was so tired. "I—I've lost my cell phone. Any messages for me?"

The clerk disappeared into a back room and returned with an express package the size of a large shoebox, addressed to Jack and stamped with security clearance. "This came for you two days ago, Dr. Garrison."

Jack's name and the address of the hotel were inscribed in unsteady cursive. It was the handwriting of someone elderly, Jack guessed. The return address was in Hebrew.

"Would you translate this for me please?"

The clerk studied it for a moment, then read it aloud with a breath of wonder in his voice. "Dr. Garrison—the sender is—was—Sol Baruch."

Jack embraced the package like an old friend. Filled with anticipation, he rushed up to his room. Tearing open the wrapping and lifting the lid, he watched old black and white photos tumble out onto the bed. There were three packets of a dozen letters, each tied with red string and bearing French postmarks from 1938, 1939, and 1940.

In the bottom was a long, heavy object, wrapped in bubble wrap. Jack cut the tape and unrolled the ceramic sign which once hung on Sol's garden wall:

SHALOM

In the midst was an envelope with Jack's name inscribed in spidery cursive.

> *Shalom, Jack.*
>
> *You are truly Ya'acov, grandson of Jacob de Louzada, a mighty descendant of Abraham! We have a saying; 'Never Forget!' But how will we who are passing away be remembered unless we are in the hearts of those who come after us? My friend Jacob and I had a toast when we were young. . .*
>
> *Here is to those who came before us,*
>
> *To those who will come after us,*
>
> *And to us.*
>
> *I pass that toast on to you now. It is my deepest prayer that in these photographs and letters. . .fragments of a beautiful life, you will find the missing pieces of your own life. May HaShem bless and keep you and make his face to shine upon you.*
>
> *Shalom!*
>
> *Sol Baruch*

So the great man kept his word to Jack. Before his death the treasure of Sol's friendship with Jacob de Louzada was carefully gathered up and wrapped to pass on to a new generation.

As the sun rose in the east, Jack spread a hundred photographs out across his bed. Young Jacob and Sol, two friends at the Sorbonne, lived their lives never knowing what lay ahead for them: photographs of the courtship and wedding of Jack's grandparents, and then afterward as newlyweds in Paris. And so very many pictures of Jack's mom as a baby, smiling in the arms of her mother.

Jack opened the first letter in the first packet. It was written in French Jack could only translated awkwardly, but the message was clear.

> *My dear Sol,*
>
> *By now you are in Galilee, planting grape vines while I remain here in moldering Europe. I am hoping for a visa to come to Palestine. Perhaps when I arrive the grapes in the vineyards of Eretz Israel will be ready to harvest. . .and again we will lift our glasses in the toast. . .I long to join you. I have met a beautiful Jewish girl here who also shares the dream of coming home to Israel Reborn.*
>
> *I taught her our toast so I do not raise my glass alone. Her name is Rachael Gold and she is the granddaughter of a rabbi. She is truly purest gold; my golden treasure.*

Jack could not stop reading. Each letter brought a new revelation. Pieces of his puzzle clicked into place one detail at a time. He studied a photograph of the little family; father, mother, and the baby girl in their arms.

> *My dear Sol,*
>
> *Though we continue to pursue every channel, our visas to Palestine are denied...We have one hope remaining...we may be able to send our beautiful little girl on a ship filled with other refugee children to America. Who knows when or if we will ever see her again? But at least we will know she will be safe. . .*

He shook his head in awe at the love and courage required by a parent to say goodbye and to give a child to a stranger's care. This was the heartbreaking reality of how different everything might have been had Israel been a refuge and a homeland for the Jews of Europe.

He kissed the image then placed the letter and photograph back in its envelope and slipped it into his jacket pocket. He would share this with Bette.

♦♦♦

This was not the news Jack prayed for.

Bette's complexion was as pale as the wall. The stats on the monitors were all going the wrong way. Blood pressure dangerously low. Oxygen levels low. Heart rate too fast.

"Abdominal wounds are especially difficult," the doctor explained to Jack outside the room. "Bacteria from the intestines. We need to open the wound again. Clean out the abdominal wall. But Dr. Garrison, you need to prepare yourself. This isn't a positive situation."

So there it was. He was saying Bette could die; that she would die, unless they operated immediately.

The roller coaster of Jack's hope once again made a roaring spiral downward. There would be no chance to share the letter or photo that brought Jack such joy.

"Can I have a few minutes with her? Please."

"Minutes. Yes. There's no time. We have to prep her."

Bette opened her eyes slightly and squeezed his hand. She mouthed, "I love you."

He stroked her forehead. Fever. "Darling, they're going to have to clean the wound."

She croaked, "I—heard—them. I'm. Not. Dead. Yet."

He tried to smile for her. "You aren't going to die. I promise you, Bette. We have a life to live together. Besides, I have something beautiful to show you—when you're better."

She nodded. "Say it—Jack. . ."

"I love you, Bette. I need you to know that. Take my love with you now. Somebody said life is a good reason to keep living. So you have to—we have to—okay?" He prayed for her, pleading in a whisper.

"I believe," she prayed. She winked at Jack. "See you soon."

The charge nurse pulled the curtain. "Dr. Garrison, you need to step out."

Jack kissed Bette. "I love you."

That was it. It was all too familiar.

♦♦♦

Handbag over her shoulder, Dodi was ready and watching for Jack as he emerged from the elevator. She waved and smiled a tight-lipped smile, but her sad eyes revealed she already knew the struggle taking place upstairs.

"Come," she said. "Come, Jack." She linked her arm in his. "You don't need to say anything."

So Jack did not speak. He let her direct him. They emerged from the hospital into the warm Jerusalem afternoon. He raised his face to the sky. It seemed deeper blue than Jack had ever seen. A flock of birds flew across the skyline of the new city, then vanished beyond the old. Every detail of this moment was distinct, as if suspended between life and death. Leaves shimmered in one hundred nuances of color. Doves cooed from within the branches. A cool breeze carried the scent of jasmine. He inhaled deeply. Had any day ever been so beautiful?

Dodi led him to the bus stop. Showing her transportation pass, she paid Jack's fare, led him like a little boy, and nudged him into a seat midway back.

He gazed at the ordinary sights of the city as they traveled. How could everything go on as if Bette were not fighting for her life at this very moment?

Men and women driving.

A young Hasidic mother pushing a pram across the street.

A young couple holding hands across the table of an outdoor café.

Two women talking together and laughing as they carried their shopping bags out of a store.

An old man speaking tenderly to his little dog as they sat on a bench.

He thought of these Jews living in the shadow of the ancient city; each life was a story made of a million little stories. They were ordinary people all going somewhere, each carrying his or her own thoughts, own cares.

No one knew what Jack was feeling, except, perhaps this old grandmother who caressed Jack's hand between ancient palms. The tattoo on her forearm spoke of a life of tragedy, loss, and suffering; but today Dodi laid aside her story to focus on Jack. On Bette. On the surgeons who fought to save Bette's life.

The bus slid to the curb outside a little café outside the Old City walls. "Our stop," Dodi said. Jack followed her. He did not know where they were.

The maître d' knew Dodi. They chatted cheerfully in Hebrew as he seated them at a table in the shade. Jack felt invisible. He was grateful.

She ordered for him. Almost instantly chilled white wine, pita bread and hummus, and creamy lemon chicken soup appeared before them.

"You must eat, Jack," she gently urged him.

"I am a shadow."

"Be here." She leaned forward and fixed her gaze on him. "Eat your chicken soup—eat as if her very life depended on you believing she will get well." For a moment he saw Dodi as she must have been: young and beautiful, sitting across the table from someone she once loved. "Eat for her and bless God. Thank God for the miracle of life. Believe God loves her and believe He loves you—the pain is real, but so is hope. There is great power in hope."

He closed his eyes a moment and nodded. "Okay, then. Thank you, God." Taking a spoonful of soup he let the taste linger on his tongue.

It was good; thick with chicken and rice and carrots, flavored with a hint of lemon.

"There. You see?" Dodi smiled and sat back. "Pick up your wine glass. I will teach you a toast." They held glasses together. "To those who came before us, to those who will come after us, and to us."

Jack repeated the words and took a sip. "I know this toast. Sol and—my grandfather."

"Jack. You remind me very much of a young man I loved. I thought so when I saw you at Sol's funeral."

"You knew Sol? He was my grandfather's best friend."

"Yes. I know. They were great friends."

Jack was suddenly aware of the numbers on her forearm. "I'm sorry."

"I was like you when I came to Israel. 1948. My heart was broken. I was hungry but I could not eat. I had lost everything. Everyone I cared about. My husband dead. Our baby girl escaped to America on a Kindertransport. But she did not know me when I returned. I was a ghost to her and she did not wish to live with a ghost. So I saved her life, but lost her, too. And so I came to this reborn Israel, like so many others, alone and grieving." She paused. "Jack? Like you were grieving for your wife, yes? Debbie was her name? And a baby too."

"How do you know—wait, what are you. . ."

"Sol took me in. I changed my name—Dodi, he called me—it means 'my Beloved'—and together we made a new life."

"But—is this real? You. . ."

"My husband had many connections, you see. And so, even though my little girl told me she did not wish to know me, Sol managed to get me news of her from America. I celebrated her every accomplishment. High School. College graduation. When she fell in love and married. And when she gave birth to her beautiful baby boy. . ."

Her eyes brimmed as Jack reached across the table and clasped her hands.

"Jack."

Trembling, he retrieved the envelope containing the old photograph and his grandfather's letter. He opened it and laid it on the table. The beautiful young mother with her baby in her arms—and then he saw Dodi in the sepia image of love and hope and pain… "It's you," he cried, "I only just found out—I opened the box Mom sent to London before she died—I was searching for you—you know that—Bette introduced me to Sol and. . .and. . .and. . ."

"And we were going to have Shabbat dinner together. To reveal it then. I packed Jacob's letters and the photographs of us when we were so very young and in love. All for you. Everything was ready—the meal prepared—and then—Sol flew away. I didn't know if I could tell you on my own. But God had it all in His plan."

Jack covered his face with his hands and sobbed silently. Dodi came to him and put her arms around him. She hugged him tightly, her cheek close to his.

"We will believe in miracles together, Jack. For Bette. We are proof—Israel is proof—even if we can't feel it—God is working things out. Be thankful and believe: where hope grows, miracles blossom."

Epilogue

J ack stood alone with Lev on the Mount of Olives. It was early morning, not much after daybreak, and the area was still deserted. "Just be glad we got here before 9:00 a.m.," Lev said. "After that you can't walk for the tourists or drive for the buses."

Thankful for Lev's support, Jack was glad they could grab a few moments alone. Jack wanted to get back to the hospital where Bette was still struggling for her life, but this was a good spot to pray.

Sunlight beaming over Jack's shoulder illuminated the golden dome on the Temple Mount, and warmed the fawn-and-amber hues of Old City Jerusalem. Below him, the slope covered with olive trees and cemeteries remained in shadow.

"It's weird to say, but even the dead fight over this place," Lev noted. "We Jews bury our dead facing the Temple Mount, so at the resurrection it's the first thing they see. And long ago, long-dead Muslims blocked up the eastern gates so a Jewish Messiah couldn't enter there—then buried their bodies on the hillside right beneath the wall to defile the ground."

"But this is a place of prophecy, too?" Jack inquired, his gaze sweeping over the Old City, trying to visualize it with a gleaming white Temple standing there.

"Right under our feet," Lev said, pointing to the shadowed canyon. "The Kidron Valley—also called the Valley of Jehoshaphat—was written about by the prophet Joel."

"Same one who predicted I'd dream dreams and see visions?"

"That's your guy," Lev agreed. "Joel 3—'I will gather all nations and bring them down to the Valley of Jehoshaphat. There I will put them on trial for what they did to my inheritance, my people Israel, because they scattered my people among the nations and divided up my land.'"

"Like the UN wanted to do in 1947 and like the world is mostly still trying to do today," Jack said. "And they don't even know enough to be terrified."

"Good point," Lev agreed.

"And Jesus? He spoke from up here too?"

"Maybe right where we're standing."

Jack shivered. After witnessing the confrontation on the mount of temptation, Jack longed to see Jesus again, to be near Him. "Tell me more."

"This is where Jesus was sitting when His friends asked Him to tell them how to know when He would be coming as King, and how to be ready for the end of the age. He told them there would be wars and rumors of wars, false messiahs, famines and earthquakes, nations fighting each other, persecution and betrayal. . ."

"All sounds pretty dismal," Jack noted.

"Have you looked at the last 2,000 years? The human record *is* pretty dismal," Lev agreed. "But He also said this: 'This Gospel of the Kingdom will be preached in the whole world as a testimony to all nations—and *then* the end will come.'"

The two men stood in silent contemplation for a moment. Somewhere in the distance a siren wailed.

Lev resumed. "That's what we're all about here, Jack. The gospel started here two thousand years ago. It mostly traveled westward—Europe, Africa, the Americas. But lately it's making its way through Asia—back here. Full circle. No more Jews and Gentiles—One New Man—home again in Jerusalem."

"And I want to be part of it," Jack said. "I belong here."

"You know," Lev said, watching a pair of Israeli fighter planes darting high overhead, "Most people remember the 'wars and rumors of wars' quote, but they forget the prophecy Jesus uttered actually began a day or two earlier—right over there." He pointed toward the Temple Mount. "Jesus' friends—mostly fishermen, country folk—were impressed by and admired the Temple; its size, its beauty, its colonnades, and its gates. 'Look at this, Master,' they said. 'Look at that! Isn't this amazing?' And He said: 'Not one stone here will be left on another.'

"You have no idea how that must have shocked them. Ruthless, cunning old King Herod died soon after Jesus was born, but he left his mark on Israel: Machaerus, Caesarea, Herodium, the Tomb of the Patriarchs—building, building, building—but most of all, right there. When Jesus walked there, the work of expanding the Second Temple had already been going on for over forty years. It was so grand—on such a huge scale—people—not just Jews, but tourists—came from all over the Roman world to see it. It was inconceivable it could be destroyed. Jack? Jack? Are you listening?"

Screams of pain and cries of rage! Spiraling plumes of smoke obscured the Temple Mount. Hordes of men marched and countermarched beneath the walls. Opposing the onslaught, defenders ran from place to place atop the fortifications.

Was this happening now? A new riot? A terrorist attack?

Was it a vision of what would happen in the future?

A breeze out of the north parted the veil of fumes like a curtain. The attackers wore helmets and carried spears and short swords—Romans.

Jack knew then he watched the destruction of Jerusalem in 70 AD.

A ragged line of defenders dropped rocks on the Romans from above, but were instantly driven back by a flight of arrows. The Temple still stood, its walls tarnished with soot, and battered by boulders flung from the Roman siege weapons.

An anguished cry was overtaken by and buried beneath a triumphant shout. "The wall is breached! The way to the Temple is open!"

Roman legionaries fanned out across the Temple Mount. Under Jack's horrified gaze, they speared men, women and children, priests and babies, young and old, without mercy.

Bodies tossed in heaps, slid down because they could be piled no higher.

A phalanx of soldiers lined up outside the Temple, carrying flaming torches. Tossing them into the interior of the building, they taunted the God of Israel to do anything about it. "Hail, Jupiter!" they mocked. "Hail, Caesar!"

The walls of the Temple were ablaze, then the roof caught and flared upward. The entire building leaned toward the west, sliding off its foundations.

Rumble and crash succeeded an avalanche of sight and sound as the Temple's roof fell in on itself, and the majestic structure toppled toward the city of Jerusalem. A cascade of stones swept across the mount, tumbling into the valley beyond.

"Jack? Are you all right?" Lev said. "Hey, man? Where'd you go?"

"The last piece," Jack said. "I saw it. The last piece. I wanted to know if Bible prophecy was true—if you could prove it was reliable. How had I missed it? Jesus prophesied the Temple would be destroyed—forty years before it happened."

Earnestly, fervently, he said to Lev: "We have so much work to do—and the time is so short. Help me! I want to understand it all—and I want to show it to the world."

An Open Invitation

I f you would like to make a decision like Jack Garrison did in the novel, consider this.

Jesus came from heaven to show us "the Way, the Truth and the Life" (John 14:6). He died on the cross for our sins and rose from the dead on the third day. He says, "Behold, I stand at the door and knock, and if any man hears my voice, and opens the door, I will come in to him, and will sup with him, and he with me" (Rev. 3:20). You can have a personal relationship with God through Jesus Christ. In a simple prayer, tell Him you know you are a sinner, and ask forgiveness. Tell Him you believe He died for your sins, rose from the dead, and you want to invite Him to come into your heart and follow Him as your personal Lord and Savior, in His name.

If you would like more information on how to grow spiritually, please go to raybentley.com.